W9-BBK-235

THE STONE HOME

ALSO BY CRYSTAL HANA KIM

If You Leave Me

THE STONE HOME

A Novel

CRYSTAL HANA KIM

wm

WILLIAM MORROW

An Imprint of HarperCollins*Publishers*

HarperCollins books may be purchased for educational, business, or sales promotional use. For information, please email the Special Markets Department at SPsales@harpercollins.com.

FIRST EDITION

Designed by Kyle O'Brien

Library of Congress Cataloging-in-Publication Data has been applied for.

ISBN 978-0-06-331097-1

24 25 26 27 28 LBC 5 4 3 2 1

For Eric, always

Let Us Part Like This

On winter nights Koreans heard infant cries
from distant wood owls. An abandoned newborn
amidst black trees, unaware
that it may be a bird. Allow us
to be like that. Let us speak these words louder
than pines cracking in the snow. Walk far from us.
Mistake us for howling animals.
That's ten of them, that's a hundred of them that we left
behind. Maybe hundreds, maybe thousands.

—Emily Jungmin Yoon

THE STONE HOME

MAY 1980

The night my mother and I were stolen, we'd been in an alley outside a go-go club in Gunsan. The air thick and gritty with cigarette smoke, studded with the scent of stale beer and dried squid. *She's sick. I need money, please.* Umma gestured to me squatting by a slick sewer grate. I wore sneakers that had once been white. The cracked rubber base let in a wash of rainwater, my sockless feet puckered and raw. My laces, gray and frayed, but bowed. I pinched the skin above my ankle, hating her for using me. Hating that we needed it. If I pinched one hundred times without complaint, she would get enough money for a meal.

I was up to eighty-seven when the police came. A net of curses, pelting, arms swatting arms. A rock I tried to slash across the men's faces. Our wrists, grabbed tight behind our backs. In the paddy wagon, Umma screamed and screamed.

Time passed in layers, until the moon slid along the porthole window, and I looked down. My yellow shirt was damp with sweat. Tears. The cotton clung to my ribs, revealing a river of bones.

2011

It's nearly noon, and I'm sweltering in bed when the doorbell rings. I twist to the window, a crowd of buildings, wind ruffling the Sincheon River, churning white peaks. The same image I've seen for years, and yet a foreboding pecks at me until I'm upright, thrashing in my sheets. I'm not expecting anyone.

I peer through the peephole to a stranger's bowed head. Tall and standing too close, blocking most of my vision. *Yes?* I ask, voice raised.

You don't know me. She keeps her head bent, so the words come out muffled. *I was told to come here.*

I don't want whatever you're selling. I told the community center I'm not interested. I open the door a few centimeters, enough to yell straight into her face.

Then, there—in her hands. A knife. She raises it between us, and fear hisses through me.

Can I come in? A smile, glinting and harsh, all teeth.

That matte blade—

You recognize it, don't you? she asks.

I flatten myself against the frame, and she brushes past, slips off her heels, and lines them up at the entryway as if she were a summoned guest. This woman walks on, barefoot. The knife, held loose, absorbs the light as she passes my living room.

Is there somewhere we can sit? She turns, the knife now an offering in her palm. Lusterless, that serrated edge like rotten teeth, that smooth black handle.

I rub my ear. This knife from my youth, now here in my home? No. It is a trick, a coincidence. I shake the possibility from me, and yet I close the door and follow her in. *The kitchen's straight ahead.*

She surveys the scoured countertops, the kettle on the stove. By the window, a round table with two wooden seats, as if I've been waiting for her all these years. She pulls back a chair. *Can I have some tea?*

We are moving too quickly. Here is this woman, thirtysomething, well-fed, tall, clearly a gyopo from America, though her Korean is nearly unaccented. A woman I've never seen before, yet a vibration bells through me.

I need caffeine. She taps the knife's handle. *I don't drink coffee.*

I rush to the cupboards, steady my hands against the knobs. Boil water, pull tins. Breathe through a new hurt in my ribs. I try to swipe glances at her face, quiet this rattling in my veins. She scans the room as she sits—a plastic bowl cupping pocked tangerines, yellow 개나리 blooms in a glass jar on the windowsill, bare white walls—markers of my paltry existence.

You're not scared, she says, and I can't tell if it is a question.

I know how to use that better than you. Unable to help myself, to resist claiming the knife as mine.

She nods, and a smoky hope spreads through me. Is it her? I bring the kettle, two cups with built-in strainers, and the tins of tea over on a wooden tray.

She sifts through pine, green, black, chrysanthemum. Her head bent, not meeting my gaze. She chooses black, I pluck pine needles, and we spoon leaves into our strainers, sink them into our cups. The stereo, I realize, has stopped. I had been listening to ocean sounds, but there's a sticky silence now, though perhaps that's the air, curdled with humidity.

She lays the knife between us. *Well, do you recognize me?* Rustles her shoulders and raises her neck, as if she's been waiting for this moment to reveal herself. A full, slightly alien face, the skin too elastic, her cheekbones angled and pronounced, a voluptuous mouth. A straight nose with a raised tip, so her nostrils show, two dark circles.

I suck in a breath, the hope a heaving in my chest now, grit on my teeth— *I think you're—*

My father died last week. I arrived here this morning from New York. She picks at her loose linen dress, the color of blood. *I should be wearing black. Part of me is still in denial.* She pulls the strainer from her mug and sets it straight on the tray. Tainted water seeps from tiny holes, flows around the tins, the kettle, into the whorled grain.

She breaks, gasping. A metal watch slides down her wrist as she covers her face, and suddenly, I understand—the man who raised her, *he* is the reason why she's here. The wrecked movement of her loose limbs. Her father is dead, and I don't know what he's told her; she doesn't know I have imagined her all these years, I never thought I'd see her again.

He used this knife for everything. Chamoes, boxes, protection, she says between bursts of air.

The cords of the past ten minutes come together—this woman with her unformed grief, this watch, her news—and no, I'm not ready. *I have some chamoes in my fridge*, I say. As if the yellow striped fruit can dam whatever else she's come to tell me.

She rotates her wrist, the knife arcing between us. I imagine the blade slicing the skein that holds our world together, the green gush of the past pouring through, making a mess on my table.

When I was young, I wanted him to get me one just like this, in miniature, so I could hold it in one hand. She laughs, a ragged bite. *He taught me to use it when I turned fifteen.* She presses the lever at the bottom of the hilt, and the blade folds at the joint, slotting into the handle. *It's yours now.*

You have the wrong person, I say, suddenly afraid.

You know I don't.

She offers it to me. An unassuming, curved handle. As I take it, our fingers touch, and for a second, I can't see her face. Only a white, edgeless fear.

She grabs my wrist with her other hand. *He gave me your name and address in his will. He wanted me to return this in exchange for the truth.*

I can't move—can't think, the surge inside me a physical crackling, scurrying acid in my throat—she is here, it has been so many years since I have held her, I want to ask for forgiveness, to run.

She stares straight at me. *Who are you, Oh Eunju?*

A sudden wash of memories, ones I've tried to cast far from myself for thirty years.

I am on a peninsula, or, to be more precise, the southern half of a peninsula broken in two. But in my mind, I am the land itself. I watch the waves, and when the tides come near, I will them to retreat, retract into their uncontained bodies.

My first mind doctor taught me this exercise, to construct a story where I am in control: *Imagine a box you can shut. Imagine a house where you can close the doors.*

Instead, I imagine a wave I try to rule with my mind.

So, she doesn't know—who I am, how the past coils us together. *Your name is Narae*, I say.

She falters, her grip on me loosening, elbow knocking into her mug. *Damn.* While she searches for a towel, I pocket the knife. The weight and feel of it a reassurance, a grounding.

Narae wipes the spill dripping over the table's ledge. Angular, impatient. Her father would have enrolled her in tae kwon do as a child, raised her in his rough way. *I know how to use that better than you*, I'd said. How stupid I was, forty-six years old with dulled instincts. A lone woman in Daegu.

But Narae sits again, her hands fluttery without the knife, her name a red stone in my mouth.

Last winter, I watched a woman in a purple-and-orange coat, startling against the New York palette of gray, tan, black. The sudden joy of such unexpected color. She stood at a sidewalk corner, her hand outstretched, cupping the sky that had started drifting snow. Seeing her, that unabashed softness, I'd yearned for Umma.

I was in the United States for the first time. Wary of every strange man, the languages blaring around me on the streets. For two weeks, I stayed in Koreatown, a teeming strip on Thirty-Second Street with restaurants, noraebangs, billiards rooms, saunas.

I had flown to the other side of the world because of a phone call. He had located me, and in my hope of finding Narae, I had come.

She sits with the wet dishrag in her lap, her youth laid out on the table like an unfortunate hand of cards. She isn't here for me, doesn't see me. A heat flares in my throat. How I had searched for her on those city streets, every woman her, if only at a slant. I stand. *Your father should have told you his own damn story.* I wring the towel out in the sink.

When I turn back, she's still at the table, resting her pale forehead against the edge. Her voice is sinewy with strength. *I'm not leaving until I know. I'll stay here until I die.*

What dramatic grief. With her expensive shoes and coiffed hair. She is a woman who has grown up protected.

Have you been sleeping? that first mind doctor once asked. I would have laughed if the question weren't so stupid. The soaking fear, crawling up my ankles, calves, as if I'd stepped into an ocean storm. I couldn't sleep, and when I could, the in-between was worse than any insomnia.

가위눌림 haunt me. Every time, my eyes are open. I am screaming, I am silent. An invisible being, some ghost or specter, is pounding on my chest, blankets shifting. I'm caught in a vengeful, titan wing. Always, there is a figure in my periphery, but who he is changes. Sometimes, I want to explain to Narae, it is your father.

Her body at a right angle, she stares at the floor. *He didn't tell me he was dying. He didn't tell me anything.*

I take out a fresh mackerel. Heat up a pan with oil. Fry. Fold laundered dish towels. Wipe the refrigerator's reflective surface. Stare at my wide-set cheeks, the lines funneling my mouth, my uneven eyes.

All the work I'd done to keep myself protected was unmade last winter, when I saw him. He was dying, and he needed me to listen, he said.

I bend over, my hands on my knees, my lungs too tight. I can't see. The mackerel skeleton. His body so lean in the hospital bed. A ravaged man, so different from the one I once knew.

Narae comes to me, in that unnerving linen dress. Her inexplicable, mutable face. *Are you all right? Breathe with me.*

The truth, he wants me to tell her the truth about the Stone Home—

False starts, tripping along the edge of my mind: I looked for you. You are a wave I cannot helm. To tell you is to reveal myself, harm you more than I already have.

Please. She tucks her head to her chest. *Say something.*

Her words in my palm, tiny seeds.

I speak. *Our stories are different, Sangchul's and mine, but I will try.*

A truth, as I remember it:

PART ONE

MAY–JUNE 1980

EUNJU

On that first morning, I woke to the sound of false bells cutting through my dreamless sleep. My face pressed against the stink of Umma's armpit. On the thin mattress we shared, I tried to orient myself. We weren't in the paddy wagon any longer, the policemen gone.

"Get up." Umma spoke, her voice tight and spiky. Her gaze mapping the three barred windows along the far wall. Thick iron, evenly spaced. Outside, a loudspeaker blared.

"Where are we?" I raised myself onto my elbows. A room of girls rousing, pushing up from their cots like sprouts. I was used to moving often, waking without recognizing my surroundings. This felt different, the air too clean, antiseptic, and vinegary. Someone unlocked the single door penning us in—a hefty halmoni who thumped her chest with a fist and hacked. "Are we in jail?"

"I don't know, Eunju. Help me fold." Umma gestured to a round-faced girl at the cot beside us, who tucked her blanket. We lifted our mattress, and the metal latticing squeaked.

A bony woman by the door narrowed her eyes. With an unforgiving face crowded by small, square teeth, she looked like the type who relished others' miseries, as tart and hard as an unpickled maesil. "Who are these new vagrants, Halmoni?"

I searched for a rock, anything to throw at this ajumma. "Who're you to—"

"Shut your mouth. She's coming," Umma hissed.

Halmoni stopped before us. She had mild eyes and kind, lined cheeks, but a bulge protruded from her throat, erasing any symmetry as it pushed against the collar of her shirt. "Welcome to the Stone Home. I'm in charge of the women, and you're lucky for that." She pointed to a set of folded clothes at the foot of the cot. A gray pullover and sweatpants. "Strip down. Bring those with you, and your shoes. Child, you get the set from the next cot over." She coughed, and the bulge in her neck leered back at me. "What're you staring at? You speak?"

I nodded.

"Is she dumb?" Halmoni asked. "What're your names?"

A hot flash of heat tore down my throat. "Tell us where we are," I said.

She smacked me, right across the cheek. "There's no back talk here."

"My name is Oh Kyungoh." Umma stepped forward. "This is my daughter, Eunju."

"In here you call me Halmoni." She touched the edge of our sloppily made bed. "Don't make us late for Washup."

Everyone besides Halmoni was pulling off their pajamas—plain white shirts and pale purple pants. Naked with the sweatsuit in their arms, they lined up by the door. The bony woman first. The round-faced one next. She seemed to be the youngest, no older than ten, and her blunt bob swung across her cheeks as she smiled. Was this a nunnery?

Halmoni sucked her teeth at us. "Now, before I strip you myself."

Umma stared straight at her as she pulled off her cotton shirt and brassiere. Her orange flower-print miniskirt. A bruise she had hidden from me spanned the space between her shoulder blades.

I undressed quickly, shucking my jeans and yellow shirt, and caught the gaze of a thin, lanky girl who nodded once before twisting away. The others stared as we approached, whispering among themselves. I imagined them parceling us into stories, injuries, potential past lives. A tall, broad girl who looked like she had eaten meat her whole life turned to me, and another unnie swiveled her head, as if a string connected their movements. "I'm Kim Bora," the broad girl said. Everything about her was bulky and soft. Her breasts flopped as she hunched closer, her nipples as round and light as dalgona ppopgi candy. "How old are you?"

"Fifteen," I said.

"You're small." She sniffed.

I squared my shoulders then remembered we were naked, my flat chest. "Better to be small than as wide as a bull."

"Careful." The other unnie leaned to me, breaking the line. A white, shiny scar worked a gap through her right eyebrow. She was slight like me, but muscled. "We're both sixteen."

"What does that matter?" I asked, refusing the polite form.

Umma stepped between us, all fluid body and bared smile. "The line's moving."

"No respect." Bora sucked her teeth. "Half-breed dust."

Umma held on to my neck, as if I were a pup, until I unclenched. "Not now."

She could pretend to be so mild, my ferocious mother. She fluctuated between extremes, a valve pressed by circumstance, switching from one person into another. Maybe it was the two sides of her, jolting from the Korean to the American, uncomfortable on either side of the divide. Umma, who kept her nails clean by running them along her teeth. She had a slim, subtle nose, with hair and eyes a shade lighter than mine. High cheekbones; a lush, round forehead; and dimples that made you feel like she was considering you fully, and what she saw was good. Even the asymmetry of her creased right eye and creaseless left was somehow charming. But it was obvious she wasn't wholly Korean, and others twisted all I thought was beautiful into something ugly, dirty, and full of shame.

We entered a large bathroom, as nice as any jjimjilbang we'd gone to when Umma had extra money. Halmoni clapped, and the others set their clothes along a bench by the door. Squat toilets to the left, sinks on the right, a tiled sunken area ahead, where showerheads jutted from the walls.

When Umma lingered outside bars eyeing men, she wore her nice dress, a dark flowered cotton whose seams showed only in fluorescent light. "It doesn't matter once one of you is naked," she'd say. Then she'd touch the crown of my head. "Not for you to worry about, anyway."

I thought that meant I was ugly, even though I saw myself in the mirror. In Umma's womb, she had given me her features, erasing the father I had never known, yet my small self had rebelled, my nose and chin cutting into sharper relief.

"What're you looking at?" Bora caught my gaze in the glass as she squatted over one of the open toilets, a stream of piss coming out of her.

"Eunju, showers." Umma beckoned. "We'll get clean, and we'll figure out what's happening here. We didn't do anything wrong."

"Five minutes!" Halmoni yelled.

I let the water stream over my face, hot and pulsing. Rubbed my arms until gray balls of dead skin formed. Dirt rivuleted down my legs and across the floor, to the drain in the center. My shoulders loosened. I caught stray lice in my hair, popped their hard bodies between my fingers, relishing the smear of creamy white guts. We would walk away clean, scrubbed fresh, and maybe that was worth the temporary unknowing. Beside me, Umma seamed her lips as she washed the reek from between her legs.

SANGCHUL

Sangchul and his older brother were rambling out of their neighborhood mart on a winter afternoon when a cop seized them by their collars. Four months before their paths would twine with Eunju's, on a day heavy with January cold, Sangchul twisted out of the man's grip and ran around the corner. But Youngchul didn't fight hard enough, his resolve splintering as the cop pinned him to the wall.

They were only ten minutes from home. Turn left at the apartment building with the glass doors, right at the elementary school, walk down a narrow alley—and they would have arrived at the house their grandfather had built after the war, where he and their grandmother and their parents waited. Sangchul peered around the corner of that apartment building, willing his hyung to run, when he noticed a second policeman step out of a paddy wagon parked on the side of the road. This cop's gait—callow, commanding—made him shudder. Their grandfather had warned them to cut their hair, remain unseen, cops were hunting for protestors, any excuse, and yet Sangchul believed his hyung would be let off with a cuff across the head.

Youngchul wriggled. "I didn't do anything!"

"You're a thief, a good-for-nothing shit." The first cop shoved as the second one pulled Youngchul's pants down. His underwear.

Sangchul watched, uncomprehending, as they flicked on a lighter and raised the blue-white glow between his brother's legs. The burning scent of fear and hair, the flame skipping up from its metal case.

Sangchul ran to them, yelling, to let his brother go.

They were shoved into the paddy wagon, belted, and handcuffed to the wall. Two others were already caged. One looked young and lost, flushed and reeking of soju. He cried openly, head tilted to the door, the wedge of sunlight thinning as the men locked them in. "My nuna is looking for me, my cousins tricked me, I've never drank before," he repeated, a prayer with no end. The other seemed older. He stank too, of dirt and the body, unwashed parts. His hair so oily it shined in the dark.

Watching those two, Sangchul noticed the monstrous feeling inside him begin to pale, fading to a clean blue. The sky. His shirt. He nudged hyung, not meeting his gaze. Sangchul could still see the flame, his brother's pale, hairy scrotum. "That one's drunk, and that one's homeless. We're not like them."

Youngchul, just as mottled and sweating, nodded. "We'll get Appa to come down to the station."

Sangchul lined his spine to the wall, relieved. His hands, cuffed above his head, were tingling. "We'll be home by evening?"

"We're in school, we're good kids," Youngchul reassured.

"Appa's going to give us such a beating." Sangchul practiced how he'd relay the story to his friends. The day they were mistaken for petty homeless thieves. How he had disappointed his father again, bringing hyung down with him. "We'll be okay?"

"I'll make this right." Youngchul gazed at the floor, the scurrying light.

How little they had understood of the world. Hours later, the paddy wagon hurtled through iron gates to the mouth of a colossal building—*The Stone Home* chiseled into the granite entrance. Disorientation rang through them. Where home was, where they were. In the cafeteria, Jae, a boy with eyes that sloped at the corners, leaned over. "We'll be in Cow's workshop together."

"Workshop?" Youngchul asked. He didn't touch his dinner, as if refusal would lead to change.

Jae gestured at the older hyungs with white bats. "Mosquito leads Leathers Workshop, Cow and Crow split Fishhooks, and they're looking for a new Keeper for Shirts." He ticked his head, determining their intelligence. "Nicknames, used among us, you got that? We address them as 'Keepers' to their faces, unless you want to be taken to the closet."

"Why two in Fishhooks?" Youngchul bunched his hands. "What about school?"

Jae shrugged. "Warden decides."

"How do we get out? Where are we?" Sangchul demanded, eyeing the locked doors, the barred windows, the white bats. If only they knew the town, the closest landmark, he could orient himself, puzzle out a plan.

Jae pointed at the two men surveying the crowd. "They say we'll be reformed in a year or two, if we work hard."

Another boy shook his head. "I heard we'll be transferred to an adult institution when we turn seventeen." Warning seeded his voice. "Of course, there's the other option."

"What's that?" Sangchul asked, dizzy with panic, the path to home disbanding with each rumor.

Jae sucked his teeth. "You can become one of them—a Keeper."

EUNJU

Halmoni, who had soaped the growth on her neck like a tender child, led us out of the bathroom and down to the ground floor. As everyone slung on shoes, I scanned the windows that flanked a double-wide entrance, the night before returning to me, split by shadows and silence. Shoved into the back of a paddy wagon. Woken by the metallic grind of the engine shutting off. Pushed up a path by police. A coldness whistling down my spine, even in my half-sleep state. If they touched me, I'd thought, I would plunge a rock into their stomachs, their eyes. A shadowed man had led us past a building that smelled of wet stone from the evening rain, a flashlight bobbing, and we'd followed to the mouth of a smaller building. We were given tea. A bed. A sleep that felt bottomless.

I blinked in the morning light. This was the ground floor of that smaller building. I glanced at Umma behind me, uncertain if I should be afraid—we'd heard of military men with tear gas and batons, children disappeared in the night, but she was right. We hadn't done anything wrong.

"He's coming." Halmoni motioned us into a line as a man unlocked the doors from the outside. He stopped with his arms behind his back, a baton just visible. Tall, with features that seemed too large for the strictures of his face, as if the skin had shrunk around his skull. "Teacher," Halmoni greeted. "The two new ones are in the back."

Umma held on to my shirt when he didn't acknowledge us, instead announcing, "Service," and leading us out. Teacher looked younger than an authority should, not yet forty.

Beneath a bright sky, a dirt path led to an imperious three-storied building made of smooth gray stone, modern with a flat roof. Rows of windows, like a school, though these were barred too. Fear gripped my throat. It was too quiet, without any marking of others beyond.

"The wall," Umma said under her breath. A shiver ran through me. At the edges of my vision was a high barricade of stacked stones. Gray, beige, jagged with crevices. The top sparked in the sun, crusted with broken glass. Flickering shards.

Teacher unlocked a metal door at the back of the large building. A ring of keys attached to his belt clicked together, sounding like a mouthful of teeth. I didn't understand. This was a school or a prison or someplace else entirely. Inside, Halmoni led the women through another entry on the left, and they followed with sloped shoulders, their ease from the bathroom swept away. Umma released my shirt, stopped beside Teacher. "Excuse me." She smiled with her lips closed, chin tucked. "My daughter and I were mistaken for others last night. We're law-abiding citizens from a good home. My husband must be worried."

Teacher examined Umma, all her washed and dressed softness. Some men loved her for her strangeness, and they disgusted me most, how they saw her features as parts to overcome. My fingers twitched, Teacher parted his lips. A glimpse of pink tongue. "Go on, children can't miss their prayers." He spoke without looking at me.

"I'll be all right," Umma said.

I walked away slowly. That man, he smelled of damp musk

and sour sweat, wood chips burned to ash, like an animal barely reined.

At the center of the room I entered alone, a cross hung, stamped with the body of Jesus. Boys kneeled in rows, split by an aisle. They wore the same sweatsuits as us, a mass of gray, like the students I used to watch run around the dirt fields in their gated schools. I slid into the last row on the right, among the girls, and the muscles in my neck loosened. We were in a church, then.

The floor was cold and hard, without padding for our knees. A man sat onstage, obscured by a podium. A priest. I had been in a church before, a requirement to attend service before we were offered meals alongside other unwanted mothers with children. I had enjoyed the music, the calm. The gospel stories with their clean grace. Umma sidled into the row after me, a sweep of hair behind her ear. Her face flat, without a hint of what Teacher might have said.

The priest swept open his arms. He was older, maybe in his fifties, with a shining, bald dome, a crusty ring of hair. Bushy brows atop indistinct features, encased in a flabby face, jowled and worn. He looked ordinary. "Good morning, my children."

"Good morning, Warden," the room shouted.

"Yesterday, we saw many of you on the Presentations line, and do you know what I felt above all? Not regret or apology or redemption, but a rotten, evil stubbornness in your souls."

As he continued, Teacher stalked the perimeter, straightened slumped stances.

"We are more than a mere reformatory center," Warden bellowed. "Teacher and I have created this home for your wayward, vagrant hearts, to lift you to your greatest potential."

"Yes, Warden," the room chanted.

"You question why the world has forsaken you without considering your faults."

Beside me, Umma tried to keep herself expressionless. I understood the pinch between her brows though. The shape and color of those words. Red and barbed and hollow-cased. This was a man who would not keep us safe. His tongue too used to blame.

A chorus of amens followed him out of the room at the end, and Teacher called us to rise. The girl beside me jerked my arm. She was all thin wrists, thin face, thin lips, the one who had nodded at me earlier that morning. "Not us. The boys run outside. We cook in Little House. Eunju, right? We're the same zodiac animal." She spoke in a warm whisper, as if we were already friends, her voice low and crackly, pleasantly deep. "Born in 1965? I'm Ahn Mina."

Halmoni shushed her as the boys exited line by line. They ranged in age, the youngest looking no more than ten, though there were some oppas too, who carried white bats. Only when they were gone did Teacher acknowledge us: "Little House rise."

The girls eased into themselves, clarifying like shined glass, once Teacher locked us back inside Little House. Not even Halmoni seemed to have a key to let us out. We were captives, and yet they unwound, breathed easier. I waited for them to explain the workings of this place, who these men were, why we were kept enclosed, to reveal a plan for escape, but Halmoni palmed the window and took off her shoes, as if we belonged. "Let's get started, then."

"That's the boys' entrance to the cafeteria." Mina pointed to a set of double doors, then twirled her finger around the corner. "We go through the side, into the kitchen."

We walked past a bathroom, a supply closet, the stairs we had come down that morning, Mina whispering details into my ear, through a door Teacher had unlocked before leaving. A burst of sound as we crossed that threshold into an expansive kitchen. Even the youngest one, the round-faced girl they called Nabi, knew what to do. The bony ajumma with the unforgiving teeth headed to the burners, yelling, "I'll start the jjigae."

"That's Ajumma Lee." Mina smirked. "She thinks she's the leader, second to Halmoni. Tiresome and mean and the best cook, so you don't want to cross her."

By a row of hooks, Bora and the brow-scarred unnie, named Areum, tied on aprons, moaning about how hungry they were. Bora sucked her teeth as we neared. "Get the rice, Mina. You're not her mother." Mina sighed exaggeratedly, but she walked away, mouthing to me: *More, later.*

Halmoni steered Umma and me to the hooks next, where she pulled pale purple aprons over our heads, as if it were natural for us to join them. "Food pantry to the left, prep counters in the center, sinks and stoves straight back. You see, there?" We rounded a corner of stacked trays, and the wall disappeared, replaced by a counter that surveyed a cafeteria. Umma and I shared a glance. No windows, no exits, Little House tightly sealed. "We serve the boys, then seat ourselves." Halmoni pointed to a clackety-looking beaded curtain. "In and out through there, as needed."

A sharp pain ran through my stomach as Halmoni brought us to Ajumma Lee at the gas stoves, where a vat bubbled already, erupting with the comforting funk of doenjang-jjigae. Slowly, I noticed the plenty, boxes of dried anchovies, sacks of mixed grains, mounds of garlic. Dirt-encrusted carrots and heaps of spinach in the sink.

"You know how to cut fish?" Ajumma Lee asked.

Umma nodded, as if she were a housewife, and followed her to a fridge.

"Help Mina prepare the mixed rice," Halmoni said to me. "We don't trail our mothers here."

I found Mina sifting a large spoon into an even larger drum.

My mouth pooled with saliva as I watched the swirling starch, the grains below. "That's a lot of food."

"You think this is enough to feed all seventy of us?" She pushed with both hands. "The boys get bigger portions, and the Keepers get double."

"Why don't you cook more?" There were sacks in the corner by the pantry, more food than I had seen in a long time.

"Watery rice, thin soup." Mina sang into a song, ignoring me.

SANGCHUL

In his first weeks at the Home, before his mind, hollowed by hunger and exhaustion, stopped seeking rescue, Sangchul could think only of the past. As they prayed and ran and worked, a memory rose, unbidden: Youngchul at eight years old, reciting an essay. Their mother's silence, their father's grunt. Still, Sangchul could feel their pride for their elder son. It was like a current, electric, invisible, too complicated for him to define. It was in the sheen of their father's gaze, the new notebooks that appeared on hyung's desk the next week, the talk of college that slipped into their conversations a few years later. Their parents mused about his future, Youngchul as a scholar. Even as Sangchul broadened into the stronger son, he never felt that current aimed in his direction, never felt its light.

Late at night in his cot, surrounded by the noise of sleeping boys, as denial ran strong through him, Sangchul couldn't shake it—Youngchul's neat mouth as he recited, that straight spine, his confidence. How hyung had dragged them here, surrendering to the cops so easily, his words in the end useless.

Now Sangchul ran around the dirt path in the early-May brisk air, the same loop for half an hour, surveyed by Keepers as if they were beasts. Resentment swelled in him as Youngchul exchanged greetings with the other runners. Beside them, Taeho, the youngest of their group, hailed everyone with his usual cheer.

Sangchul sighed at the droning rhythm of their days, four months ticking by with the weather their only marker. Though Morning Run was their time to trade secrets with those outside their groups, to consider escape, they were careful. From his office on the third floor of Big House, Warden kept watch, and unlike Teacher, he never had to make himself small. His presence a constant reminder: outside the wall were the cops willing to bring them right back. Inside was the threat of isolation in Chapel, a room that was more effective than the wall that surrounded them, where boys returned with Warden as their savior—and the fear deeper within themselves that they really were unwanted.

With a low whistle, Youngchul led them to the other side of the path as they ran past Rat's Keeper post. They had come together in the same paddy wagon: Youngchul, Sangchul, drunken Taeho, and oily-haired Rat, before he had flipped into a Keeper as soon as he turned seventeen. Now he oversaw Shirts Workshop. Rat had broken the thread tying them together, and for that, they hated him.

Rat jogged up to them anyway, smacked Sangchul across the head. "Pick up your feet, slug."

Youngchul nudged Taeho, and they detached, ran faster. Their protocol: to detract attention and keep themselves safe. Alone, Sangchul let his head judder the way Rat wanted, though it coiled inside him, all he wanted to do, his palms slick and hot with want.

"Your mother disown you after seeing that shit stain, #27?" Rat pulled Sangchul's collar, revealing his birthmark. Snickered. Still, Rat didn't strike as hard as some of the others, a thorn rather than a hammer. He boxed Sangchul's ear and pushed him away.

"If I got Rat alone," Sangchul panted as he rejoined his group, "I'd pack his face in."

"Not worth the aggravation, all right?" Youngchul bumped his elbow.

"I'm fine." Sangchul shrugged off hyung, picked up the pace so they'd have to quicken their strides. The insult of being called by his number lightened only by the nickname he rolled around in his mouth: Rat, that oily-haired stink, unkempt traitor.

Jae caught up with them at the next bend. Though he was the fourth in their Fishhooks group, he floated during the runs. Their intel gatherer, the perceptive one who served as a counterweight to Taeho's guileless fumbling. Jae, with his pleasing face, eyes that tugged at the corners, casting him with a shine of sweetness, hiding his true discernment. "New additions came last night, a mother and daughter," he said.

The loudspeaker buzzed, and Mosquito, the Head Keeper, corralled them from his post closest to Little House. "Head count!"

"I heard the new ajumma's a mixed-blood," Crow said, his squawky voice easily overheard as the groups made their way to their lines.

"If only Warden let us patrol the women," Mosquito said with a smirk.

Cow gave a crooked grin. "I'd have lots of things I'd want to do to them."

Rat snorted. "Right. You can barely manage your group, idiot."

"I wonder where they got picked up," Taeho said as Youngchul steered them to their Keeper, Cow. Their group was always last, Cow mumbling in a dejected way as they waited to enter Little House.

Jae spoke. "There's something wild about the girl."

"How do you know?" Sangchul asked.

Jae tilted his head, and Sangchul was once again disarmed by how shadowy he made himself, easily floating out of the mind's eye, yet absorbing everything. "They were at Service this morning."

Cow rapped his bat as they entered the cafeteria. "Shut up, you idiots."

When they reached the serving line, Sangchul searched for them, like everybody else. Halmoni with her goiter kindness. Bora and her jeering confidence. Areum, with her chiseled stare and scarred brow. Young Nabi, cheery-faced. Mina, who Youngchul glanced at too often, her thin wrists a match for his own. Then there, beside her, the new girl. Jae was right, of course. She had a feral air, all eyes and hungry mouth. She looked Korean, no glimpse of foreign blood in her. Sangchul searched for her mother. She must have been in the kitchen with Ajumma Lee, beyond the wood-beaded curtain they weren't allowed past.

The new girl. They would call her that among themselves until her name was revealed. Warden never branded them with numbers. Halmoni saw to that. At night, when Sangchul couldn't sleep, he ran through their names like a prayer.

EUNJU

The boys arrived sweating, veiny, and foul, through the double doors at the back of the cafeteria, framed photographs of Park Chung-hee and Chun Doo-hwan above their heads. A dictator who had called himself president, and then was killed. A man everyone said led our country now. I shivered beneath their gazes. They looked ordinary too. In silent lines, organized by some system I didn't comprehend, each boy picked up a tray and utensils. We served mixed rice, banchan, soup. When one boy stumbled, Mina grabbed a fistful of rice from his bowl and stuffed it into her pocket. She was right. The amount we made for breakfast wasn't enough.

Their faces seeped into my mind like tea coloring water. A boy with a shaved head wiped his wet eyes. Another cracked his joints, sharp pops gouging the silence. An oily-haired oppa with a white bat grinned with a glint that made me want to kick him between his legs. The space swarmed, too many bodies wedged together at long tables, a rotten sadness oozing between them.

"You may eat," Warden said from beneath the dead dictator. Teacher, who was taller but hunched, squinched his eyes, looking prickly in his own body.

Umma and I received our food last. A shallow bowl of doenjang-jjigae with one tofu slice each. The hardened rice from the bottom of the pot.

Mina whispered as soon as I sat down, all jittery energy and crackly voice, "You see those oppas? Mosquito, with the strong nose, is Head Keeper. Rat's the one with the greasy hair, given that nickname because he hoards food during meals. He's the newest Keeper, and he's closest with Crow, the muscled one. Wait until you hear his voice. The last one's Cow, with the big eyes and chin dimple."

"Which group are we part of?"

Mina shoved braised tofu into her mouth. "We stay in the kitchen. Though Cow only has four boys now in his Workshop. A few were aged out last month, you know? Sometimes Teacher recruits us if production slows."

I stared at the oppa she called Mosquito: sharp nose and eyes, a white bat tucked into the back belt loop of his pants. His boots, laced to the ankles, shined. He looked unassuming enough. "How'd Mosquito get his nickname?"

"He's always buzzing in Teacher's ear, making sure he's the favorite." She picked a doraji strand from her banchan plate, grasping the question on my face. "Keepers are the only ones who get those bats. New boots, a watch too. The best of them becomes Head, and I heard he gets his own room."

"Is Bora going to be a Keeper?" I asked, low enough not to be overheard.

She laughed. "Halmoni's our only one. She holds all our secrets for us. That's why her tumor's so big."

I held the nooroongji in my mouth, the toasted flavor of scorched grains. The food, the showers, the new clothes, the warmth of the kitchen, they weren't enough to keep us here. Umma and I would leave this reformatory center. We didn't need their help.

A crash. At the far side of the cafeteria, a boy struggled on the floor.

"What happened to him?" I asked.

Mina jabbed acorn jelly with her chopstick. "Chapel. You don't want to end up there."

I thought of the morning's gospel, Warden's loud voice and blameful speech. I tried to yoke together everything she told me, but questions scurried through my mind. "What's Chapel? What happens to the others, the ones that don't become Keepers?"

"You'll figure it out," Bora said between slurps. "Enough guiding, Mina. Didn't you hear what I said this morning?"

Mina sipped water, shrugged. "Fine, unnie."

I ignored Bora, and Mina too. We didn't need them. The tofu slice disintegrated on my tongue, and I wished I had another. Most of the boys had finished eating, some scraped at the sides of their metal bowls, twisting to look at us, their hunger keen. Their faces dry and flaky. A glimpse of green beneath a stray sleeve. A bandaged arm. At the far end of the room, a different boy with purple darkening his cheeks.

SANGCHUL

Sangchul heeled the nearly dead grass and tried not to touch the back of his neck, where the skin had blistered. It was eight in the morning, and the sun stung already. All week, Teacher told the Fishhooks boys they were lucky to be outside, chopping wood for hours. Now they had to haul the stacks across the property, and this was supposed to be better than Workshops.

"At least we're exempt from Presentations." Youngchul lifted his face to the light.

"Sure, hyung," Sangchul managed. So they wouldn't be on the daily lashing line if they didn't make quota. A minor reprieve for sun rashes and scraped hands. His muscles shook as if he were swimming in bone marrow soup. He knew Youngchul must have felt even worse. Yet he joked with Jae and Taeho about Cow's noxious farts, boosting their spirits. Sangchul sucked his teeth. What they should have been doing was strategizing: Youngchul would turn seventeen at the end of June. Less than two months, and the path forward remained hazy.

As Teacher headed to the front gates, Cow and Crow divided the field. Their group had only four boys to Crow's six, but they would be responsible for the same loads. "We'll be at the trucks timing you." Crow pointed to his watch.

"You'll have to work faster to catch up," Cow said.

Crow slung an arm around Cow's shoulders, his muscled weight toppling his slighter partner. "That's right, now let's go." He jeered about the new additions as they left, wondering if anyone had seen the mother, if she was pretty or strange or both.

Jae and Sangchul hefted five logs each, moving slowly to give the others time. Jae was sinewy, sturdy like Sangchul, while Taeho was scrawny, not grown into himself, and Youngchul, well, athletics didn't suit him. Cutting through the heart of the field, the dirt path and trees, they rounded Big House to the front. Despite the weight, Sangchul jolted at the view. Two trucks, parked at the mouth of a paved road that curved downhill. The glass-topped wall. Beyond, the swaying gold-green barley.

Teacher sat to the side, reading a newspaper. His spring-loaded baton flat across his lap. Rumor had it Teacher had stolen the baton from a Japanese officer as a youth, though no one dared ask if that was true. Cow whistled from his truck.

"Come on." Youngchul dumped his logs onto the flatbed and helped Taeho unload.

"Do you think she could be from my hometown?" Taeho asked Youngchul.

"Who, the new ones?" Cow asked.

"You think they're from your hometown?" Crow's voice veered high. He jumped from his truck into Cow's. "Maybe Warden will open the gates and she'll take you with her." He grabbed Taeho's hand. "Say it: *I'm so dumb.*"

Taeho winced as he smacked himself across the face. "I'm so dumb."

"Again."

"I'm so dumb."

Crow laughed, releasing the grating squawk that gave him his name, his voice a contrast to his thick, muscled form. Teacher rustled his paper. Sangchul swallowed his spit. The Keepers were pathetic, sucking satisfaction from these small acts of power.

"All right, they're my boys," Cow protested.

Crow landed one more cuff across Taeho's ear. Cow shrugged. He was the dumbest of them, a lumbering dope with a chin dimple and round eyes. Sangchul didn't understand how he had become Keeper.

"They're the idiots," Jae said, when they were at a safe-enough distance, returning to the field. "I'll find out where the new ones are from, Taeho."

"There's a chance," Youngchul said, stoking a hope that would have been better extinguished. He wrapped his arm around Taeho. "You were right to ask."

"Probably not." Sangchul moved between them. Taeho was naive, a sheltered only son who had grown up well off, unlike the rest of them. While visiting extended family, he had been teased into drinking soju until he was frayed, wandering the streets, easy prey. It irked Sangchul, how simply he saw the world. "Even if they were from your hometown, what would that change?"

Taeho sucked his cheek. "I was only wondering."

"We all were," Youngchul said softly.

"Do you think they've figured this place out?" Taeho asked.

Everyone had their stories. On their first night, Sangchul, Youngchul, and drunken Taeho had slid their hands across the walls of their room, searching for a secret exit. It was Jae who had intervened, coaxing them to their cots. Jae had arrived three months before, he explained. Kicked out of his home and on the streets for a week before the police caught him. The rules here shifted, he said, but the most important was to be unobtrusive.

Sangchul always imagined the new ones' first nights, how quickly the reality of the Home cast their truth in clear light. A month ago, a new boy had tried to escape during Morning Run. Before they'd gotten to learn his name, he'd sprinted to the front gates. Mosquito caught him halfway down the drive; he was Head Keeper for a reason—merciless, especially when his position was in danger. He cracked his bat against the boy's shins, knees, the frail bones of his face. If there was a Keeper whom Sangchul hated more than Rat, that traitor who had arrived with them and immediately clambered to Keeper status, it was Mosquito.

And that poor boy. Warden had sent him straight to Chapel. It would have been better if he had tripped and broken his neck.

Teacher whistled, a sustained call for the two groups to take their five-minute break. The boys dropped their logs right there at the edge of the field. Sangchul heaved, his back tight enough to splice, the undersides of his arms raw and tender. The blood beneath singing.

"Six." Jae pointed, and they searched. There, at the base of Youngchul's favorite tree, with branches like a blown umbrella revealing its skeleton, a cicada clung to the near-black bark. Its shell split down the middle, the pale brown nymph wriggling within.

"Looks like the last molt." Taeho knelt on the ground, giddy like a child much younger than fourteen. "I love maemis."

It was defenseless, hunched and vulnerable and in the middle of transformation. "Where are the others? Don't they move in broods?" Sangchul asked.

"Maybe he's a loner like you," Youngchul teased.

"A leader like me, you mean," Sangchul said, though that made them laugh. Youngchul was their head, despite his gentleness. It was that electric pull, that current, his belief in the goodness of others, that he used to harness them together.

"It's a sign that summer's coming," Jae said. "Already too hot for spring."

"The maemis will drive us mad." Sangchul hated the way they buzzed the brain.

The whistle blew. The boys gathered their logs. As they returned to the front, they searched for other maemis, the round holes they made as they escaped the earth.

"Seven," Jae said, hours or minutes later. A beetle. He was the best at this game, trained for any slight movement in the dirt.

Sangchul was better at locating the birds. Follow the call, search the blue or gray or white above for a shift in texture. There. A wing. A creature in flight.

EUNJU

The boys left behind a fetid scent, the stench of their sweat yellowing the air. Something cracked after Breakfast, the easy camaraderie among the women dissolved, replaced by a jagged quiet, sharp-edged and discontented. Umma washed alongside Ajumma Lee, elbow-deep in gray water. I followed with stacked trays, but I felt Bora's and Areum's stares from the drying station. Spiky pricks, as if I were a found insect, defenseless and exposed. "I know you're talking about me," I said in my loudest voice.

Ajumma Lee sniffed. "She's a mouthy one."

Umma gave her a slip of a frown. "You seem like a childless woman."

Ajumma Lee reared, her tiny teeth snarled. "You said you were caught at a bar, didn't you?"

"Were you a hostess?" Bora widened her eyes before smacking her lips into a twisty laugh.

I stepped closer, my distaste flipping between them. *Bora* was the mouthy one. I had heard her mocking my scrambled accent, my mixed-blood mother. Her insults were lumbering, and still Areum laughed. I'd even seen Mina smirk.

Areum spoke to Bora, ignoring me. "Maybe it won't happen this time."

"What won't happen?" I turned to Nabi and Mina. They shifted, preoccupied with their greasy knuckles.

Halmoni shushed us, her head cocked—the sound of the front door unlocking. "He's here." She nodded to Umma and me. "Dry your hands."

The wood-beaded curtain clacked as we walked through, but I caught the girls whispering, Bora's smug *See?* and someone else's assent. Halmoni led us down the aisle to Warden. Up close, he looked old, with grooved pores and stained teeth. Muddy featured, his moods controlling the workings of his face. The top of his shirt was unbuttoned, revealing a damp, spotted throat. A gold chain, a swinging cross. He didn't hold a baton or have Teacher's height, but my spine tightened as we sat before him.

He examined Umma, his gaze raking her hair, her bared neck. Too keen, too coiled. His breath heavy and strained. "We are a welfare center for wayward boys, but we have space for the most vagrant women." He sneered. "Mixed-blood scavengers."

I shoved my hands beneath my thighs. "We don't want to be here."

"A prostitute and a bastard child. Sinners." He made the sign of the cross like a man who believed his words. Umma had taught me—that type was the most dangerous.

Still, I couldn't help myself. "You don't know us," I said.

He caught my chin—the tender give beneath my jaw. He pulled me like a drawer, and I jolted to the edge of my seat, a gasp tearing out of me. "Halmoni, the shears," he said.

"I'll get them." Her voice weak. She was diminished, only a Keeper.

Warden let go. He had hurt me, and Umma sat in silence. I bit down on my words. Held in the heat behind my eyes, refusing to touch, feel if he had broken skin. *Shears.* He would cut us into pieces, have Halmoni cook us into a soup. Shred our clothes. Sever our tongues and wear them as a necklace.

Halmoni returned. "I can cut their hair, Warden. You must be busy."

I twitched. "Our hair?"

He smiled. "You are the property of the Stone Home now."

"We'll start with you first." Halmoni repositioned Umma at the foot of the bench, and I waited—for Umma's rage, her resistance.

She folded her hands in her lap, and it was only after Halmoni lopped off a sheet that she finally spoke. "My daughter's right. We don't want to be reformed."

Warden pushed Halmoni aside, and I watched his hand rise. The slap a hot noise. Umma jerked, her hair swinging like an uneven dress.

I tried to stand, but Umma—her voice rose: "No."

"That's right, you tell her to shut up," Warden said. "Mixed-blood filth." He slapped me too, the sound a bubble in my ears, an unexpected relief as Umma struggled to stand, Halmoni holding her back. Spit, in the corners of his lips. "Do you want to end up like your mother, girl? Without my help, you will, naked in a shack with men between your legs."

With that, he left.

"Eunju," Umma said, her voice a flicker.

I lifted my chin, as I had seen her do. "It didn't hurt. See?"

She wrapped her arms around me, but I wriggled out of her grasp. I wouldn't cry, not with the whisperings from the kitchen rising like a tide. "How long until we're released?" Umma demanded, her gaze on Halmoni hard and dark, the way I knew her.

"I've been here since the start." Halmoni held up her shears. "Three years."

I hinged forward, clutched my sides. Three years was too long, time I couldn't gather in my mind. The sounds of cutting. The clink of the shears landing on the table. I looked up to see Umma, bobbed above her ears. She touched the blunt ends. My mother was vain, and I loved that about her.

"We can't stay," she said.

"I know it, and still, here I am." Halmoni came to me next. My hair was short already, chin-length to avoid tangle. She parted my strands. "Lice. We'll have to do a full shave. Nabi! Get the clippers from the closet."

"We can kill them with vinegar," Umma said.

"Can't risk that lice getting to all of us." Halmoni scissored by my ear. A crisp, metallic sound. A prickly rainfall. The clippers came next, buzzing my skull until my teeth chattered.

"There." Halmoni leaned back. "It's not so bad."

I didn't want to see what I looked like. A monk. A leper. One of the boys. "Do I get to run instead of cook?" I joked.

Umma grazed my head as if I were a broken egg. "My girl."

"Halmoni." I touched her arm. "We haven't done anything wrong."

She palmed my crown. "You talk too much. Kyungoh, return to the kitchen. Eunju, you'll help Mina clean the cafeteria."

Before Umma trailed Halmoni, she knelt in front of me. I wanted to tell her our hair would grow back, it was a useless part of our bodies anyway. I wanted to ask how Warden knew about us, and if he had the power to imprison us. She pinched a cut strand. "Give me your wrist." She tied the thin black line into a bracelet. "So we remember who we are."

While Mina unearthed dustpans from the supply closet, I peered through the barred windows by the entrance. The same dirt path, abundant pines. "There's a field past the trees. Three Workshops on the far side. Is it true, what he said about your mother?" Mina whispered the last words. "She's really a prostitute?"

A gray bird hopped across a branch. It was scenic here, empty and quiet and green. The bird spread its wings and took flight toward Big House, cresting on a gust of wind. Umma—she took on whatever job she needed, and sometimes, it was with men. "Does it matter?" I asked.

"Ajumma Lee thinks so." Mina shoved a broom at me. "Take this."

I thought I heard yelling, a scream pitching higher. "Do you hear them?"

"It's probably Crow. His group is doing fieldwork." Mina whistled in my ear, her breath startling against my cold, shaved head. "Better?"

I touched the back of my neck, the shorn hair prickling my palm. Mina hadn't warned me about Warden. Still, I felt a heat in my chest at her attention, her crumbly low voice. I hadn't had a friend in years, my life tightly honed to Umma, our ways of surviving. I squinted at the field. "Why the Keeper nicknames?" I asked.

Mina laughed, soft. "You seem smart enough to figure that out."

I nodded, sadness streaking through me, the slurs we'd whisper among ourselves such paltry retribution. "Why are you being nice?"

Mina cracked her neck as I followed her back to the cafeteria. "The first week is the hardest. Warden wants to put new arrivals in their place. We don't get naked in the room every morning either. It's just ritual, for the newcomers. I know it doesn't seem like it, but we're better off than the boys. Here, sweep the hair and I'll wipe the tables."

"Where are you from?" I asked.

"Gangneung. It was my fault." Mina spritzed cleaning solution. "They caught me at the bus station. I was going to hairdresser school. I wanted to be a lady."

I gripped the broom. "They can't keep us here."

She rubbed a few grains off a tabletop. "Remember, if you see any food, you eat it."

I gathered our cut hair into the dustpan's mouth. Mina hummed. We would eat every day. We wouldn't have to rub dirt off our arms with our own saliva. I wouldn't have to beg women who hitched their noses at us. Umma wouldn't have to sell tteok and limp vegetables at the side of the road, disappear with men whose eyes were too empty for their faces.

Mina watched Umma as we returned to the kitchen. "They don't like the weak ones."

"Who's they?"

"Everyone. Us."

"She's strong," I said.

Mina handed me a crumpled napkin we'd found caught beneath a bench, millet grains stuck on white paper. I peeled the sticky smear off with my fingernail and slipped it into my mouth. "Good girl," she said.

• • •

All day, we chopped, seasoned, scrubbed. From her corner between the pantry and the stove, Halmoni considered a small calendar, shouted orders, complained about stretching the spinach to last three days. The work a slow drain that surprised me, wiping questions from my mind. The depth of exhaustion unclear until I bent over the bathroom sink and found my fingernails throbbing. In the bedroom we shared, I dropped into my cot, my face still wet. Mina's cot was in the first row, beside Bora and Areum. I tried not to look their way.

"Eunju." Umma spoke low, beneath the current of the others' talk. "We need to leave."

I stopped. All day, I had watched as she had. There were no unlocked doors, no amount of time when we weren't monitored. "How?"

She crouched with her elbows on her knees, as if the curve of her spine could protect me. "Keepers don't have keys, Halmoni only has the one to this room."

"Teacher has them all," I said. "Warden too."

"We need to find their weakness. Hawk eyes. Sink our anger until we know more."

The wrinkle between her brows. Her chin cupped in one hand. My mind a jumble.

"I should have, I'm sorry for—" she started.

"We got two meals today. I made a friend." I nudged closer so she could stroke my hair, then remembered I was shaved.

She ran her fingers along my scalp. "You don't want to stay here any more than I do." She pressed into the tender spots at the backs of my ears, where the lobes connected. "You don't need to protect me, Eunju."

"They think you're soft," I said.

"You think I don't know?" For the first time all day, she smiled. "We use that foolishness to our strength. Until then, we eat. Sleep. Figure out the workings of this place."

I pressed into her touch. She knew me, and I her. Her fury had once thrown a man onto his back. Burned the hair off a street vendor who'd cheated us. She was a protector, a winged woman.

She was my mother, and she would get us out.

2011

Narae stares at her fingernails, the irregular grain tentacling across my wooden table. Her tea cup drained, leaves clumped in their strainer. Behind her, the sun casts its smoky orange glow. Hours have passed, and I have only begun. *I don't understand how they could keep you locked up.* She shakes her head. *How was this enforced?*

I rise, pluck chamoes from the fridge. *Outside the walls, there was violence. Inside the walls, there was violence.*

What are you talking about?

It was 1980, I say, thinking that will be enough, but this woman, her mind is made of the United States, and she knows nothing of our history. *Park Chung-hee was assassinated the year before. Chun Doo-hwan staged a coup. The Gwangju Massacre began as we settled into the Home.*

A massacre?

Umma and I didn't hear of the killings, and yet we felt their current. The smokescreen and rumors within the Home a reflection of what was happening throughout our Korea.

Tell me what happened to my father. Tell me in a way I'll understand, Narae says. As if time is not folding in on itself around us.

I peer out the window at a line of children holding on to one another's backpacks. The neighbor's daughter, her pigtails swinging. *Your father was worried about his hyung. He cared for Youngchul*, I say, wanting to be kind.

I didn't even know he had a brother, Narae responds, bitter.

What does it mean, to construct another's story? There is what he told me, and there are the gaps. The stories I harbor and the ones I am unraveling with time.

EUNJU

Two weeks passed, and still everything felt askew, the walls slanting around us. Umma and I tried the locks of Little House, memorized the order of the hours; there was no gap for us to slip through, the Home securely seamed. Fourteen days, checked against Halmoni's calendar. Fourteen days, and a peculiar current infused the air, not from the late-May heat or the recent thunderstorms, but from the women. Their barbed words spreading through me like a stain.

"Sometimes I wonder if Kyungoh even understands us." Ajumma Lee laughed, her seedy voice traveling the kitchen. "She's the product of a yanggongju, after all."

"Forget her." Mina plucked the stems off the mushrooms I plopped onto the counter, her cheeks reddening as if she were the one insulted. I snorted. We smelled like the earth, all soil and fungal damp, and this was supposed to be better than the life we'd lived earlier.

"They don't bother me." I tore my gaze from Bora smirking her way out of the kitchen. Flipped over a white cap and tried to fill its gills with water. My fingertips were pruned, bits of rubbery flesh. Since the first night, Warden's words followed me. *Do you want to end up like your mother, girl?* It was true I had seen a path, hazy, but a line forward, despite Umma's efforts at putting me in school, her promises that I would be different. *Naked in a shack.* So what if I did become like her? Maybe I wanted it, and yet Ajumma Lee's and Bora's sneers confused me.

Mina sighed. "I have to help Nabi. Can you wash the fruit?"

Alone, I dunked my hands into the sink, scoured red strawberries. *With men between your legs.*

Ajumma Lee laughed again. "Those yanggongju filing into military camps! My mother spat at those girls, and now look at the company I have to keep."

No matter what Ajumma Lee said, Umma only concentrated on her work. This ploy of allowing others to speak her name into the ground, it accomplished nothing, I wanted to shout. I squeezed, bumpy seeds bruising.

"The day can feel so slow," Areum said as she came to rip the green tops off the washed fruit. I eyed her in silence, startled. She passed me a berry when Halmoni turned her back, and despite myself, I nibbled the sour flesh. "Better than Teacher checking on us. Trust me."

I fumbled for a clever comment. Before I could speak, Bora returned from the bathroom. She'd claimed to be sick for the third time this week. "You must have a frail stomach," I called out.

"Wash these next." Bora thrust a basket of chopsticks at me. "Or do they seem clean enough to you?"

"I've got my own tasks," I said, sucking my teeth.

"She's your elder. You don't get to use the casual form with us," Areum said, turning stern, as if her muscled presence would change my mind, and for a second, I wavered. The white line above her eye, her compact form. The way she moved so surely. She was striking, this unnie who had spoken to me kindly only a moment ago.

"She's not my Keeper," I said, softer than I expected.

"Do you think you're special because of *her*?" Bora dumped the chopsticks into my sink. "There are no men here for her to influence."

I turned to Areum, the pressure behind my temples quickening. "Bora's pretending to be sick to shirk her work." My voice veered high, contemptuous. "She's fooling you."

When Areum spoke again, her voice was quiet. "You don't understand what's happening, Eunju."

"Forget it," Bora said, so close I could feel her breath on the back of my neck. "What else should we expect? She's the bastard of a half-breed prostitute."

I charged, her name a ripple in my mouth, my hands against her gut, a fast straight drive, but Halmoni came between us, suddenly and all at once. "Not in this kitchen." When I growled through bared teeth, she let go, like I wasn't worth the effort. "Kyungoh," she called. "Leash your daughter before I put her down myself."

I walked out of the kitchen. The women screeched, not caring that I could hear—about how mannerless I was, untamed and crude and wild. Yes, I wanted to shout, I was all of those things, and shouldn't they have embraced me? Hadn't Mina said they hated the weak ones? "They're the kind this place was built for," Ajumma Lee said.

I whipped around, the desire to collapse my hands into someone's body coursing through me again. Umma yanked me into the closet by the stairs, squeezed us between brooms and plastic jugs of vinegar. "What's wrong with you?"

"I was defending us." I narrowed my eyes. "What's wrong with *you*?"

She grabbed me, her nails piercing the tender skin behind my ears. "You don't talk to me that way."

I pushed harder into her grip. Let her hurt me. At least I would know there was fierceness still in her, that this was truly an act.

"I didn't raise you to be cruel," she said. "We don't strike someone weaker than us."

"They think *we're* the weak ones. You let them bad-mouth

and—" I looked away, the heat behind my eyes teeming. I searched for a truth, for the stone that would hurt her the most. "I don't want to end up like you. A whore. Naked in a shack like some used rag."

She released me, her shoulders collapsing as if I'd plucked out her spine in one clean move.

"It's not decent." My voice wavering, more fragile than I wanted. "You hid that from me, you made me believe what you did was work like anything else."

I waited for her to hit me, throw a dustpan in my direction. Instead, she pointed to her feet.

I kneeled, flinching as she grabbed my head, but she only stroked my scalp, the buzz of hair I had grown in the last two weeks. "Seeing us reminds them they're alone. They're jealous. Ajumma Lee was kicked out of her home for having an affair. Why do you react to her plain hurt?"

"How do you know that?" I asked, fingering her shirt.

"Control," Umma commanded. "You make it harder, for no reason but pride."

I rolled up her sleeves, revealing pale wrists. A dark bruise. "When did you get this?"

"You're angry with me," she said, pushing my hands away. "I'm protecting you, even if it may not seem like it. That's what we need to focus on. You trust me?"

Between us, her voice had regained its strength. Still, her expression from moments before flared through me. The hurt in her gaped mouth as I had called her indecent. I kissed the round bone of her wrist that jutted out like a pearl of barley. The women confused me, with their talk skirting shame, their spit-laden words. I believed Umma. I wanted to, at least.

SANGCHUL

Pain like a viney weed choked through Sangchul as Teacher hit him across the ribs, calves, thighs. Sangchul retched. A rope of green bile. He palmed the hallway floor outside their room, but his elbows buckled. Hurriedly, Youngchul and Jae raised him to his knees, and he clasped his hands, the bones in his body wrung by a ghost and pieced back together with rice glue, spit. He knew what to say. "Forgive me, Teacher."

"When you defend a corrupt one, you are corrupt also," Teacher snarled. Minutes before, he had pulled them out of the line for Morning Washup without explanation. Clawed at Taeho's sleeve, revealing a tumble of cigarettes. He turned to Taeho now. "Pick them up, #26."

Taeho scraped and cupped the contraband like an offering. Snot running down his face. Annoyance flared through Sangchul's ribs. Taeho cried freely, without shame, when he got in trouble, and yet Teacher only flicked open his baton for Sangchul.

"Did you injure yourself?" Teacher asked, his voice thin and level, his final words so laughable in these exchanges, as if their answers provided absolution.

Taeho and Sangchul shook their heads. "No, sir."

Teacher sighed, suddenly looking tired of them, the effort it took to crush their spirits. He lurched to Youngchul and Jae, crammed against the wall as commanded. "You know what kind of stick this is? A tokushu keibo. I picked it out myself when I was in Japan. That's right, while you have never left this country, I have—more than once—and here I am with you." He perched his baton against the hollow between Youngchul's collarbones. "You disappoint me, #28."

"Sir?" Youngchul asked, his voice shallow.

"You may never see your brother again, and yet you act the same," Teacher said.

Youngchul squeezed his thumb and forefinger together, and Sangchul shut his eyes, unexpectedly wanting the vibration of Teacher's baton against his legs, if that meant he'd leave hyung alone. His seventeenth birthday, coming in five weeks. "I know what you're insinuating," Youngchul started. "I'm reforming, sir. I'm—"

Teacher groaned. "Do you think meeting quota is enough?" He grasped Youngchul's throat, gentle, with control, before releasing him. "I'll be watching. Act like the elder you are."

They gathered around Taeho as soon as Teacher left, as if Sangchul hadn't been the one beaten and Youngchul hadn't been threatened with his leaving for the first time. "You need to stop falling for Dal's requests," Youngchul said gently to Taeho, because even without explanation they knew it was that thick-necked squealer who had conned him.

Sangchul tunneled his forehead into his hands and spoke into the floor. "I won't defend you next time. I'm sick of Teacher beating me for your mistakes."

"Sangchul," Jae chided, turning back at him. "That's cruel."

It had been Sangchul who'd stepped in to take the worst of the blame. Not hyung or Jae. Yet Youngchul was their leader, Jae their intel gatherer, and what did that leave for him? Their dumb might?

"I didn't mean to get anyone in trouble." Taeho, snub-nosed and yielding, hated confrontation. "Dal hurts me if I say no."

A flicker of anger—a feeling that fit the contours of Sangchul's body more easily. Dal was a leader of a group of squealers who traded Rat secrets for cigarettes and turned back to sell them for favors. A boy who blinked too often behind sliding glasses, as though he were entering from dark to light. "If Dal bothers you again, ask me for help," Sangchul said. He grinned, an idea coming to him. "I'll show him."

He quickly found Dal's shirt in their shared dorm room and returned to the clump of vomit in the hallway, its sticky, sharp scent of bile. He gathered the green mush with the squealer's shirt, laughing as Taeho cackled, excited, but Youngchul grabbed the ruined top from him. "Dal isn't our problem," hyung said.

Sangchul snorted. This was what irked him about hyung, how he thought the world would adjust to his views, that ignoring anger could cure it.

Youngchul sighed, exasperated, as Mosquito blew a whistle from the bathroom. The signal for Service. "Get in line. I'll put the shirt back."

Throughout Service and Morning Run that day, Sangchul didn't speak. The pain was a good excuse. At Breakfast, he limped through the line, his legs gnawed to the bone. Warden rounded the cafeteria, stopped beside Dal, and spoke into his ear.

"Maybe he'll get in trouble," Taeho said.

Jae dropped his gosari namul into Taeho's bowl, and Sangchul felt a streak of jealousy at his generosity. He pushed his calves against the bench's legs, the pain almost thrilling. He had rolled up his pants to peek before they'd sat down—the blood was already pooling beneath the skin, a dark sticky color.

"Here, you need the energy to heal." Youngchul picked out a

chunk of flaky fish and set it in his brother's bowl. It was a peace offering, food the only way they knew how to apologize. Hyung had been distant all morning, and Sangchul hoped he felt guilty for not stepping in earlier, for believing he could appeal to Teacher's compassion. Sangchul ate the fish in one bite.

"Looks like Warden's coming this way," Jae said, below his breath.

Warden caught Sangchul's head, the heat of his soft palm unexpected and alarming. "I heard what happened, #27. You're resilient, intelligent. A good worker. Don't waste your strength on those who are weaker."

Sangchul shifted, his birthmark flaring. Embarrassment opened up in him, how pleased he felt at Warden's words, though he wouldn't ever admit it, though it was only for a moment. Despite everything. The pleasure a viscous honeyed feeling in his stomach.

"I told your Keeper to give you five extra minutes at Evening Washup." Warden spoke loudly, enough to carry to the tables around them, acting as a salve to Teacher's outbursts.

When Warden departed, Sangchul felt a coldness coil in his stomach. Youngchul, stiff beside him. The others, avoiding his gaze. He knew: Warden revealed the parts of himself he disliked, and in doing so, he made him foul to his friends. "I hate him," Sangchul said.

"It doesn't mean anything, that he came to you." Jae reached for him across the table.

"He's a liar," Youngchul said. "Acting like he's the generous one when he controls us."

Sangchul stared at his soup, an empty clamshell at the bottom of his bowl. What did it matter if he was strong, or a good worker, when his brother was right?

EUNJU

All day, Bora claimed she was sick, that my shove aggravated her nausea. When we trekked to Big House to clean the boys' floors, Halmoni tasked her with wiping the showers while I was given the toilets covered in flies, dead and alive. My punishment, even if Halmoni didn't say so.

The stink of shit still coated my nostrils as I scrubbed my hands during Evening Washup. I raised my stained, grimy nails to Umma. "I'm disgusting."

"After all your complaining about the kitchen," she goaded. "Didn't you say you liked going over to Big House?"

I scoured harder, pushed my thumb beneath the nails, trying to ignore the girls soaping together at the other end of the bathroom. Black grit crumbled into the sink. "That was before," I said. The initial thrill of being in Big House while the boys were in Workshops, of entering their private space and searching for a way out, had worn off. Big House was more closely monitored with Teacher's and Warden's constant presence. Cleaning the boys' bathrooms, with their rolls of dead skin and stray pubic hairs, only another weekly chore.

"Sullen girl." Umma toweled her cheeks. "I'm going in."

Even she had been stony today, though I had apologized, said I believed her promise. I watched her leave. By the door, Mina pointed to a beauty mark on her left breast, making the others laugh. Little Nabi jumped on her toes, her desire to be part of their conversation so obvious. I turned off the faucet. Slivers of white soap, anemic half-moons, sat in a milky puddle. At least I wasn't Nabi. At least I didn't mind being alone.

"Eunju," Halmoni called from the showers, where she squatted on a plastic stool, her breasts hanging like gourds. She motioned to the washcloth on her dimply knees. "Help me."

I caught glimpses in the mirror as I walked over. My flushed cheeks. My flat chest and hairless body. My shorn head. Even Halmoni felt bad for me.

"Sit," she commanded.

I soaped the cloth and rubbed it across her goiter, which was firm and smooth, and instead of repulsing me, I felt a tenderness as I washed it for the first time. Halmoni stared at her shaking hands. "Are you in pain?" I asked.

She clenched and unclenched, her palms a ruddy flash as if she were holding a crab, an apple. "Scrub harder. You don't need to be afraid."

I rubbed around the bulge and into her neck creases, where sweat collected in gray rolls. "I don't care if I'm alone," I said.

She snorted. "We need each other. I've learned that much at my age." I pulled the washcloth down to her hips in rhythmic strokes. "Three years, and still a vagrant." She laughed, mostly to herself. "If they say I'm rehabilitated, they'll have to train someone else, and they know no one will take me with this growth."

"What about me? I'm still young." I made circles beneath her shoulders. The girls had left, and in the silence, I heard Halmoni sigh.

"When you cause trouble, it makes it difficult for your mother. She has enough to manage. Is it so hard to be obedient?" She craned her neck at me. "It's better here in some ways, isn't it?"

Some days, we had slept on street corners, beneath store eaves,

Umma's eyes rolling in their sockets, the funk of hemp and a cottony feeling invading my mind. Here, we slept on cots. Here, we had a rhythm to our days. We weren't beaten like the boys. Mina told me Park Chung-hee himself had sanctioned this place. He was dead, a dictator, a president. He had been educated. I was nobody's daughter. What did I know? But Umma and I, we had eaten and woken when we wanted. When we had enough money, we rented a room of our own. On my tenth birthday, we slept on our warm ondol floor until noon, and she treated us to soda and ramen, and we had walked into a department store. She had bought me a sweater. Gray with a colored argyle pattern that I had thought made me look grown-up, proper.

Studying my feet, I asked Halmoni, "What does it matter if she was a prostitute?"

"Gossip tucks itself into corners." She tugged my earlobe gently. "We come in with our ways of surviving. I don't blame anyone for that, but some don't approve of her methods."

I shook her away. "I hate this place."

She heeled a knot of muscle beneath my wing bone. "When I can't stand the idea of dying here, I remember the ugliness outside."

I closed my eyes, and that night came to me—when I was eleven, when we'd had our own room for more than a year. Umma's taut voice, telling me to get dressed. "As many layers as you can." As I put on three pairs of underwear, pants over my pajamas, a shirt, that argyle sweater, now too tight, Umma grabbed our one kitchen knife. A sharp-edged wing. Then, I heard him. A man raging at the door—our only way out. The handle breaking, a beast coming in, stinking of alcohol and power. "Run." Her only word. Too scared. I couldn't leave without her. "Now," she yelled, as the man came. His fists. Umma slashed the air until blade touched skin. Then we were fleeing, red on her face and hands, on me too. Beneath my nails, the blood looked black.

"She's put you in danger," Halmoni said, staring at me, intent.

I tried to smooth my face into blankness. It was unlike me to misstep, to reveal the porcelain under the glaze. "No," I said. "She protects me." I was Umma's burden. She had hurt a man for me, taken care of me, put me in school whenever she could. She hadn't cast me out, as her grandparents had to her mother, pregnant with a white man's seed. She was mine, and I hers.

"Dip forward," Halmoni said.

I tucked my chin to my chest, and she washed my head beneath the faucet. The water shockingly cold. I wanted to say the women were wrong to judge us, that by ridiculing, they were only diminishing themselves, their shame leaving no room for someone like me, but I couldn't explain it. The words stuck in my throat, all garbled, more feeling than form.

SANGCHUL

Beneath the shower in the evening dark, savoring his five extra minutes, Sangchul tracked the purple borders of new-blooming bruises. Across his ribs, rivering down his coarsening pubic hair, to his thighs and calves. The tender parts of his back. If only he were home, where his mother could have rolled a warm egg over his skin, pulling out the pain. No, they didn't speak of home here. They didn't think of it.

As he returned to his cot, Sangchul tried to listen to the passing conversations the way Jae did, gathering information like a bird caches nuts, but his mind wandered to Warden: *Don't waste your strength on those who are weaker.* It was that last cut that bit Sangchul with shame. He wanted to understand what made it clear that he was capable of callousness. He pulled back his sheets, still trying to shake Warden's praise, when Dal's shirt fell from the foot of his cot. Crusted with vomit, stiff around the collar. "What's this?" he asked, though he understood immediately. Hyung.

Youngchul remained supine, his voice stern. "It's your vomit."

Sangchul shook. "You couldn't let me get back at Dal?"

"It's my stupid fault," Taeho called from his top bunk, his knees to his chest. Jae shifted above them too, silent and watchful.

"It's not about you," Sangchul nearly shouted. He trembled,

hating how hyung refused to see the boulder tumbling toward them. His chest tight, he pushed out the words: "Do you really want to leave me behind?"

Youngchul squeezed his fingers together.

"Well?" Sangchul asked, fiercer this time. "The way you're acting, you're going to end up being transferred to an adult institution."

Slowly, Youngchul rose. "I want to stay here with you."

Sangchul crumpled Dal's shirt, the crusted vomit releasing its odor between them. "Then stop acting like you're better than me." He wanted to sound harsh, but even he could hear the desperation, the grasping. There was only one way to remain, but to want it, to work for it—he leaned his forehead on his brother's knees, feeling a liquid surging within, spilling before he could catch himself. "We're not home anymore, hyung."

Youngchul pushed himself back, a huff deflating his chest. It was true, though, and it was time for hyung to hear. They had never spoken of their parents' undiluted favor of him. A black pool from which Sangchul lapped at the edges.

"They thought you were immaculate," Sangchul continued. "It's because of you that we're here. You're the one who didn't run fast enough, who told the cops we were guilty for something we didn't do. You're responsible."

He'd said it, the truth. So why did he feel a pit caverning between them? Ice, from their friends above, from hyung. Sangchul shut his eyes, and he felt Youngchul shift. Then, a weary drip of words: "You think I don't hate myself? But what can I do, brother? I'm not like you."

Sangchul returned to his bed, those words cracking harsher than any of Teacher's blows. He rolled onto his stomach and shoved his head into his pillow. Concentrated on his ribs, puckered with pain, as if sewn together all wrong, skin rubbing skin. Anything to avoid the sweep inside him: disbelief, sour agony.

• • •

The click of a knob. The door, unlocking. Keepers. The boys' ears pricked at the sound, hackles raised, like hounds, alert on entry.

Silence weighed them down as the others, their twins in purpose, cried and held on to their selves. Some Keepers beat with a ruthless need, faceless beneath masks, though over time, Sangchul guessed who they were, based on scent, height, predilection. Mosquito. Crow. Sometimes, Rat.

The burst of pain behind the eyes at the shock, the hitch in your lungs as the air flattened through you, your head pushed into a pillow already soaked with sweat. The praying praying praying that it will stop, you will not die, you will die. Floating into the sky, the blue-black ether.

They had all been beaten, at one point or another. But a deeper terror snaked through Sangchul—sometimes, the Keepers dragged one out. Those boys always begged. Always, they were silent when returned, clutching their waistbands with a new caginess. Never comforted, never looked in the eyes when the sun broke through the windows, though the haunting would linger on their bodies, the stench of violation coming from their skins. What happened out there, Sangchul didn't want to find out.

He heard someone approach. The white bat, its rubbery smell, rattling against his cot. Quickly, he pulled on the sullied shirt. The stink of vomit a wish, an armor, another kind of protection.

2011

Was there any goodness? Sunset bands Narae with stripes. Her linen dress is wrinkled, and I lace my fingers to stop myself—from touching her arm, asking her to sit. She must be thirty years old now. She seems a child.

Tomorrow, I will have to go in to my shift at the restaurant. Tomorrow, I might never see her again. *How long will you stay in Korea?* I start to say.

How did you know about me? She cuts me off, and I feel the room shift. A wetness hits my face, a gyring wave. She narrows her eyes. *Were you in contact with him?*

Sangchul told me he gave you up, I say, betraying him. My old instinct to preserve myself rising to the surface. *He lied to me.*

What do you mean? Narae asks. *When did you see him?*

I pull at my earlobes. *Last winter, at the hospital.* The words crumble like sand.

I know I should be grateful. Our meeting now is only possible because Sangchul called me, because I flew to New York on a glacial morning, because I sat by his side and listened. Yet I think of the time she and I have lost, my fury its own mania. I collect the dregs of our teas and dump them in the compost.

How? she demands.

You asked if there was any goodness. I tilt the room further. I can tell her—how everything changed the day I met those four boys and their laughter. *Will you come back tomorrow? So I can tell you about Pentecost, your father?*

EUNJU

Despite the rising heat, the air around us felt loose, gauzy, the clouds feathery against a bright sky. "It's the best day of the year," Halmoni shouted as she surveyed our makeshift counter. It was Pentecost, the one holiday when Warden allowed a picnic feast, and for the first time since my arrival three weeks before, we would have a meal beneath the sun. The winds shifted, scented by the meat we had browned at dawn, the miyeok we had simmered in broth. The trace on my hands, lifting from my skin. The boys jostled between two narrow tables set on the grass, their smiles revealing dimples and pallid teeth.

Mina tiptoed as she dumped mixed barley rice into bowls, scanning those waiting their turn. All morning, she'd been distracted. "Who're you looking for?" I asked, surprised at the ease in my voice. "A boy?"

A laugh tumbled out of her. "No one you know." The surprise hit me in the chest: that she could have feelings here, even in this place. A grin split my teeth, and Mina elbowed me. "I won't reveal a thing."

"Your cheeks will betray you," I teased, a new warmth filling me. I'd never bantered with her so effortlessly, with Areum and Bora smirking along.

"Look at them acting like kings," Areum chided, motioning to

Warden and Teacher. On a straw mat beneath the shaded trees, the men devoured the san-nakji we'd prepared. A few meters away, the Keepers' table had been laid out with their own vat of miyeokguk, banchan, juice.

"At least we're not the Chapel boys," I said. On the other side of the field, forced to face us on their knees, those boys were shirtless, arms raised above their heads. They wouldn't receive a thing. No miyeokguk or juice. Not even water. They would fast for our sins, Warden had said.

Bora squinted at me. "Who asked you?"

I sighed loud, exaggerated. "You're so tiresome, unnie."

Mina bit her lip, but Bora seemed satisfied by my use of *unnie*. We watched Teacher rise, a camera in his hands. Snapping photos of boys waiting for the meal to begin, pretending we were a real church community. Mosquito followed, doling out red carnations. Beneath the cicada drones, the scent of seaweed, anchovy, and beef made my mouth water. A sticky pool I spit into the grass.

"Thank you, Mina." A low whisper that stilled even me. We weren't supposed to speak to each other.

"It's o-only rice, oppa," Mina said, her voice sliding down her throat.

I looked up as she colored, her stammering so obvious my stomach twisted too. So, this boy. I recognized him, Youngchul-oppa. He was from Cow's group, tall, not especially striking, with a kindness in his eyes.

"Thank you too," Youngchul said to me.

"Her name's Eunju," Mina offered.

"We know." A stone-faced oppa nudged from behind. "Everyone's waiting."

It was true. They were the last ones, holding up the start of lunch. Cow beckoned, anxiously eyeing the Keepers' table, where the others had gathered without him. Behind the stone-faced boy, another oppa with thick lashes pressed his lips into a slim smile before moving on. "Time to eat," the last one, a gentle boy I recognized as Taeho, said.

As soon as Cow's group sat down, Warden blessed the meal, speaking of the fifty days that passed since Easter, urging us to eat and converse and remember God's grace. He didn't wait for Little House to serve or seat ourselves. Bora sucked her teeth. I wanted to believe it was willful of him, some display of power to exclude us, but he returned to his picnic mat and lay back like an unburdened man. The closer truth was we didn't matter. He burped, and I imagined a chunk of octopus stuck between his teeth, the wet salt scent of his breath.

That morning in Service, Warden had approached one of the Chapel boys, who was crying in a careening, uncontrolled way that made my skin tighten. "I have not forgotten you," Warden said, loud enough for us to hear. I almost wanted to believe him, the blame lacquering his every word. How easy it would be to accept instead of see—he twisted faith without knowing it himself. Our country was full of men like him who believed in their goodness, their worth.

"Never mind Warden." Halmoni sighed, the hurt of being unacknowledged quickening her words. She was our true Christian, after all. "Enjoy the meal you've created, the sun."

I picked a bowl with four chunks of meat, a curl of miyeok. As Mina moved to the table where Bora and Areum were settling, I hooked her elbow to the left, where there was just enough space next to Cow's boys. Panic squealed through her. I pulled, determined. It was a holiday, we were allowed to have some fun. "This is our only chance," I said. "I saw you, eyeing that oppa."

Mina whined, "What would I say?"

I settled beside Youngchul with an unceremonious thump, as if it were natural for us to sit so close. Mina took the seat opposite, beside the stone-faced one.

"Me too." Nabi scooted onto my other side. "The unnies said

I was annoying." She peered at the oppas. "I see you didn't wait for us to eat either."

"The soup's good," Taeho said, rueful and oblivious. "You should eat before it cools."

I slipped my spoon into the bowl, the miyeok gleaming like a handful of clean, dark hair. Glistening dots of sesame oil floated on the surface of the broth. I ate, relishing the near-foreign, ear-tingling taste of meat. The miyeokguk was delicious, fatty and briny and filling.

"We were going to sing 'Happy Birthday,'" Taeho said a few minutes later.

"It was supposed to be a secret," the stone-faced boy said, the grind in his voice clear.

"I'll be seventeen in four weeks," Youngchul acknowledged. "This is my dongsaeng, Sangchul."

"Seventeen?" Mina asked, brows furrowed.

"Does that mean you'll become a Keeper?" I asked.

"We don't know." Sangchul bit his words, his lips shiny. He had a rounder face than his brother, and his ears didn't stick out. A birthmark peeked from beneath his shirt collar, like a wisping cloud. Some boys ate in gulps while others sipped slowly, stretching the meal to its edges. Sangchul was in the first group. His bowl empty besides a slick of oil. Youngchul, in comparison, still had two pieces of meat, a third of his rice untouched. I wondered about them, here for months without figuring a route out; pity swarmed me, they were a warning. Sangchul tugged at his shirt and glared. "What're you staring at?"

"Don't mind him," the quiet, thick-lashed oppa with the delicate face said, his eyes laughing. "I'm Chung Jae, and I bet you're better singers than us."

"That's probably true." Nabi elbowed me for my dureup namul, and I gave her the bitter greens, even without a trade.

"*Happy birthday,*" Taeho began. He smacked his spoon against the bowl's rim, and I smiled, despite myself. I knew his type—gentle, like a new animal, exuding a vulnerability that made people want to take care of him.

We sang along, Taeho leading, confident in the noise around us. Nabi raised her arms in crescendo but knocked into her bowl—a chunk of meat and miyeok spilling onto the grass. She stopped, the cheer draining out of her. "I was saving that."

Youngchul picked the meat from the ground. In his fingers, it looked grotesque, brown and ridged and leaky. "Trade."

"You can have mine, Nabi," Mina offered, too late. Youngchul popped the beef into his mouth, despite the boys' groaning.

"I thought only hyung would be noble enough to give up a perfectly good piece," Jae teased.

Nabi scooped the fallen miyeok before Youngchul could, a long and wet-seeming strand, with a blade of grass that squeaked between her teeth. The groans came again, almost good-natured. Nabi smiled, and I tamped down the suspicion biting at my toes. I didn't know this oppa or his friends, and whatever he wanted in return was something we didn't have. I pulled at my ear. Mina's ease had returned, and she chattered about the early hours of preparing the soup, the slippery feel of miyeok as it plumped in a bowl.

Later, as we opened our juice pouches, Youngchul tried to give Nabi his last bit of rice, but Sangchul swiped the spoon. "Hyung, you need to eat." He didn't acknowledge us, this broad-shouldered younger brother, and when he did, it was only to make Nabi flinch. "Enough for you, little girl."

A sudden knowing passed through me. Sangchul was like me. The truth of how I would have acted looked ugly coming from this other person. I pushed my tray into his. "Who are you to talk to her that way? We have a whole pot of miyeokguk inside. You have nothing compared to us."

I scraped rice into my empty mouth, the giddiness from the morning sapped out of me, leaving me shivering. Raw, prickling, filling with all I'd been trying to ignore for the day—Bora's continued sickness, the flare of glass on top of the wall, unsure if it was true, that I made it harder for Umma with my back talk, if I was the problem that had led us here. Beneath our gratitude was a well too dark and bottomless. How easy it was to please us. We were grateful for an hour in the sun.

SANGCHUL

Glutted, broth sloshed in Sangchul's stomach as they began Workshops. Even with Eunju's terseness, the girls at lunch had been a reprieve from the silence that had burrowed between him and hyung. Ever since their confrontation, Youngchul had been distant, their jokes brittle.

Now, they sat at the rectangular table that columned the center of the Fishhooks room: Taeho and Sangchul on one side, Jae and Youngchul on the other. Cow on the swivel stool by the door, a new comic on his lap. They'd make six hundred hook-and-lines each, group them into piles of ten. Tuck them into slim cardboard packages with Japanese writing on the sides. Sixty packages. If they didn't hit the quota, lashings at Presentations. A simple, inescapable system. Already, Crow's high, squawky voice vibrated through the wall. *Idiot. Faster.* Crow's group were the youngest, no boy over thirteen, a solemn set flattened beneath their Keeper's muscled watch. Some, like Honggi, often dragged out by his Keeper in the night, held a blankness behind their eyes that twisted Sangchul's insides. But Cow had eaten well, which meant they would have an easy day. Erratic and insecure, occasionally he even let them chatter. Sangchul knew he should've been grateful.

Taeho ripped open a box of fishhooks, and they listened to the dry rasp, the tinkling of metal hitting metal. "The girls were nice," he said.

"You could have been kinder to them," Youngchul chided his brother.

Sangchul turned to the snell knots. The pads of his fingers were flat and calloused, the act—of slipping the line through the eye and down the shank, looping five times before pulling the tag end down—its own sort of mind-numbing gift. So, he had been curt. It was stupid of Youngchul to give away his food. The girls worked in the kitchen, surrounded by meat and miyeok, with their easy hours, without the pressure of Presentations.

"Eunju brought Mina to our side." Jae smirked. "I saw them hesitating between the tables."

Youngchul squeezed a hook, sheepish, shoulders hitched to his neck. As if talking to a girl once would erase the fact of this place.

Sangchul worked the acrid taste in his mouth into a pat of phlegm. He imagined hyung staying for her. "We have other matters to worry about. Your birthday?"

"It's out of my control," Youngchul said, organizing his nylon lines and the silver-plated rods he'd bend into hooks. "What do you want me to do?"

Sangchul sucked his teeth. He didn't know, but Youngchul was the elder, and he should have been able to figure a hole in the system, something, anything, so they wouldn't have to spend the next four weeks staring down a fissure, waiting for an unknown creature to devour them whole.

"Shut it." Cow stood, and they tensed as they heard it too—footsteps, the doorknob rattling. Even with a wall between them, they recognized his heavy tread.

"Boys!" Warden entered with outstretched arms, feigning, a jovial uncle. He brushed past Cow, rubbed Taeho's ear as they bowed. "You have met your quotas for the past two weeks."

"Thanks to you for encouraging us, Warden," Cow said.

"Starting tomorrow, you'll be responsible for six-fifty each." Warden paused to pierce each of them in turn. "I will be adding two workers from Little House. As the oldest group at the Stone Home, you need to be leaders."

Little House? Taeho mouthed to Jae.

Warden's attention landed on Youngchul, the space between them flinting. "Did you hear what I said, young man?"

Youngchul caught his brother's gaze. They blinked, trying to level the shifting space, the panic braying in their silence. Cow spoke for them. That was the rule.

Warden moved down the room, his movements sleek, as if cutting through water. He rested a hand on Youngchul's collarbone. "We are preparing because of you."

Youngchul shook his head, and Warden snorted. "Are you saying no to me, young man?"

"Please." Youngchul slowly lowered to his knees. Clasped his hands together. "Let me stay until my brother turns seventeen. I'll meet quota every day, sir. I'll be good. Let us transfer to an adult reformatory together."

The broth in Sangchul's stomach clotted. His brother, a statue. The distaste of his entreating. It was the wrong move, entirely. Warden hated weakness. If only he could seize hyung, wring sense into him.

Warden cupped Youngchul's cheek. "You show me, whether you want to stay or go."

EUNJU

The sun deepened into a dusty orange as we broke down tables, folded cardboard mats, and broomed the grass as if it were a kitchen floor. I stacked Warden's and Teacher's wares into a tower—the banchan plates into the rice bowls into the soup bowls, with the shot glasses on top. Mina rubbed a rag over a smear of kimchi brine staining the straw mat.

"Youngchul-oppa seems nice," I said. "Unlike his brother."

"Sangchul's protective." Mina shaded her eyes with her palm, looked beyond me. "What do you think he's saying?"

I followed her gaze. By the dismantled serving area, Warden spoke to Halmoni, his posture rigid, his convictions stacked in his spine. I didn't understand it, how he compelled us to obey. His presence as ordinary and threatening as the parasites that wormed through our bodies, creating a fear we couldn't place. If only I could uncover its burrow, I would root it out, dig until I was free. He pointed at us.

"Do you think we're in trouble for talking to the boys?" Mina asked.

Worry prickled my neck. "We better do a good job of cleaning."

She sighed, considered the stain as she got to her feet. "I'll get some vinegar."

I watched her go, the reedy shape of her. I imagined us outside of this place, her in a miniskirt that showed off her legs, me in bell-bottoms and a bright shirt, picnicking in a real park, without anyone to obey. A silly vision. I had never owned bell-bottoms, even during Umma's best days. I turned to the mess everyone had left behind, so content in their knowing that we would clean up after them. Toothpicks scattered on the grass. Juice pouches ripped open. An empty soju bottle tucked into the roots of the nearest tree, the metal cap curled around the glass neck.

A cicada shell hugged the bark of the tree trunk. Translucent and detailed, crisp. I imagined crunching it in my mouth and shivered. The first time I saw cicadas emerge from the ground, I had been six. On a humid afternoon, we had found a wise alder tree off the side of the road. Beneath its shade, we unfurled a brand-new bamboo mat. Smooth and cool to the touch, bordered by a bright orange fabric hem. Umma had plucked one of the burnt-brown cicada husks littering the grass and placed it in front of me. "Isn't it beautiful?" she asked. I counted the number of ridges on its tail until I could nod. It was a ghost creature, hunched and clinging to an imaginary life.

Balancing the dishes on one hand, I picked the shell off the tree, careful not to crush its feet, and dropped it into my pocket. Bora hated bugs.

2011

Narae breathes in quick forceful bursts as we tread wooden planked steps, through a glade in the trees. Behind us, my apartment building looms among a cluster of identical sister structures. Ahead, a wandering path, shrouded in green. She wanted to walk along the Sincheon River. I brought her here instead. My clothes smelling of oil, garlic, the spicy crunch of scallion. My face sheened with sweat from the hours in the restaurant. *So you met my father and he was brutish*, she says. *What next? You became friends and escaped together?*

No, I say, astounded by how simple she thinks it could be. *We were in a reformatory.*

Appa never spoke of any of you. Her American impatience, her want to find a neat answer she can hold upright in her palm.

I'm telling you what he wanted you to know. I point to the deepening sky, as if the answers are written. *You need to recognize who we were to each other, in order to see how we changed.*

She shakes her head. *I have a life to return to.*

I know, I say, unable to keep the terseness from my voice. She has told me so little of herself: a high school teacher, single, living in a one-bedroom apartment in Queens. She asks me to unveil my past, while I am given only bones.

She wipes her face, and I soften: somehow, she loved the man who raised her, and for that, I should feel grateful instead of whatever it is I am feeling, this slurry in me like wet earth and stone and seed.

We found each other, and it felt like relief, and we didn't know better, we didn't prepare— I stop.

Narae sits, heavily, on a wooden bench. Her nails rattle against her phone case. *For what?*

SANGCHUL

Eunju and Mina slipped into the routine of Workshops as if they'd always been part of the group, a refreshing distraction even in the chafing heat—now, the boys didn't care about the cramped quarters, the oppressive start of June, Cow's fatty farts, the haze cast over Youngchul's future—all of it lessened by the girls' slim fingers forming hook-and-lines. The work went quicker, despite the higher quota. Cow's dumb fumbling the greatest satisfaction.

At the five-minute break, the loudspeaker buzzing, their fishhooks hit the tables, the tinkling of metal on metal a pathetic opening chord. They stretched tight calves, squeezed shoulders to crack spines. As Sangchul banged his wrists together, Mina reached over, and unexpectedly, she was touching him. Her skin surprisingly cool as she pushed into the supple space between his thumb and forefinger. "Got to loosen this muscle," she said, taking his other hand.

"Can you do me too?" Eunju asked, like their touching was nothing.

Sangchul managed a glance at Cow, who was watching. Wide-eyed. With the girls' arrival came his hesitance. They lay beyond his jurisdiction, and somehow, their protection rippled to the rest of them too.

Still, any pleasure Sangchul felt withered as he realized she was only kneading his palm because she was too scared to touch hyung. It was obvious, in the mottled way she looked at him. He didn't want to be their conduit, some vessel for their idiotic love.

"You know what I dreamed about eating last night?" Taeho asked.

"Naengmyeon?" Mina let go of Sangchul's hand.

"Bet it was jjajangmyeon." Eunju thrust out her palm. "Me next."

Mina squeezed onto Eunju's seat, knees knocking against Youngchul's chair. "Do you want a massage next?"

"Sure." He nodded, looked at Taeho instead. "Was it bindae-tteok?"

"Or kongguksu?" Jae asked.

Sangchul glanced down as relief threaded his wrists, down his spine. Their grandfather had told him that everything in the body was connected, so that pushing into the tip of the middle finger could cure a headache. Halabuji once instructed him to burn dried mugwort at the base of the thumb to ease stomach pains, showed him his moxa sticks. Sangchul couldn't remember now what the other parts of the hand represented.

"Hyung?" Taeho pressed, waiting for Sangchul, who hadn't guessed.

"I don't know," he said. "What was it?"

Taeho shook his head, the memory of his dream playing across his face, delight enough to stamp Sangchul's churlishness. "Fried chicken and bananas." He laughed at his own joke, and Sangchul stared at this rich kid who knew the taste of imported fruit, dumbfounded again at how Taeho had survived so shielded.

"I've never tried either of those, you prince," Eunju said.

"Only Taeho." Jae pressed his lips together.

"My nuna will buy all the bananas we want when she finds us." Taeho smiled. He was the only one of them to speak of his family. Always, his nuna. There was no social code with him, no protective layer. He called up the precarity of their world, and they willingly listened because it was him. Their tender one.

"Describe it to us." Mina reached for Youngchul's hand, but Cow clapped his comic shut.

"You're making me hungry. Break's over." He bit his lip, and it occurred to Sangchul, with a hint of awe, that Cow could be jealous.

Mina returned to her seat, mouthing *Next time* to Youngchul, and as they began their hook-and-lines, Sangchul laughed. It was silly to envy them. He couldn't even recall the facts of his childhood. The smell of the moxa sticks, the moxibustion points of the body. He could only conjure hills, a blue wing. A crumbling road without end.

At the seventh hour, tendrils of heat cramped his fingertips, a lightning strip up his spine. Hundreds of fishhooks to go. This happened, the sudden crunching of time, pushing against a deadline that seemed impossible.

Youngchul clenched his fists. "Think of those bananas as our reward."

Taeho hummed the tune to "Butterfly." The song a familiar comfort, as if they were only children playing at work. Mina joined, lilting back and forth, and then they were all singing "Half-Moon," "The Mountain Rabbit." A ragged musical band, glancing at Cow to see if he'd stop them, knowing too that he wouldn't.

"You have a nice voice, Mina," Youngchul said.

Jae and Taeho raised their eyebrows. Eunju pushed back her seat so Youngchul couldn't catch the laugh gliding over her face. Mina only smiled. "We should convince Warden to let us sing at local churches for money," she said.

"Use it as a cover to escape," Eunju added in a whisper.

"Our lord, he heals us with grace," Mina sang over her, voice crackling, frowning slightly. To mention escape was a step too far. Eunju shrugged and mouthed along. From the way her lips didn't match the rhythm, Sangchul knew she didn't know the words. She sank a glare in his direction. He threaded a line without looking away and missed the silver eye. She must have had sixty packages already, her fingers the quickest of them all.

"All right, enough." Cow lobbed a piece of cardboard at them, and when it landed halfway down the table, he pushed himself up. Flicked Eunju's packages, the closest he would get, and stopped in front of Taeho. "You better hit that quota, the way you're talking."

"You could slow down for us," Mina sulked to Eunju as Cow returned to his seat.

Sangchul's eyes tightened. "Why don't you trade us a package to even us out?"

"I worked for these." Eunju scratched her ear. "Aren't we all trying to make quota?"

"She's our minder," Youngchul soothed. "She keeps us on track."

They worked the rest of the day in silence, Eunju's completed hooks outdoing theirs. Sangchul felt like a dog, nettled, full of needled energy. Still, Eunju would beat him. She'd make quota and ask for more. Win Rewards. Ten minutes to wander the property with one Keeper after Dinner, to examine the darkening light in peace. He wondered if he'd give that up for his friends, if he could maneuver a way for Youngchul to win, so he could taste that freedom, work harder to stay. Sangchul sighed, hunched over his fishhooks, their simple shapes, his simple existence. He remembered now. If the tip of the middle finger was the head, the center was the heart.

EUNJU

"Eunju-unnie, come join!" Nabi waved from the circle of girls squeezed between Bora's cot and the corner, the barred window above blueing their faces—and I felt myself entirely as I walked over, the short hairs prickling my ears, the limp towel slung over my neck, the collar of my wet shirt. They were calling for me.

Mina pulled up her legs, making room. "Here," she said gently.

I settled beside her, smiling despite myself. They sat in this corner until Lights Out every night, and though Mina had invited me before, I hadn't ever come, unsure if she meant it, if the others would shun me. Embarrassed to show my want. "Kitchen work go well today?" I asked, my mind blanking as I drew my knees together.

Areum dipped her head so Ajumma Lee, returning from the bathroom, wouldn't overhear. "We were asking about Workshops."

"She means the boys," Nabi whispered, as if I didn't understand.

The scruff growing from Youngchul's cheeks came to mind. I knew they wanted other details. Areum and Bora were sixteen, growing breasts and bleeding according to the moon, but the boys held no allure for me. Their sweat foul, bodies crude and lumbering. I preferred Areum's compact form, how her oval face shone in its beauty because of the scar, rather than despite it. Those sparse black brows, the white meat of mended skin. "Are they good to you?" she asked.

I picked at my nubby towel, nodded. I had learned so much—how the three Workshops ran, with Cow the kindest Keeper, unlike brutish Crow in the next room, who treated his boys like spinning tops. Strike quickly, and watch them flail. Those boys, like Honggi, a square-faced one with light brown hair I'd thought meant he was like me, not fully Korean in blood, seemed stamped by surrender in a way I didn't understand.

"They're kind," Mina said. "You know Cow's group, they're real oppas."

"We know who *you're* talking about," Bora said with a smirk.

Mina kept on despite the teasing. She spoke of Youngchul, but also irritable Sangchul, naive Taeho, and watchful, wry Jae. Nabi lay her head on my knee, and I brushed her glossy hair, the soap she hadn't cleaned trailing from ear to throat, as Mina described the surprise of pricking her fingernail with a hook. She didn't mention how I'd challenged her to touch Youngchul that afternoon, the way we'd laughed after at Cow's unease, our exhilaration at the boys' yearning. I bit my cheek, willing myself not to boast. We would leave that as our secret, a fine yellow pearl to savor on our tongues.

"What I want to know," Bora said grudgingly, "is what Rewards are like."

It was a release. The best part of my day. The rope I held on to when my mind spiraled to the unknowing depths of this place. But they wouldn't ever receive Rewards while in the kitchen, and Mina wasn't as fast as me. "It's like a drug," I said, trying to sound confident, yet knowing too that wasn't right. Before the Stone Home, Umma had smoked hemp one night and laughed and laughed, her mouth so wide I feared it would unhinge, that her red tongue would swallow me whole. "No." I shook my head. Tried harder. "It's like an extra breath."

"I can't imagine it." Bora sniffed. "Mostly because you're not describing it well."

"I hope I get it." Mina tucked her chin into her knees.

"It's not so great," I said quietly, though I couldn't meet her eyes. "As soon as it starts, you know it'll end and Mosquito's there, so I have to be on alert."

Areum gave a dry smile. "Nice try."

"If I were you, I'd survey the field. Figure a way out," Bora said.

I caught her gaze, forced her to look at me. "Who says I'm not already?"

"Enough boring talk," Nabi cut in, gathering her sweetness to halt our bickering. "I saw what you did today, Bora-unnie."

"What now?" Bora said, straightening slowly, though her cheeks were pink.

"You stole something during meal prep!" Nabi teased.

"I did not." Bora sucked her teeth, but Nabi insisted. It surprised me, how she provoked, without fear of Bora's barbs.

"Show us," Areum chided. "You know Nabi catches everything."

Bora groaned, and though she glanced at me, she didn't tell me to leave. From her pocket, she pulled out a bundled cloth. Inside, a pale, sandy powder. "Red bean and rice. I ground them down," she said. "I'm going to rub it on my face tomorrow morning."

Areum snorted, and Mina snickered. Nabi whined, "There's a rice shortage."

Then we all laughed, even me. It was stupid to waste food. It was true, though, that Bora's cheeks pimpled along the jawline. I hadn't thought she was the type to care, constantly nagging on me for my delicate face, Umma's preening.

The lights flickered on and off. Halmoni's sign. Our circle segmented. Umma watched with sleepy eyes as I approached, her wet hair spread out like a dress. "You won Rewards again."

I lay on my belly and reached over the gap that separated us. Squeezed a drop of water from her hair into my palm. "I walked to the northern edge. It's all trees until the wall."

She turned to her side. "Those ten minutes, they're yours. Breathe the air, touch the dirt, do whatever you want. I'll figure out a way."

I nodded, smelling the stink of my breath against my pillow. "I only want to help."

"You're a good girl, Eunju." She yawned, and even the pink of her mouth seemed beautiful. She was my mother, and she wanted to protect me. "Sleep now," she said, and the desire swept in, a warm weight over my eyes and limbs.

• • •

I woke to a rustling in the dark, a flick of water. The haze of sleep pulled off me like a blanket in the night. A swing in my stomach as I opened my eyes. Her cot was empty. There, between the rows, she crept to the door. The sight so familiar it made my stomach clench. My mother, her back against the wall as if that would conceal her.

Slowly, the door opened from the outside. A silhouette: squared shoulders, leaner and taller than Halmoni. A man. A hand reaching for her, too rough. A dark streak, made of her shadow.

The key locking in place behind them, a shiny click of metal on metal.

I couldn't breathe, the air sucked out of me. Fumbled for my clothes, for her. Slowly, I crept to the door on my knees, unwilling to wake Ajumma Lee with her scorn. The handle, locked.

She has enough to manage, Halmoni once said. *Some don't approve of her methods.* The bruise on her wrist. Umma's silence, when I'd asked, *When did you get this?*

I'm protecting you, she'd said, and I had ignored the signs, unwilling to see, admit the truth. I crept into Umma's cot. I would wait for her. When she returned, I would tell her: this was my fault. I was the one she needed to care for. A constant pest. I was the reason she had been on that corner begging when the police came. I had been trying, Umma—so hard to be good, to work and stay quiet, to change myself to fit into the space allowed me here, hoping we'd be protected, at least, from men and their desires.

But as time passed, sticky, slow, another feeling lit my body too. *Yanggongju. Half-breed. Do you want to end up like your mother, girl? Naked. In a shack. Men between your legs.* This was why they hated us, why Warden's words burred into me, why I'd grown up seeing a straight path ahead, why the shame the women planted in me unfurled with the days—because in this place, where we had food and shelter, Umma acted the same.

SANGCHUL

Sangchul was under the showerhead when he heard the shouts—Teacher and someone else's cries. He sank into the flushed blur of his lids, the water running down his face, not wanting to know, the sleep not yet rubbed out of his eyes, when someone jerked his arm—fingers slipping against soap-slathered skin. Jae, speaking in a rush, "Your brother and Taeho."

Sangchul ran, grabbing someone else's towel, leaving a wet trail as boys scooted out of their way, Mosquito yelling from the sinks, "Don't you go out there!"

In the hall, Teacher wrenched Taeho by the wrist. In his other hand, a book of matches. Contraband. "I didn't do it," Taeho said. "I promise, it wasn't me this time."

"It was them." Youngchul pointed to Rat and his squealer Dal, smirking behind Teacher's back. He turned to Cow, pallid-faced in the corner. "Tell them."

Teacher pulled shirtless Taeho higher, onto his tiptoes—stretching his arm to a frightening height, the newly growing patch of hair sprouting from the pit like a furious mouth.

"Wouldn't you rather stanch the problem at the wound?" Youngchul, too forceful, stalked over to Rat. Teacher pulled him back by the hair.

Sangchul returned to his body with that sudden touch. He tried to step forward, his throat constricting. It was too much—Teacher's erratic anger, his compulsion for control. Youngchul's righteous insistence. It was a book of matches, he wanted to scream.

"You think you can pass me, you think this is the way?" Teacher spoke to Youngchul. He laughed, a smeary sound. "Maybe it's time, then." He turned to Cow. "Let's see here, what #28 will do when faced with his final test. Unhook your bat, Keeper."

"Teacher, please." Cow knuckled the meat beneath his eyes. "I'll do better."

But Teacher forced the bat from Cow, gave it to Youngchul. "Make a circle around them. Let's have a little tussle between Keeper and boy."

Suddenly, Cow and Youngchul were surrounded. Suddenly, the other Keepers stood sentry. Things were moving too quickly, Jae and Taeho trembling beside Sangchul. He blinked, and a knowing passed through him, what Youngchul would have to do to earn his Keeper spot. It seemed fitting, to have to beat another. But it wasn't time. They had three weeks left until hyung turned seventeen.

"I'm tired of this group causing trouble," Teacher shouted. "Who's to blame here, the incompetent Keeper or the one who doesn't understand his place?"

"It wasn't right, Teacher. I was only pointing out—" Youngchul stopped, an animal caught in the light, squinting as if he was seeing the white, hefty rubber bat in his hands for the first time.

A scythe through Sangchul's stomach at hyung's slick panic. Their mutual pleading as they caught each other's gazes. Hyung's lips mouthing his name. Why was it always on him to step in, receive Teacher's berating?

"Should we?" Jae whispered.

"No," he heard himself say. This was how hyung would learn. Hyung would have to act, admit the truth.

"What if—?" Taeho asked.

"Shut up," Sangchul hissed, a fine heat spreading through him. He shut his eyes—the sound of his brother's pleading, a whimper, and then, slowly, the swish of a bat. A light thwack, barely a hit at all. *Harder.* He would have to hit harder.

"I think we should—" Jae started again, but Sangchul held fast.

A bat, rising. Sangchul's surety too. Then, Cow opened his mouth: "Protection!"

A sudden flush, the other Keepers rushing in. Their bats smashing into Youngchul's shins. Teacher watching. Hyung hitting the floor. Sangchul didn't understand. Was this part of the test, some vile initiation?

"Enough," Teacher said.

Keepers, returning to the shape of boys. Cow, crying. Youngchul, coughing on the ground.

"You see? You are the wound, and I decide how we fix problems here." Teacher toed Youngchul's side. "Take him to Chapel."

Chapel? Sangchul struggled, his arms wet, slippery. His voice, careening jumbled words. Jae and Taeho pulled him back as the Keepers jostled Youngchul down the hall. Tile, beneath his feet. The moist air of the bathroom. His face wet. How bizarre. Yesterday, he had been thinking about the heart.

EUNJU

Cocooned in the shower at first light, I filled my mouth until the water bowled my throat, wetness running over my lips. I'd felt the skim of dust on the floor last night, the cool metal of the handle. The black shape of Umma's absence. Smelled the earthy melon scent of her sheets. It hadn't been a dream, yet I woke in my own cot. My blanket tenting my head and tangled between my knees. Beside me, Umma sleeping like nothing had happened. When she'd opened her eyes, she'd stretched her arms and rubbed her cheeks. Cocked a look at me, as if I were the one acting strange.

Where did you go? A hot question in my throat I couldn't ask. *Who did you go to?*

"Are you trying to drown?" Mina turned on the shower next to me, and I dropped my head to release the water, a heaping gush. She stepped back, scrunching her toes. "What's wrong?"

Milky soap drifted between us. More than anything, I wanted to ask if Umma was doing it for me, whether she was going to be this way forever, if this meant she'd given up on leaving this place. I imagined her disappointment in seeing me in her cot, the knowing now that I knew. Lifting my sleeping body in the night. What did it mean, then, that she hadn't said a thing this morning?

Mina picked up the soap and ran it between her breasts. They were larger than mine, though my nipples were darker. We were both growing. The pale lightning marks of stretched skin around my armpits declaring themselves more insistently with each week.

"Eunju?" Mina asked. "What is it?"

I touched the pink muck that gathered on the tiles every few days, no matter how well we scrubbed. Slick, slippery. "I saw my mom leave last night."

Mina pushed a wet strand behind her ear. I knew her tics—she stuttered when nervous, set her jaw when unsure, the slim profile of her hardening. She played with her shower handle, swinging it cold and hot. Her black hair clinging to pale shoulders in clumps.

"You knew," I said, a new accusation rustling through me.

She tapped the handle. Shrugged. "I didn't want to embarrass you."

"Embarrass?"

She stared at the tiles, pink crawling up her throat. "You know, that she was using her body, even here. Doing that sex stuff." She smiled at me reassuringly. "I don't judge you for her actions."

I turned off the faucet. Reached over to shut hers too. Her skin chickenfleshing immediately, revealing the weak person she was. A sudden and deep force filling every crevice in me. As if she knew me. As if she dared. "You think that's what I feel?" I asked.

Her eyes stretched with surprise. "What do you mean?"

I pulled on my ear, focused on her spindly shoulders, her clavicle. Those thin wrists. All the parts of her I could break because I wouldn't let her see me cry, wouldn't let her know. How her words cut, stripped me to the bone. How much I hated her for seeing, how much I hated my own shame. "You think she's disgusting."

Mina reached out, her hand wavering. "Eunju, I didn't mean—"

This time, I was the one who stepped back. My skin aflame. No, I wasn't ashamed, I was angry, all white heat and flame, and with that, I walked away.

SANGCHUL

Chapel meant dark rooms on the third floor, enclosed and dank with only a bucket to shit in. Chapel meant three days of isolation. A fractured body or a disappearance, a transfer. A hot, clenched panic threaded Sangchul's spine, into the base of his skull. The air in the Fishhooks room too sharp, a shock of water up the nose. He lay his forehead on the Workshop table's ledge and choked down a rope of spit.

Taeho touched the back of his neck. "You're sweating."

Sangchul reached toward him, knocking into packages and lines. "I can't think."

"Breathe," Jae said.

He gripped a hook to stop the room's spinning. For the first time, he wondered at Teacher's and Warden's stupidity. How easily he could prick their eyes with these sharp points, slash until he punctured their reality.

"Get up." Cow treaded the front of the room in a tight loop. "It's not my fault he got himself into trouble. I mean, did he think I'd give up so easily? That the other Keepers wouldn't protect me?" He scoffed, and Sangchul's mind lunged, though his arms remained limp. Watery. Mina and Taeho held on to his shirt just in case. To pass the Keeper test, Youngchul had to beat Cow, but what they hadn't understood was that Cow would have the protection of the others. A nearly impossible task.

"Focus on the quota," Eunju said, stern. "It'll make you feel better."

Sangchul hated her, with her efficiency and short hair and silver strength. He grabbed a line. Youngchul was in Chapel. A cup of water and dregs from the bottom of the soup vat. No sunlight. No hygiene. Nothing except your disintegrating thoughts.

Sangchul's mouth flooded with the coin taste of his guilt. Youngchul had hit Cow, but it was Sangchul's voice he remembered. "No," callous, final. He knew his brother, what he was capable of, and he hadn't stepped in.

When taunted in high school by a trio of boys, Youngchul had insisted that Sangchul ignore them. "They'll forget me," he'd said, stanching a cut on his cheek. How mercilessly they'd beaten him a week later. Sangchul found the leader, a tall teen with a crooked nose. Pushed him into an office building until the glass doors shuddered like loose teeth. Only after Sangchul stepped in did the boys stop. His brother's weakness was his fault.

"He'll be okay," Taeho said, but the words sounded false, even in his good mouth. He'd been trembling all morning, holding his tears to focus on Sangchul. His guilt a medallion around his neck, brilliant and obvious and ornamental.

Sangchul rubbed his eyes, unsure of where to place the feelings inside him. "I'm going to kill Dal and Rat. Tonight, after Lights Out."

"That won't—" Jae said.

"I don't care," Sangchul spat.

"You won't." Mina's voice shook. "Who knows if that could cause him more trouble?"

He stared at her lips, bitten up, and understood—she believed in her pain too. All of them with their glances, as if he couldn't feel their alarm. But he was Youngchul's brother. His only family.

"I think you should do it." Eunju thrust her chin in the air. Sliced a glare at Mina. "I would, if someone betrayed my mother."

"It's my fault." Taeho pushed his head between his knees, abandoning his hook-and-lines.

"Enough." Cow leaned over Youngchul's empty stool. His fleshy, hairless arms, the sheen of sweat on his upper lip. Sangchul swallowed his spit, his desire to punch him square in the mouth. "Look," Cow said, shifting his tone. "We have a quota to meet. Teacher only discounted half of Youngchul's load, which means you'll have to make extra. Do you want to end up on the Presentations line? You're so focused on yourselves. I'll get in trouble too, you know?"

"That's going to be impossible," Jae said.

"Why can't you ask the other Fishhooks room to take some on?" Eunju asked.

Cow pointed to the wall, Crow's insults vibrating like a new signal. "I could be like that. You're spoiled, that's what it is."

Four hours later, Sangchul's eyes watered, his right arm streaked with dried tears. Eunju had been right, in her way. The attention to numbers leashed his panic. Whenever a jolt ran through him, he bore down on the quota.

Mina stared at her completed packages. They were nearing the end, and she didn't have enough. "My hands keep cramping." She pressed her fingers to her cheek, and they juddered, brimming with a life of their own.

Jae checked for Cow before sliding one of his finished packages across the table. She pushed some of her incomplete hooks and lines back to him. He carefully gazed past Youngchul's empty seat to Eunju. "Why don't you give some to Mina too?"

"I can share, nuna," Taeho said.

"You might not even make quota." Sangchul pushed one of his own packages to Mina.

Eunju's shoulders rose to her ears. "I don't have enough."

A bulb buzzed above them. They had an hour left. "You know you will," Sangchul said.

Eunju swept the packages closer, as if they would steal them. "I said no."

"She'll get a lashing," Jae said, stern.

"She won't." Eunju's voice was small and stiff. "They don't lash girls at Presentations."

"Is getting Rewards that important to you?" Sangchul asked. "Ten minutes outside over your friend? You don't know if you'll win."

"Who says she's my friend?"

Mina laughed, a spiky stutter. "It's my own fault."

"We help each other here," Sangchul snapped, reaching over the table. "Why are you being selfish?"

Eunju lunged, her arms a round sweep. "Keeper! He's trying to take my packages."

Sangchul recoiled. The shock dropping out of him. Taeho and Jae scraped their stools.

"Hey." Cow pushed his bat into Sangchul's ribs. "Shut up and focus." He worked his jaws on his round, mottled face. "All of you."

Eunju scrunched her lips into a tight bud, her lashes flat and spidery against her cheeks. Her arms around her packages. "*We help each other here*," she mocked in a low voice. "You think my ten minutes is selfish? You're the one who let your brother get hauled off to Chapel. Take a look at yourself."

• • •

At Presentations, they toed the white line rimming the gymnasium floor. Clasped their hands behind their backs. Formed a rectangular border, and at the center, Warden called up those who hadn't met quota. The boys from Shirts, Leathers, Fishhooks. Mina too. She stepped forward, and they jeered. It was ritual, they had to, and yet Sangchul felt a perverse pleasure in it most days. The thrill of ruthlessness, of turning against one another, even for a moment.

Warden cut the air with a branch before calling each sinner individually. He was eternally calm, as if he were doling out communion wafers. The first boy bent over and balanced his hands on his thighs, his butt in the air. His pants rolled above the knees. Warden spoke to the crowd: "You question why your family has forgotten you, when the answer is clear, because if the group is slothful, so are you."

Keepers rammed the shoulders of anyone who looked away.

"We are all witnesses," Warden shouted.

Mina wept when called to the center. The wet shuddering enough to rattle Sangchul. Warden raised his whip. The women, brought in from Little House for this special occasion, screamed with her, their cries splintering the air.

Sangchul searched the sliver of moonlight sliding in through the windows. Unclenched his fists. *Take a look at yourself*, Eunju had said. She didn't understand. They were the same. In her, he saw his own foulness. His desire to hoard his work, reach for Rewards. No. He had offered Mina his packages. He wasn't like her at all. "She's not a loyal person," he said.

Jae softened beside him. "She's a child, like all of us."

But Jae was wrong; Sangchul was sure of it. No one was a child in here.

EUNJU

Even from the field, I could hear Mina crying, the ruckus of Presentations winnowing through the gym windows. So, she had been called to the line after all. Acid rose to my throat at the thought of her, the boys and their judgments. I wanted to erase the last ten minutes of Workshop, when Cow had counted her packages with his tongue at the corner of his lips. A pause as he looked away. No girl had ever been whipped before. A glance at my side. He hadn't counted mine yet, but we knew I had enough. "I'll walk to the window and back," Cow said below his breath.

I felt Mina's gaze on me, her fingers clattering on the table. "I don't want to get hurt."

"Eunju," Jae said, warning and pleading, and for him, I nearly wavered, but—my arms were around my pile, and I couldn't move them. A ditch, a wall. Her tilted head, condescending, when we had spoken in the showers: *I didn't want to embarrass you.* Mina had betrayed me first.

Here I was now—in the open air, the bright scent of pine and wet earth from a humid afternoon, with only Mosquito as my guard. Umma had taught me to protect myself before all others, and I had forgotten. So focused on befriending Mina and the boys, I hadn't paid attention to finding an escape, to what was happening to my mother. Time blurring together—today was our twenty-eighth day here, or twenty-ninth, I didn't know, my throat tight with my own negligence.

A bird flew overhead, a gray smudge against the sky. I had thought, in some dumb way, that it would work out. Umma, safe. Mina too. Youngchul. All of us. Or maybe I hadn't thought that at all; maybe I knew what I was doing.

"Slow down," Mosquito called from behind as I reached the northern edge of the property. I knew, at least, what face he was making—brown eyes scanning left and right, brows raised, forehead creased with lines. The shadow of his strong nose. My watcher, Head Keeper.

On my first Rewards, I'd kneeled in the center of the field, pressed my fingertips against the warm, loose earth. The wind grazing my short hair, my bare neck. The fading light of sky. Something within me split, an invisible hand cracking open my ribs. On my knees for the full ten minutes, I watched the sky thread itself with pinks and rusty oranges, navy bands of dusk rushing in, leaving me in the dark.

It was a false freedom, I knew that. Still, the awe didn't go away. I would take that sheaf of space, the loosening in my body, whenever I could.

"Not too far," Mosquito warned.

I bent over, my lungs tight. I didn't want to consider the boys, their anger. Youngchul in Chapel. Mina's whipped calves. Her words that saw through me: *You know, that she was using her body, even here. Doing that sex stuff.* Umma had taught me sex work was a type of trade, like the tteok she sold in the market, the beer she served at the bar, the factory jobs she sometimes secured. Still, she had hidden what she was doing here. Why, if she wasn't ashamed? If she was, then I was a shame too. A constant marker she had to carry.

"Do men ever come here from outside?" My voice light, mild. As if I had plucked the question like a flower from a branch.

Mosquito leaned on a nearby trunk. He wasn't as muscular as the largest Keeper, Crow, but he had big hands, a solid frame, more man than boy. I knew facts about him now. He had seven sisters. He was the youngest, the favored son. He was from Soŏ-san. He never called me "mixed-breed" like the other Keepers. When he thought I wasn't watching, he massaged his right elbow. He was given the weakest name; he was the most biting. I saw no anger in him. He inhaled, wary. "Why are you asking?"

So he didn't know either. The shadow who had jerked Umma by the arm. He could have been Warden or Teacher, or another.

I picked up a stick. In the weeks we had been in Workshops, I had won Rewards six times. I now knew the property's shape, with Big House to the south, Little House to the east, Workshops to the west, the center field our eye. Behind Workshops, azalea bushes clambered over a metal fence, the land sectioned off. North of Little House was open. Whatever route I took, I found my way to the edge—the wall. If he noticed, he didn't say.

Mosquito gestured at the stick. "You know you can't keep that."

I twirled it, made my arms appear clumsy. "I'm just playing."

"You'll drop it when we leave." He had a severe, unusual face. I didn't know how long he had been here, what he had done to become Head Keeper. What I did know—he released branches before they broke while I swatted leaves with my stick and shredded them at my feet. He was the only one who handled Rewards. Maybe he could help me and Umma before that shadow returned, before I saw again the blackness she left behind.

"Do you ever think about going home?" I asked.

Mosquito glanced at his watch, my words gliding off him. "We should head back."

The wall rose, the top studded with glass. Before Rewards, it had felt mythic, but when I touched the cool stones, it became only what it was. A man-made enclosure. Six meters at most, enough to hem us in. Could I get my fingers in those crevices? Could I convince Mosquito to smuggle Umma out too? I threw the stick up in the air. It only reached halfway.

"Wait." I pulled out the cicada shell I'd found at the Pentecost picnic. I'd picked it up from my cot after leaving Mina at Morning Washup, my skin still damp and agitated. I cleared a space by the wall, flattened the grass. The cicada had crumbled, one of its legs broken, the body brittle and translucent. I bordered it with stones.

"What're you doing?" Mosquito asked.

I shrugged. A gesture—for not sharing my hook-and-lines, for not witnessing Mina's lashings, for knowing I was right. I had confided in her, and she had hurt me. How could it be my fault she hadn't made quota?

We turned back to Big House. On the third floor, blackened windows absorbed the night. "That's where Chapel is, isn't it?" I asked.

He appraised me. His right hand worrying the handle of his bat. "You're too curious."

At the other end of the third floor, Warden's office shone. Not a barred window, a clear pane. Maroon curtains framing a wooden desk. "Warden must buy special bulbs," I said, nodding at the gilded light, so different from the harsh white cast we lived beneath.

Mosquito followed my gaze. "I never noticed. Made of honey, I suppose." He smiled before heading to the door. "Let's go, before we both get in trouble."

I spoke in a whisper, catching the back of his sleeve, my voice softening. "You don't seem that bad. Maybe we could help each other, oppa."

"Don't be stupid." His voice immediately changed. Rusted and hollow. He jerked away. "Of course I am, like the rest of us. I do what needs to be done."

2011

Ajumma? The hostess, a twentysomething with flyaway hair, calls me from the door. *Someone's here for you.*

Me? I touch my face, hoping, despite myself, and enter the dining area—seated by the window, whitened by the sun, it's her. *Narae?*

A shy smile, a strand tucked behind her ear. *I wanted to see where you worked.*

I dip my head.

Oh. She rises. Touches my arm, hands me a paper napkin. *Are you all right?*

The well inside me, gratitude and something else—I had thought after our last meeting, my betrayal of Mina, my weakness. I had thought she wouldn't come. I try to explain, but I don't know if I'm making sense, if I'm saying the right words.

You were a child, Narae says. *You understand that, don't you?*

Ajumma! The hostess motions to the kitchen.

I should get back to work, I say.

Take one. Narae gestures to the box of chocolates she's brought. A fine silver package with an embossed bow. She lifts the lid. I pick a sweet, though they make my molars ache. I am unstitching this story, the threads all knotted together, slippery in my hands. I must reveal the circumstances of her birth, expose her father's treachery, and, in doing so, change the shape of her past. Why does it feel like I'm the one unraveling?

SANGCHUL

Four days, and Youngchul hadn't returned. Sangchul clenched fishhooks. Where was his brother? Three days in Chapel was standard. Cow clapped, yelled the quota into the air. Taeho held his pliers in demonstration, as if Sangchul had never done this work before.

"Leave me alone, Taeho." Sangchul's voice laced tight.

Mina sucked her teeth. "Don't be an ass."

Sangchul twisted, ready to yell, but she stiffened, and he remembered her legs, the pink welts that had burst after Presentations.

Her shoulders rose into her neck. "I'm saying we understand, we're worried too. Don't take it out on Taeho. We already have enough trouble here." She didn't look at Eunju, but he understood. They had shut her out, or she'd shut them out, he wasn't sure. Eunju, who worked with her chin tucked. Not saying a word about hyung, though he'd been the one to welcome her.

"Youngchul will be all right," Jae said. "Maybe he'll show up at Dinner, or after Washup."

Mina knotted a fishing line. "Maybe they put him straight on another job, like when you were on lumber duty."

Sangchul nodded, though he didn't believe it. The window outlined storm clouds, and all the groups were in Workshops. There was no extra job, no outside hire.

The possibility slunk toward him—Youngchul could have been

hauled off to an adult institution without a goodbye. He pressed his toes against the roofs of his sneakers, anything to ground himself. His hands slipped, too wet. They were good citizens, with family searching for them, they didn't belong here, not with these children abandoned by their relations. His throat seized, tongue hot and lolling, and then he heard Taeho's whine, Mina calling his name.

"You're bleeding," Jae said.

Sangchul stared at the silver hook, this foreign object in the meat of his palm.

"Pull it out," Eunju said. "What are you doing?"

He closed his fist, pushed until the round loop disappeared, until he felt the hurt and his stool fell sideways, his body loose, wild.

"He's injured!" Taeho called to Cow.

Sangchul was crying. Bleeding. Full of liquids he didn't want. He got to his knees.

Cow stretched his palm flat like a map. Pain lightninged up his arm to the backs of his eyes. "We're behind already." Sangchul spasmed as Cow tried to pull, black crowding his vision. A sigh. "Come on, we'll wash you up."

Jae and Taeho helped him stand, and he cupped his hand like a bird to his chest as he followed his Keeper. "What if it's hit bone?" he asked, now waxen with pain.

"Better hope it hasn't. I'm not calling Teacher."

Out in the sun, the hook looked bizarre, the silver gleam an alternate terrain. Cow listed to the side as he followed the path of a hawk in the sky. Sangchul glanced at the wall, imagined climbing it one-handed.

"You know what would happen," Cow said mildly. He yanked Sangchul's elbow.

They stopped at the outdoor pump on the side of Little House. Earthenware jars of cloths and bandages, a bar of soap in a plastic container on the concrete ground. A window reflected them back to themselves. Sangchul was pale, eyelashes dark with wet.

He concentrated on a sun glare blanching the trees as Cow flattened his palm. A squelch as the hook released. He sunk his hand beneath the spigot, and the shock of the cold, clean water ate up some of the pain. Beneath the blood, stringy layers of muscle. A line of white. Bone or fat, he didn't want to know. "Hyung," he said.

"You call me Keeper," Cow said.

"My brother." Sangchul watched him through the window glass. "Is he still in Chapel?"

"They don't tell me anything." Cow twitched. "You know I'm the worst Keeper."

"He's my only family." Sangchul raised his hand to his ear, as if he were saying hello American-style. "You could help us."

Cow stuck his tongue beneath his lower lip and teeth. Wrapped the gauze tight, though blood seeped through right away. Another layer, carefully this time. He stuffed extra into Sangchul's pocket, his fingers sliding across Sangchul's thigh. "You need to be careful. Output is everything for these people."

"'These people'?"

"Come on," Cow said. "The others will be falling behind on quota."

But when they reached the center of the field, Sangchul stopped. Turned to Big House. There, on the third floor. The blackened windows. He had to believe his brother was there. Sangchul raised his bandaged hand above his head. He waved.

EUNJU

Four days, and Mina hadn't spoken to me. Not at the bathroom sinks, Service, Workshop, or the walk to Little House. The crunch of dirt beneath our feet, the high whistling wind that pronounced a coming storm. I kept my voice silent in my throat as Teacher returned us to the kitchen. Mina's hair swinging across her shoulders. Her hate a clear stream I wanted to drown in.

Mina headed to the rice station without turning back. In the corner by the storeroom, I found Umma scrubbing rags in a basin of soapy water and hugged her from behind. I was angry with her; I needed her; I wanted the press of my skin to tell her all of this. She only patted my hand. "Look at this stain." She raised one of the rags, the center splotched with green.

I rubbed my earlobes, as if I had touched something too hot. "I met quota."

"Spinach is the hardest." She hummed as she scrubbed the rag against the ridged slats of the wooden washboard.

Four nights, and Umma hadn't left again. When I woke with a jolt in the dark, she was always asleep, lips parted. In the mornings, rubbing the corners of her eyes. Four days, and I hadn't yet asked her. Once I unpeeled the rind, there would be no return to original shape. No whole fruit for us to pretend to carry in our hands.

"Umma," I started.

She shrugged me off, her neck tensed. "So much work. Halmoni must be looking for you." She was newly muscled from her time here, her arms sinewed. Freckles spreading across her nose. I opened my mouth, but I could only picture the pocked skin of an orange, how I loved to dig my nails in as a child, releasing that citrusy oil. The spray of scent in the air.

I reared back on my heels and watched the line of her spine. The strip of exposed neck before her shirt collar. I would never not be her child. A burden. My stomach lurched with the weight. It wasn't fair. How hard she had to work, how little I could help. It was because of me that we'd ended up here, that a man took her away in the night.

A man with square shoulders, lean and tall. Four days, and I cycled through the possibilities. It must have been Teacher—with his keys, height, his too-large eyes and voice like cigarette char. His emotions a hot flame. His squeezed, lonely self.

"Umma," I said again. I was fifteen. I could take care of myself.

Mina's laugh ran toward us as she and the unnies rounded the corner, carrying a vat of jogaetang. The brackish scent of clams and anchovy broth.

Umma eyed them. She had noticed the silence between us, my refusal to join the girls for their evening chats. She touched my cheek with her own. "What did you fight about?"

She must have guessed—Mina's punishment, my Rewards. What was the use in saying it aloud? I pushed against Umma once more, breathing in the scent I knew so well. Tart and clean with a whiff of earth, like melon and grass. A new texture lifted off her, smokier, a burning. I wondered if I smelled the same, if scents were passed down from mother to daughter or picked up somewhere along the way.

SANGCHUL

At Dinner, Sangchul gave his rice to Taeho. Watched the door. Picked sesame seeds from kongnamul banchan. Anxious. Maybe Youngchul would arrive at the end of the meal. Whole and unbruised. Maybe he would appear at Presentations, broken-armed but upright. Sangchul's veins felt tight, dried up, his blood supply diminishing. Please. Any news. He spooned jogaetang and held the empty clamshells on his tongue. The slippery ridges with their briny, iron bite. Imagined the meager nutrients streaming to mend the cut on his hand. A trick Youngchul taught him when he was young, scraped-kneed after climbing a tree.

Hyung couldn't leave because, Sangchul understood now, he had so much to apologize for—not stepping in, stepping in too often, the blame he cast, born of his own self-hatred.

He felt a knock on his back. The round pulse of a bat. Cow swiped a soybean sprout from his dish. "Confirmed, he's in Chapel," he whispered.

Sangchul spat out a clamshell. The relief and shame in asking his Keeper swarmed him. Maybe he had been wrong about Cow, all of them. He avoided his friends' gazes. "What happens next?"

Cow picked at Jae's eggplants. Shrugged as he moved down the table.

Sangchul squeezed his injured hand. The shock forcing a rush of blood to his throat, as if he could throw up a lake of red. His brother was still here, and there was nothing he could do. He searched the crowds. Looked for the narrow face of his hyung. He had kind eyes. A long, tapered nose. He smiled often. Enough for both of them. At the women's table, Halmoni raised herself up. Her slow, effortful gait. Sangchul felt the space behind his nose prick as she reached him.

He raised his palm.

She unwrapped the gauze slowly, until she got to the last layer. Clucked. "It's stuck."

The white knit was embedded in the wound, and she ripped it off without warning, making him gasp. Pink meat flamed in red, crusted in dried blood. She pulled out a tube of ointment.

He felt her methodical tapping, the gash cooling around the edges at her touch. "Can I see him, Halmoni? Could you ask Teacher or Warden for me?"

She sucked her teeth and glanced at the door. It was time for Presentations. "You need a salve as a barrier. I'll tend to the cut again tomorrow. Find new gauze after you wash."

He held on to her shirtsleeve, his voice shrill and pleading. "It was my fault, and I can't—maybe you could go up there to check on him."

Halmoni pressed his shoulder. "I don't have that sort of power." She spoke slow, as if he were someone to pity. "Finish your meal and mind yourself."

He watched the ugly hump of her leave. The bulge at her throat, her thickset hips. If she didn't have any power here, who did?

EUNJU

Mina spat into the bathroom sink after Dinner, her sallow green calves rebuking me. The words that would lead to forgiveness squirmed in my stomach, refusing to rise. She had been wrong too. I turned on the faucet beside her, willing her to stay, airing my voice until it was light, cheery. "The jogaetang was extra tasty today, don't you think?"

Water gushed through the pipes around us, a wet din, and I pretended her answer was lost in the noise.

"I wonder where Youngchul-oppa is," I tried.

She turned off her faucet and pulled back her shoulders, as if putting on a new dress. "Is there something you wanted to say?"

I felt the heat rising from her as she shifted, the ends of her wet hair slapping water across my cheek as I searched for some topic to hold her to me. "Chapel," I started. "Tell me about Chapel."

"Chapel will melt your mind," she finally said. "The first day I arrived, a girl went in for trying to escape. She killed herself after she got out. In the kitchen, with a knife." She spat into the sink, though there was no more foam. No more pretending. "That's why Halmoni only lets the ajummas use them now."

The mirror above the sink was fogged, streaked with toothpaste. A white spatter erased my right eye. She was talking to me. Chapel had killed a girl. Youngchul might still be there. Teacher was taking Umma out at night. Mina had been beaten because of my own selfishness. Again, I'd won Rewards. If only I made tiny movements, I wouldn't break.

"Maybe I could talk to my mother, see about Youngchul," I whispered.

"No one wants to go up there." Mina wiped her neck. "There's nothing we can do."

She walked away. Her slender spine, the horrific blue of her bruised calves. She wasn't the type to hold a grudge. Not like me. She toweled off by the door alongside Areum. Bending to slip on fresh underwear, skin taut against the curve of her ribs. She hadn't forgiven me. I knew that, and I turned from their laughter. The grout between the floor tiles was black with grime. My toes curled. We were never truly clean in this place.

Ten minutes later, I walked into a vibrating room, everyone knotted beneath the windows. Fear pulled at my ankles. Bora was on her knees, slamming her head against the wall.

"We'll figure out an answer," Halmoni said, holding her from behind.

Bora moaned, frantic. Her gaze searched, slid off the others until she found Umma. Accusation hurtling through the air. "Why couldn't it have been her?"

I moved closer; whatever was happening, I wouldn't let her blame my mother. Mina stopped me with an arm across my chest.

Halmoni cupped Bora's face. "You think if I punish her you'll feel better about your life?"

"You should have protected me," Bora screamed. She rocked on her knees, and I knew: her hands cupping her pelvis. The bowl of her that made her a woman. "What am I supposed to do? Tell me, what am I supposed to do?" A howl, drenched in desperation.

Areum rushed to her at that sound, Mina too. The girls mashed together, but I couldn't cross. My skin clammy, coldness in my chest. Saliva in my mouth. I slid to the ground and hugged my knees. Chosen every time as Chapel Meal carrier, Bora had whispered about bound wrists, ice buckets, the stench of bodies giving up. A window through which she slipped trays of food, and how the boys lapped the soup like dogs. She had been harmed, and yet she hadn't ever said anything about herself.

Halmoni pulled her close. "I'm sorry." Her words splitting like a chestnut burr.

Bora was only a year older than me. We weren't protected here. Not her, Umma, any of us.

"We'll find a way," Halmoni said. "There are methods."

Umma came to her. Sleek and sound, like an otter pulling up from the river. "Let her breathe," she demanded, and the group cleaved.

"Oh god." Bora splayed her legs. Wept. "What am I going to do?"

Umma cupped her head. Held her like a daughter. "I'll kill him," she said. "I'll kill him, I will."

2011

In bursts, I bring dishes to Narae. *Service*, I say, laying out haemul pajeon, mandu, gamja jeon, gejang, tteokbokki. She has a fondness for fried food, salt and plenty. In between plates, I rush out what happened next, fear raw between my ears.

Narae rises, a crab leg in one hand, a smear of soy sauce on her lips. *No*, the rage in her a bright and powerful thing. *You can't tell me like this. Am I Bora's daughter? Is that what you're trying to say?*

I . . . That's— But—

You can't, not like this. How could you—? She slams the door.

I trace the sound of her voice, listen in the sunlight's dark to the silence left behind, standing on my two withered feet. Stare at the remains on the table. Oil oozing on the plate, a discarded oyster heart, the jagged edges of shredded potato, that crab leg dripping onto the box of chocolates. She has given me a gift, and in return, I have thought only of my country—how we disappeared in the night, hundreds of us.

For all these years, I imagined the families.

Searching for the missing.

Searching for ghosts.

The fog of us lingering in the air, on their tongues, inside their bones.

In focusing on my hurt, I have forgotten hers.

SANGCHUL

He was returned to them before dawn, the door lurching too early. The sounds of stumbling. A body. A 귀신. A bruised and swollen thing.

Jae and Taeho scrambled from their top bunks, rushed to help him to his cot. Sangchul couldn't move. A cold grasp around his throat. This was his brother?

A purpled face, eyes swollen shut. The skin around the wrists and ankles raw and red. Youngchul collapsed onto his pillow, making no sound. The silence pulsing in Sangchul's ears. He clasped his brother's hand. It was so frail. The bones shifting from the lightest pressure. Connected to an arm and torso and legs and head whittled to a new gauntness. This was his hyung.

"Strip him," Sangchul said.

"Maybe we should let him rest," Jae suggested.

Sangchul pulled Youngchul's shirt to his throat. Swatted hyung's clawed hands away from his waistband, pulled down his pants. He needed to see. Witness. What they had done to him. What he would have to do to earn back his brother's trust. He would destroy them. Warden and Teacher. Bind them by the ankles and hang them from the wall. Grind glass into their gums, down their throats, until they shat crystals. He would make them see.

EUNJU

Nabi sang in a low voice, a gentle mumble as she poured clean water into a vat of rice. By her side, Bora sifted the grains with her fingers and tipped the starchy liquid back out. "Just like that," she murmured. "You want to wash until the water's clear."

"You'll have to decide soon," Halmoni said, trying to gather her attention. "The earlier we act, the safer it is."

"Another rinse," Bora instructed.

Nabi poured again, and their fingers touched among the grains. I watched from the other side of the counter. It had been two weeks since Bora's reveal, seven days since Youngchul's return, and still, Bora wouldn't tell us what she wanted.

"There isn't much time to do it with herbs," Halmoni pressed.

"I'd get rid of it," Ajumma Lee said, her words as clipped as the scallions on her board.

Areum nodded. "You're young. We could get out of here one day."

I held a clump of washed soybeans, pretending to dry them when I was only listening. Waiting like everyone else.

"I knew a girl in my town who died giving birth," Mina said. "But you can die from trying to get rid of it too."

Halmoni pushed her tongue against her teeth, chiding. "You don't bring up death in a time like this." She came around the counter to Bora. "Think about it tonight, and let us know tomorrow, all right?"

Bora hummed us out of her ears.

Umma pulled her chopsticks from the bowl where she was mixing eggs. Orange yolk clinging to the metal ends. Bora looked up. Ever since that night, a line connected them together. A warm flicker in my ears as I flitted between jealousy and pride. "It's your decision," Umma said.

Nabi dried her hands on her shirt. Squinted at us. "What are we talking about exactly?"

The loudspeaker rang. The boys would come from Morning Run soon. Halmoni told us to ready breakfast. "Mina, Eunju—grab a fishhook today, just in case," she said.

"Why?" Nabi asked.

"If Cow refuses, tell him I need a word."

Mina and I hesitated. We hadn't ever stolen one before, the numbers for each package exact. Mina nodded though. I did too. The bright glint of a hook that fit in the palm of my hand. That could fit inside a woman. My body clenched at the thought.

"No," Bora said, her voice surprising me with its calm. "I'm going to keep it."

"Are you—" Halmoni started.

"It's her decision," Umma cut in, fierce. Slowly, Halmoni assented. Ajumma Lee too. All of us, gathering together like a net pulled out of the water. Bora at the center our holy bounty.

"You decide," I said, an echo of my mother.

Ajumma Lee brought over a pot of tea. Poured into our one nice ceramic cup. Fragrant and woodsy. She had been an herbalist. The thought bloomed in me. All the things I didn't know about these women. "It'll be difficult, but we'll help you," she said.

Bora looked up, a smile on her face. The first in weeks. She took the tea and brought it to her lips. Her eyes wet. "Thank you."

SANGCHUL

Sangchul nudged hyung, still lying belly-down on his cot. The fresh welts on his legs from yesterday's Presentations leaking pus atop the Chapel bruises. "It's time to get up."

Youngchul curled into himself, his hands between his knees.

"Now," Sangchul said, severe. He grabbed hyung beneath the armpits. The line to the bathroom was moving quickly, Taeho and Jae trying to stall Cow at the door. He hauled hyung off the bed, bony knees landing with a thud. So, he was a little rough. Every day, he dragged hyung to waking, circled arms around his bird-frail chest as they stumbled through his refusal, the haunting that had stamped him since his return.

How quickly Sangchul's relief had been replaced with frustration. It was exhausting, pushing his emptied brother to sprint, ignore the abrasions on his wrists and ankles, to eat, work. To pretend they should continue as before. Without Youngchul trying, there was no way to deny their circumstance.

Yet the past and future refused to clarify in Sangchul's mind. What had happened in Chapel? What would their lives become, once separated? In two weeks, they would see. He tried to picture the days and failed. Saw only blankness behind and ahead. He didn't know. He didn't want to know.

EUNJU

"Nits." Halmoni sucked her teeth, peered at the pale of Bora's scalp.

"I don't want to be shaved." Bora's voice shook. She'd cried that morning over the color of her nails, sure the white marks were a sign of malnutrition. "Didn't we say the less attention on me, the better?"

I watched from the wooden curtain dividing the cafeteria from the kitchen, a rag and sudsy bucket in my hands. For the third day this week, we hadn't been taken to Workshop, and I hadn't won Rewards. Inside Little House, I didn't have to see Youngchul's drained face, his listless hands hovering over incomplete hook-and-lines. The panic in Sangchul twisting into something ugly and hard. Still, it felt strange to see Bora in this delicate form.

"We can't let the lice spread," Halmoni said.

I stepped forward. "I know how to get rid of them with vinegar. Let me get a bowl." I hurried to find the items, skipping over Bora's reaction, not wanting to see if she was grateful or annoyed.

When I returned, Halmoni patted Bora's cheek. "You'll need to be stronger now."

Bora didn't look different, not yet, but she had changed. Fear replaced by calm replaced by a loose, shifting basket of feelings. I saw it in her hesitation, the way she yielded, closing her eyes and tilting her head so I could parse each strand. "Thanks," she said, quiet.

A few nits caught in between the comb's teeth, and I dunked them in the bowl of hot vinegar. The smell so sharp it pricked my eyes. It was easy work, soothing. I pleasured in popping lice between my fingers. The brief thrill that came with killing an inconsequential life. "Why didn't Halmoni do this instead of shaving us?" I asked. "When we first got here."

"It's always about you, isn't it?" Bora scratched her scalp. "You know, I used to go to school. I had a normal life."

I pushed a nit into the bowl. No matter what I said, she shaped the conversation into sharp points, a reason to fight.

"I lived with my aunt and uncle and grandfather. One day, when the men were out, Gomo married me off to a stranger. She had been planning it for months."

"How could she?"

"She blamed my mother for her brother dying." Bora scratched a spot on her arm that was pink and flaking.

I caught a roving louse between my fingers. Squeezed. Imagined the bug as her new husband, her aunt. "That's terrible," I said.

"I thought that was the worst that could happen to me, and I ran away."

The dead nits floated on top of the vinegar, skimming the surface with dots. I didn't know what to say. There were too many stories. Was it only our country, broken, that held such grief? Or was it the whole of us, all the nations squirming with too much life?

"This is the first decision I'm sure of." She rounded her arms, clutched her sides. That movement, the tiniest of gestures. "This is mine," she whispered.

"Do you feel anything?" I asked. "I can't picture it. I'm not bleeding yet."

"I feel her, like a fish blowing bubbles." She scrunched her nose, shook her head, revealing her youth. She was only a year older than me, she was going to be a mother. "It's hard to explain. She's telling me she's here."

"Have you been dreaming?" I asked.

"That's how I found out. A 태몽 in the night," Bora said. "Chestnuts and persimmons. A fat orange fish nibbling at the fruit." She held herself tighter. "She's mine," she said again.

I let go of her hair. Damp, vinegary, now clean. One last louse flailed in the bowl before surrendering, dead.

Bora squinted at the wood-beaded curtain. The sounds of the others—water gushing from the faucets, the clacking of bowls being put away, a cut of a song shared in the air. "You worry for her," she said, "but at least you have each other."

I homed in on Umma's voice. For the first time, I realized Bora was jealous—of Umma and me, how we had come together. I shook my head, confused. This was bull-shouldered Bora, who had taunted and jeered, marking a line between me and the other girls. "All done," I said.

Bora raised her chin. An expression I couldn't decipher crawled across her face. I cupped her shoulders, hugged her before letting go.

2011

I arrive at Narae's pension house as the sun tucks itself behind the trees. It feels as if I've been holding all the air in my head. I can hear it leaving me, a pin releasing in my ears as she opens the door.

What do you want? A crackling edge to her voice, though her eyes soften—at what?

The shape of me, the stained chocolate box in my hands, my repentance wringing itself into a sound. *Bora isn't your mother.*

She steps back, and I enter, before either of us can change our minds.

She leads me to the living room. Sparse, absent of personality, as these rentals usually are. A rain jacket hanging from a hook. A door ajar, leading to a bedroom. On a low black lacquer table, scattered photographs. It stuns me, to see an image of Sangchul grown, smiling, his arm around a young child I know to be Narae. Instantly recognizable. With that flared nose, her punchy cheekbones.

We sit on floor cushions, and I return the gift to her—the squares of chocolate with their liquid centers. How can I explain? Every night, after she leaves, I lie awake waiting for her return. I imagine a wave, Narae pushed up to the crest. A tiny and flailing creature.

What she doesn't realize: we were the vestiges of a country

trying to reshape itself. It was easier not to see, to let us disappear. I don't know what to make of it then, her arrival, my desire to share.

You are making me witness, I say, *but I will be careful, I will try not to hurt you.* It isn't a lie, not wholly, because I do not want to hurt her, even if I know I must.

SANGCHUL

Warden shouted from beneath the cross at the center of the pulpit: "In two days, we will have a reckoning. I have witnessed your hard work, and I have news."

Sangchul breathed in shallow bursts. In two days, Youngchul would be seventeen. Maybe this was how Warden would announce a new truth, maybe hyung would become a Keeper after all, or he would stay as he was—quota demanded workers. He focused on Warden's tie, the blotches that looked like blood.

"An Inspection is upon us," Warden yelled.

Sangchul scraped his collar. The red blotches blurred, seeped into the black silk.

"This Inspection will allow us to receive the funding to feed, clothe, educate you. Today and tomorrow, we will have no Workshops." Warden laughed. "That's right. Instead, we will clean our home from the entryway corners to the ceiling light fixtures." He strolled the aisle, the smile on his face unnatural, as if he had never learned the taste of happiness. "There will be foreigners among us who will inspect your progress from filth to working members of society."

Teacher followed. "There will be benefits."

"Who will be our representatives, who will get the honor of

meeting our French nuns and American humanitarians?" Warden bellowed.

"Who are our star reformers?" Teacher asked.

The tempo of the room shifted, frothing excitement. Cleaning instead of Workshops. Benefits. Outsiders. Maybe the nuns would save them, a call to parents across the country, a mass release. Beside Sangchul, Youngchul was the only one who remained unchanged, his disinterest a dark, sucking hole. Sangchul looked back at Warden. His tie, they were poppies, not blood—the red flecked all over fine silk. Irregular petals with black, gaping centers.

The cafeteria thrummed: Warden and Halmoni gestured by the wood-beaded curtain while the Keepers huddled by the doors, ignoring their groups for once. Everyone chattering about Inspection. Sangchul tried to hold on to this fizzing thrill, but he could feel it vaporizing. Youngchul's emptiness was too unplumbed. He wanted to ask, and yet he was afraid to know: *Are you angry with me, can't you tell me, or shove me across the room like any other older brother would?*

Jae touched the wing bones of his shoulders together. "You know what this means."

"What?" Taeho asked, spooning chunks of white fish into his mouth.

"Don't draw attention to yourself, don't do anything to end up in Chapel." Jae glanced at Youngchul. "They don't want to be embarrassed."

"What about the benefits?" Taeho asked. "It could be fun to be a representative."

"I'd rather be locked together in our room than paraded around for some foreigners," Jae said.

Youngchul sliced through the fish at the bottom of his bowl.

White, slimy slivers. "I turn seventeen then," he said, his first words all day.

"Let's focus on getting through Inspection," Sangchul said, as gentle as he could manage.

"Maybe they'll be so busy they'll forget," Taeho said. For once, his naivety a relief. A gift Sangchul wanted to consume whole, like a dark cherry, pit and all.

"I don't want to go to an adult institution." Youngchul's voice cracked, cratering the space between them. "I don't want to be alone."

They looked at one another—Sangchul, Jae, Taeho. The fact of Youngchul's leaving was a boulder pushing against their spines. Hyung had refused to face it directly, and now here he was crying.

A hush from behind. A lingering gawp from the next row.

Sangchul could cup hyung's face, the way their mother had in the mornings when blessing them on their way to school. He could lie and say they would stay together. There were kindnesses he could extol. Anger rose in him. He wanted to scream: *Don't you see, how tired I am?* For weeks, he'd carried his brother's life. Watched him at all hours with a stony pit of fear in his stomach.

Taeho reached over, rubbed Youngchul's ear like a pearl, a wing. Sangchul pulled at his collar, his pulse ticking in his ears, hating Taeho's easy giving, while something in him refused.

EUNJU

I dreamed I crawled into the mouth of a snake, stinking hot and wet. Jagged teeth and pulsing tongue. Gliding down a ridged throat. Inside its stomach, I placed my hands on the pink wall of muscle and pushed until a curve revealed itself, solid and rounded as a tooth. This was no tooth, though, but the bone that made us women. The rib shifted, writhing beneath my palm, and raised its fanged tip, pierced through to attack. Even the snake would devour itself to hurt me, I thought sadly.

I woke gasping, an ache in my side. Liquid darkness, everyone asleep. Umma, her hair mussed. My skin clammy with sweat. Ever since Bora's reveal, nightmares unraveled me. Sometimes, I was bound at the wrists, mawing for food with a gummy, toothless mouth. Other times, I dug a hole by the stone wall only to find tiny Youngchuls pushing their way up from the soil, all wriggly limbs and high-pitched screams. More and more, as one month here turned to two, I felt like I was losing my grounding, the boundaries of my knowledge dissolving into fractured dreams.

I breathed. Concentrated on the snores and murmurs of sleep. A shifting beside me, the smooth sliding of sheets. Umma. The slightest creak as she rose.

I crawled onto the floor. I would confront her. I would save or shame her. I wouldn't let her go alone. Following on my knees, quiet and small, dark and unseen. Ajumma Lee, asleep by the locked door, arms flung above her head.

The rasp of a key in the hole. As Umma slipped out, I skated my hand through the gap, grabbed tight. I didn't want to stop, think.

The hallway was dark, and I felt a strange teetering, as if I were facing the edge of a mirrorless lake. Someone pulled her along. I knew already, the tall build, the sloping shoulders. The one who took Bora to Chapel Meals. Teacher.

My feet slapping against the floor. I ran to them.

"Eunju?" Umma's alarm. "What are you doing here?"

It was Teacher who hurt the boys, wielding his baton, fist, the Keepers. Warden lectured about God, disappeared into his office, and returned for his daily display of power at Presentations. But Teacher, he prickled with a fury barely contained.

He wrenched us both by the hair. Down the hall. Past the bathroom. A jolt at the thought of him flinging us down the stairs. He stopped and shoved us into the last unused room to our left.

A hot loud slap. "What were you thinking?" I couldn't see, the textures of black on black, a man hitting a woman.

"I didn't— I'm—" Umma said.

The room was stuffed, clangy with items I tripped over as I searched for a light switch. Finally, I toggled it on. Brightness. Is this where it happened? In between cardboard boxes, his flat eyebrows and Umma's open, weeping face. Her body a bent line.

"I'm sorry," she said.

Umma, who was once lean with anger, had changed into a woman I didn't recognize. Rage studded through me. Where was she, the one from before, who'd made the landlords and street vendors who cheated us recoil?

"I snuck out," I said. "She didn't know."

Teacher stared. "Are you as stupid as your mother?"

I imagined swinging his baton at his head, the electric spray of blood bursting from his eyes, the satisfaction.

"Neither of you matter," he said. Spit on his chin, a white dribble.

"Byungchul, please. She doesn't know."

His eyes flitted to her at the sound of his name. He lunged. Caught her by the neck and slammed her against the metal frame of an upright cot. "You think only boys go to Chapel?"

I charged. My fingers scratching his shirt and arms, thin hairs getting caught beneath my nails. He flung me off, and Umma drank in air.

Teacher towed me by the sleeve, his face filmed with sweat. I lifted to my toes, my shoulder loosening in its socket. The skin beneath his left eye twitched. I wanted to pierce him there with a fishhook, right through to the creamy meat of his brain.

"I'll tell the nuns," Umma said between gasps. "I'll tell them everything if you hurt her."

He carried my arm as if it didn't belong to my body. I tripped over my feet, fear ripe in my throat, colliding into a cardboard box, a stack of paint cans. "Whatever happens to her now is because of you," he panted.

Outside, down the hall, back to our room. He unlocked the door. Shoved me in.

I fell onto my knees.

Ajumma Lee woke. "Eunju?"

It was only as she hugged me, cradling my arm, whispering that it was going to be okay, she would return soon, I should try to sleep, they wouldn't hurt her right before Inspection, that I tasted her absence. Umma was still out there, bent over and searching for breath, her throat wrung red.

SANGCHUL

He dreamed he watched hyung leave, disintegrating into a green-dusted landscape. The air chalky with his remains. Sangchul rubbed his collarbone, and when he looked down, the brown stain he'd hated all his life was snaking down his arm, looping his elbow, settling in the meat of his hand, a sudden coiled puddle. He understood then, had known all along: he belonged here, alone, worth less than the weight of the fishhook in his palm.

In the gym the next day, Sangchul knuckled his eyes in surprise. He'd woken from his nightmare sure he'd see the morose husk of his hyung. Yet it seemed Youngchul had changed overnight. Grinning, full-teethed, energetic. Hyung joked about Rat's group's haphazard poster hanging, Crow's boys' streaky window washing. They'd all been given specific tasks, with their group to push towels crusted with wax across the floor, leaving gleaming strips of pale wood in their wake. Sangchul watched his brother banter. Suspicion gnawed his toes. Why was hyung so . . . happy?

Jae shrugged, the same question on his mind. "It's better this way, isn't it?"

Perhaps. Sangchul was glad for not having to badger, but there was something frenetic beneath Youngchul's demeanor, a brightness he didn't believe, some inner working chirred to life.

"Look at that leech sidling up to Rat." Youngchul pointed at

Dal at the far end of the room, smirking behind fogged glasses. He had been squealing more than usual since the announcement. Spilled soup, shirked work, a shoddy job, a stolen bite of rice. Anything was enough.

"He'd give up his own mother to be a representative," Sangchul said. "Just to parade around some nuns."

"I'd rather be in the room with you all." Youngchul smiled. "Right, Taeho?"

"I heard we'll get treats," Taeho said, and Youngchul laughed. Sangchul eyed Jae. Tomorrow was Inspection Day. Maybe hyung had decided they should enjoy this time together. Sangchul tried to ignore the unease smearing through him as Taeho pretended to follow the poses on the posters hung on the wall, black-and-white images showing how to stretch different parts of the body. It was absurd, them exercising or playing in here.

"What do you think the foreigners will be like?" Youngchul asked.

"Some of us were talking about pushing the bunks against the windows," Jae said. "We could get a glimpse."

"I want to see." Youngchul nodded, then cocked an eyebrow. "Race?" He sped off, pushing the waxy towel, his heel showing through a hole in his sock. Calloused and thick, with a ledge of crunchy white skin.

EUNJU

Halmoni warned us while straightening bottles of soy sauce, vinegar, how well Warden and Teacher would hide their violences. How easily deceived the foreigners would be. Our job was to cook. Feed and smile and not speak. Add sugar and less gochugaru, their faint foreign tongues weak. As she spoke, the bulge in her throat gleamed, firm and smooth, like an egg. She waved us to our corners, prayer worrying her lips. Scrutiny on the men meant their scrutiny on us.

Umma held me before going to her station beside Ajumma Lee, a nod between them. I didn't know if Ajumma's kindness would evaporate with the night, if she would betray us, but no one glanced at my aching shoulder, Umma's shifting agitation.

Next to Mina, I held in all I wanted to say—about Teacher's choking grip, the fear he'd kill Umma in a rage, the room with boxes and stacks of paint cans, a spare cot, how he hadn't used a key, only jiggled the knob, and his name, Byungchul, a knowledge intimate and potent, my only reserve—and it hollowed me, how I had no one.

Mina soaked namul, rubbed dirt off leaves. Pulled thready roots. Silent. I ripped steamed eggplants into shreds. Their soft, pale meat so hot my fingers burned. "Do you think the nuns will be kind?" I tried.

"You're bruising them." A shake of the head. "Can't you be a little gentler?"

I saw Teacher's hands around Umma's neck, his fingers white with pressure. Sweat rolling down my chest, the backs of my knees. I had never seen Umma that way. I squeezed the eggplants harder.

Mina's eyes narrowed. "What's Warden doing here?"

I turned—in a suit and dark tie, at the kitchen entrance. Panic. My skin latticed with bristling heat. Before I could find Umma, or say anything to Mina, Warden pointed. "Come."

"Me?" My voice small. Had Teacher told him what I had done? I raised my palms. The eggplants I had handled too rough now a liquid mush. "I'm making gaji namul."

"Is something wrong?" Halmoni asked. "There's so much to do."

Umma stepped forward, shaking. "She's my daughter."

"Come," he repeated.

She stopped before him, and I followed. "Umma," I said. "I'm sorry."

Warden examined her face. His lips twitching at the red of her neck. He grabbed my arm and pulled me out.

We walked across the empty field, the sting of cut grass underfoot. He had forbidden shoes. "You won't need them," he'd said. What did that mean? Halmoni's prayer came to me, her whisper in my ear as he pulled me away. *Like a wing, shelter this child.*

Was he taking me to Chapel? *Neither of you matter,* Teacher had said. Maybe he was right. We had already disappeared, and no one had found us. I almost slipped, trying to match Warden's quick strides. It had turned bitter overnight, the warmth gone like a sleight-of-hand trick. Too many clouds, a harsh wind.

He stopped in the center of the field. Beneath an indifferent gray sky, the glass on the top of the wall a relentless reminder. "What were you thinking?" he asked.

I rubbed my hands before him, *I'm sorry* the only words I could form.

"Kneel," he said softly.

I bowed. Touched my head to the ground in full prostration. My lids into the earth. "I'm sorry, Warden. I repent."

"When you disobey, you not only harm yourself, but your mother." He heeled my neck, his leather shoe's hard sole crunching me down. Grass in my eyes, nose. My face wet. "She has many tallies against her, so much she must erase from the stain of herself, and here you are, adding more."

"I won't cause trouble," I whispered. My tongue grazing dirt. "I'll be good."

"Should I forgive you?" A rougher thrust. Pressure, pinching my eyes. *Like a wing, shelter this child.* He would crush me. Pop my skull off my neck.

"Please," I begged. Dirt against my teeth, in my throat. Pain, starbursting behind my nose.

"You cannot hide from me, do you understand?"

Chapel. Umma disappearing in the night. Warden's silence. A horde of nuns. All this time, I had been wary of Teacher. His erratic anger. It was Warden who held us in his power.

He released his foot, air a gift.

"Clean my shoes," he said.

I looked up. Backlit, a faceless man against gray clouds.

"'Do you see? I entered your house; you gave me no water for my feet, but she has wet my feet with her tears and wiped them with her hair.'"

"I don't understand," I said, my hands gritty, my mouth too. "With my tears?"

"Your tongue."

I shook my head.

"Give me your obedience."

His red tie. The paunch of his stomach. A brown belt with a double-barred buckle. The muscles in my neck refused.

"Now."

I opened my mouth. Animal meeting animal. Silt and salt collecting on my tongue. The laces waxy. My stomach roiled, and I swallowed a well of vomit.

"With meaning," he said.

I licked around the vamp, down to where the ridged welt met the sole. The tangy scent of spit, sour wetness on my nose and cheeks. He sighed, and I gagged.

"Open your eyes."

When I finished, he raised me by the armpits as if I were a child. His touch a radiation. I swallowed the sludge in my throat, the smell of leather in my nose. "You will be a good girl now."

The skin around his narrow eyes wrinkled, and a colorless fear ran through me. He believed himself to be right. He gestured to the east, where the sun shone through a gap in the clouds. A bright, silvery light. "I'll accompany you to Little House."

No violence had come to me, but I felt raw, harmed, afraid as I walked ahead.

"Stop," he said as we reached the edge of the field. I saw the trees, the dirt path, Little House in the distance. The wind harsh, riotous. If only a bird would sing, that note could save me.

He slid his shoe between my feet. Up my ankles.

I shuddered, chickenfleshed and alone.

"Fix your crooked walk."

I cried, a hard, loud weeping. I had been crying all along.

2011

Narae holds me. *I'm fine*, I try to say, but the words don't leave my mouth. Shame. Invisible insects scurrying beneath my skin. Clawing out of my eyes, nose, the space below my tongue. He made me feel shame. I shift back on my heels, not recognizing my surroundings, until, slowly, it comes to me: I am sitting in Narae's pension house. I am telling her our story, despite wanting to paint over sins, make us appear brighter, cleaner.

You don't have to tell me everything, she says. Her touch a forgiveness of its own. I concentrate on her orange-painted nails, the red floor cushions beneath us, the framed painting of a wave on the wall. *Not if it hurts you*, she says, leaning into my neck.

I nod, though she isn't right. She must hear all of it in order to understand the story of her life, why her father wanted us to meet.

Wait. She drifts through the kitchen. Brings me tea and a sleeve of Ace crackers, those buttery, flaky squares I love so much. Clears the chocolates with intention, as if this act will save me.

I wanted to burn myself, I say, *but there was no time to act because what happened next—the disaster of Inspection Day, and Youngchul—we changed.*

EUNJU

Halmoni gathered us in the kitchen. More than our room upstairs or the cafeteria where we served, this was where we felt whole, protected. We linked hands, and she prayed for little Nabi and me, thumbed a cross on our foreheads. Ready in our new tracksuits, crimson with white stripes running down our limbs. Mina kissed my ear. Bora touched my cheek. "Don't be dumb," she chided. "Protect Nabi."

"I will," I said.

Umma circled me, her breath warm against my crown. "Today isn't the day to be brave." She leveled her face with mine. The crease over her right eye deepening as she spoke. "Stay in sight of the nuns. He won't be able to do anything in front of them."

I wanted to tell her everything—about Warden, my humiliation. His bulbous nose, that flabby mouth, his leather shoes. There had been no time yesterday, Nabi and I chosen as representatives, kept for hours to practice our cues. All night, we had perfected raised hands and straight backs. Open-mouthed smiles. "Foreigners like teeth," Teacher had said while I sat empty, my mind eaten up by what Warden had made me do.

"I'll be invisible. I'll be good, Umma," I said.

Halmoni called us to the entrance leading out of the kitchen. It was time. "We'll be waiting. You return as soon as greeting duties are done."

Nabi nuzzled her face into Umma's apron. "I'll bring unnie back to you."

Umma cupped Nabi's head, wiped a stuck strand from her lips. "Bring yourself back too."

We left for Big House, following Teacher's quick strides. The new tracksuits cool to the touch, made of higher quality than our usual garb. The fabric shone beneath the sun, swished against our skins. Nabi swung her arms, just to hear that slippery sound.

Inside, the other greeters waited. Teacher steered us into two lines flanking the new carpet in the main hallway. Nabi the head of one, me the other. "Backs straight. Smiles on. Warden will bring our visitors from the gates." A forced grin on his face too. Practicing, like the rest of us. "Greetings, an introduction, lunch," Teacher reminded. After, the next group of representatives would be fetched from upstairs. Sangchul had been chosen for Lessons. Not Jae or Taeho. Not Youngchul. The rest of us meted out, controlled.

"It's time." He opened the doors until they clicked in place, a mechanism latching them like a drunken mouth, the carpet a long flat tongue. The day's brightness spilled in waves, so white I couldn't see, my vision adjusting too slowly. Beyond, a paved road sloped down a hill to closed metal gates, the stone wall hemming us in. Three parked cars, dotted figures stepping out. The gates, we could climb or pry them through sheer force. I glanced at Nabi, but Teacher zipped his baton up my spine.

The group approached, slowly and then all at once. So many, a rush of new smells and noises and bodies. We clapped with stretched smiles. Women in black dresses, heads covered, faces pink. A man with notepads and pens. Another with a camera. One tall, thin-limbed Korean man. The interpreter. The foreigners spoke in their tongues, a jumble of greetings. I wanted to hate them, these adults who would easily believe Warden's and Teacher's sugared words, but even I felt gummy with excitement, caught in their eager hellos. We bowed, hinging our bodies, "Welcome to the Stone Home!" reverberating against the walls.

They remarked on Teacher's neat classroom, with its freshly cleaned blackboard, the wooden two-top desks with matching benches spaced out in rows. The walls decorated with plaques, framed newspaper clippings. One nun pointed to a heading—*The Stone Home Rehabilitates Vagrant Citizens*—with the interpreter. The sounds of satisfaction and approval obvious across languages.

Nabi led her group into the second row, and I led mine into the third. As the visitors found their seats in the front, Warden spoke, the interpreter beside him, translating into French and English and back to Korean. I tried to dissolve my mind. Warden was too enthusiastic, feeding on the admiration of an audience. I almost laughed as Teacher brought in poster photographs of the Pentecost picnic. We were smiling, bowls of miyeokguk and rice aplenty. We looked nearly healthy. How easy it was to deceive.

"Now we will hear from some of our best citizens." Warden stepped to the side.

A boy from Shirts stood, cleared his throat. "I was once a homeless vagrant, stealing food and defecating in the streets. At the Stone Home, I have learned how to be a productive member of society. I'm skilled at sewing buttons, and I have become rehabilitated thanks to Warden Kang and Teacher Chung." He bowed and sat back down.

Another boy next. Pocked face and a squealer. Nabi turned to me, a quick suck of teeth. This one was dramatic, eager. He spoke about drinking alcohol and brawling on the streets. "The Stone Home offered me shelter and hearty meals."

One after another, lies spilled from their mouths in silky layers. The interpreter transformed words into new meaning. Finally, Nabi stepped forward. "I have friends who care for me here," she said cautiously. "I've learned to cook and wash laundry." Her smile faltered. "I was brought here because—"

"Can she come to me?" the interpreter said, then nodded to one of the nuns. Nabi approached, and the nun touched her face. Her hair. Murmured to the woman next to her. They thought she was pretty, with her round cheeks and blunt bob. Foreigners favored freckles. Nabi fiddled with the hem of her tracksuit. We had heard of adoptions, children sent abroad, but she already had a family, a mother she'd lost in the market when she had wandered away, drawn to a red plastic lunch box. Soon, we used to say when she woke in the night. Soon your umma will find you.

"Thank you," the nun said through the interpreter. "She's lovely, a little China doll."

Nabi returned to her seat, and I touched her spine, our secret language. I wanted to stand, shout, but no, I would protect myself and her.

Warden spread his arms. "The Stone Home is a welfare center, and our goal is to transform our country's wayward souls into reformed, productive citizens. We feed, educate, and instill religious faith in them. We welcome you with God's grace."

The interpreter spoke without the emotion that rustled through Warden's words. I listened to the double rhythms of their two voices, the visitors interjecting questions. They paid no attention to us, our stiff effort. One man snapped his camera. I stared right at him. My gaze clear. If they didn't understand, they were idiots, willfully ignoring us.

"We recently took in a teenaged woman who is pregnant out of wedlock. Kicked out of her home. The baby's father a mystery. We ask for your prayers especially for our Bora," Warden said.

My right eye twitched. How did he know about Bora? Nabi turned, alarm blotching her cheeks.

"We can take her with us." The interpreter gestured to a nun with wire-rimmed glasses. "We have a home for unwed girls, and we find proper families for the babies."

They couldn't make Bora give up her child. I pulled on my ears. Warden warned me with a glare. I wouldn't say anything. I wouldn't bring attention to myself. Wouldn't give him a reason. My tongue, his shoes. I tried to squash the memory into dust, my mouth dry and gritty, but the smell flooded me. Musky leather and grass and sweat.

Warden led us out: the visitors, Teacher, the representatives in our two lines. "We'll take a tour of the grounds and have lunch in Little House." He pointed to the running path, the Workshops.

Nabi mouthed, *Bora-unnie.* We had to warn her. I shut my eyes. The smell of him inside me. We would have lunch soon. Rice, kimchi, gyeran-mari. Jangjorim, miyeokguk. Maybe the foreigners would forget about the pregnant girl. Maybe Halmoni had hidden her away. Maybe Bora would believe what they promised—a better life for her child.

He continued on. "After lunch, Teacher Chung will bring you back to the classroom, where our brightest students will discuss their educations."

The wind was quieter now, a wisp that swept the hems of the nuns' habits. I clenched my fists. Bora and her swollen stomach. Warden and his leather shoes. The nuns and their ignorance. I needed to find Umma. She would tell us what to do.

A scream.

Warden tripped—his teeth shiny between parted lips. Scanning the group, Teacher stalked our way—but it wasn't us, we were silent and good.

"What's happening?" the interpreter asked, and I didn't know if he was speaking for himself or for someone else.

Again. A pitched strangling, streaking through the air.

We turned. The noise was coming from behind—Big House, from above—a boy on the second floor. Small fists, landing on a window. A dark head of hair. A long face. Screaming and screaming. *Help us. Help us. Get us out of here.*

SANGCHUL

Sangchul plucked at the sleeve of his new tracksuit, a deck of hwatu cards on his lap. The plastic casing untouched. All around them, laughter. Bunks pushed aside, the remnants of cellophane-wrapped cookies sweetening the air. By the windows, Dal performed a simple, exhilarating trick with a yo-yo. He had been chosen as a representative too. Sangchul nudged his brother's cot. "Want to play?"

Youngchul spoke into his pillow. "You're ruining everything."

"Hyung." Sangchul touched his shoulder. "I didn't mean to."

"Then how did you get chosen?" Youngchul asked, accusation barbing each word, yesterday's giddiness stamped out. "You earned it somehow."

Sangchul flinched. He couldn't help it if Warden picked him for a role he didn't want. Maybe hyung would've said no, but Sangchul couldn't, hadn't—and he liked the new tracksuit, the rewards. That was winning too, extracting moments of pleasure where they could.

Youngchul snorted and stood. Jae held Sangchul back. "Give him time."

He shrugged. If hyung wanted to sulk, so be it. Sangchul ripped open the cards, the red plastic clacking together. "Let's play a round."

A laughing shout came from the hallway as they set up the game. The Keepers, making sure no one would run downstairs and reveal the real workings of the Home.

Jae glanced at the locked door. "I heard they got Apollo Candy."

"Really?" Taeho asked, wistful. "Those are my favorite."

Sangchul dealt out seven cards each, feigning indifference. The reps had received Apollo Candy too. Last night, as they practiced their lines, Teacher handed out the short pastel straws. Three each. Not enough to share. Sangchul and Dal had stopped outside their room, sucking the sugary insides coated in pink, yellow, green. Tossed the emptied tubes into their new pockets. The hit of sweetness, the false fruit flavor a euphoric high.

He flipped over six cards in the center and stacked the rest. So, he'd received Apollo Candy. He deserved it, for memorizing lines, for being forced to soon lie to a bunch of foreigners.

Jae slapped a pi card, but his gaze wandered to Youngchul and a few others pushing a bunk to the window. Honggi, from Crow's group, climbed and grabbed the bars.

"Asa," Sangchul whooped, sweeping four cards, yet even as he gathered them, he knew there was a mistake—with him and hyung being here, with a world that allowed such captivity, and he turned by instinct—drawn like a ghost to its body, knowing before he heard—he had always been connected this way, to hyung—

Fists on panes.

A shadow blocking the sun.

He jolted, realizing too late. Youngchul: screaming, *Help us, help us*, the glass refusing to break.

Hoarse and brave and idiotic and relentless.

A flash, and Sangchul saw him covered in blood—what they would do to him, the Keepers, surely, the men.

"Get him down," Sangchul yelled, scattering cards, running. Honggi banged on the window too. Another joined, and another.

Sangchul climbed, the bunk unwieldy, reaching for some part of his brother he could pull down. Hyung kicked him away.

Behind them, the door thudded: Keepers, shouting to let them in. A horde holding them back. Dal screaming, "The boys are blocking you!" A traitor through and through.

No hope. The Keepers were older, stronger. The door opened too soon. Sangchul clawed hyung's waist, twisted fabric. Begged, "You have to get down," but he couldn't hear his voice, hyung's response. The din too loud. He looked down—Mosquito was on them. The sound of snapping—

Sangchul hit the floor as the bunk split. Lattice caving in. Iron in his mouth. A white bat, aiming for Youngchul's legs.

Later, others told him, voices bowled low with admiration, about the nuns. The confusion on their faces—and also, the fear.

Eunju said the chaos upstairs became contagious, tainting the air and traveling to the chosen ones outside. Nabi begged a nun to find her mother. Warden pleaded with them to move on. Teacher lost control.

Sangchul didn't witness any of that, and he didn't care. He only saw Youngchul—the determination spilling from his mouth, invisible and hot, the emptying as Mosquito dragged him out of the room. How hyung's eyes rolled, revealing yellow snaked with red. That image, he would remember forever.

What had hyung seen? Were the nuns listening? Surely the ragged sound of desperation, the hollowed ring of fear, crossed languages.

Why hadn't they all screamed? Why hadn't he moved to protect his only brother? He turned that day over in his mind, an endless, excruciating circle. He would never know.

2011

Narae rings the bell at noon. I watch her unzip supple leather boots, loosening metal teeth, surprised at her lightness after yesterday's reveal. She heads to the kitchen. A purse and netted bag of groceries swinging from her hands. *Come on, unnie. I have news and fruit.*

Unnie. How unexpected to have come to this intimacy in a week. I follow, and she makes a noise of pleasure at the dishes I've prepared. *Let's eat. Chamoes and news for dessert*, I say, wary.

I'll see if I can wait. She holds the high wooden back as I sit, her warm fingers briefly raking my neck before she takes her seat.

Narae waits until I take the first bite and then begins her usual devouring. Bowls of white rice, gyeran-mari dotted with scallions, jangjorim, kimchi, miyeokguk. I make the same dishes at the restaurant, overheated in the back kitchen. I've made the same dishes for years.

There's more, I say, glancing at this woman, unmoored by her steady cadence. Perhaps this is what it means to be American, to take such a story as mine in stride. *Are you ready to find out what happened next?*

Not yet. She looks young when she eats, the skin beneath her eyes plump. The child she once was revealing herself, and it aches me—the years I didn't know her, what I've learned of her now: she teaches English literature, coaches the girls' soccer team, hates ice cream, the cold traveling through her teeth, she broke up with her partner a year ago, she cannot drink vodka any longer, the clear substance of her high school youth.

When her rice bowl glistens, she pulls a folder from the purse by her feet. *I've been doing some research.* Her voice pitches, eager.

Last night, I dreamed of waves, the white froth of their tails. Woke to silence in a darkened room. The knife, open and ready, in my hand.

I slice a gyeran-mari. *I don't want to hear it.*

I know. She quiets, but from her narrowed gaze on the papers, it's clear she doesn't understand. *The Stone Home wasn't the only one.*

Fear climbs my stomach.

She flips through a stapled packet. *This building here, on this island outside of Seoul, was used as a reformatory during Japanese colonialization. The same situation, children and teens disappearing from the streets. It's an artist retreat now.*

She slides the article to me. An accusatory headline. A photo of a building. No children, not even shadows. *That would have been years before I was born*, I say.

Exactly. Narae moves her bowl out of the way. *What does it mean, that the same sort of institution existed fifty years before?*

I shake my head. An impossible thought and somehow fitting, to continue what our colonizers created.

She riffles to another article. *The Brothers Home in Busan operated the same time as yours. They say the government was involved, maybe Park Chung-hee. What if Teacher and Warden had been told to open the Home by someone with real power?* Her voice ramps up, her painted nails tacking the tabletop.

Real power? Anger flares in me. *All of their power was real.*

That's not what I meant.

My chopsticks clatter as I stand. There had been others—other buildings. Other boys and girls. Other families broken apart by unaccountable men. I blink away the cavern opening inside me.

Narae kneels. Her bare knees on my wooden floors. Her leather shoes in the entranceway. I see myself before Warden, in the field. No, she is only gathering papers. I concentrate on the tail of an unraveled egg roll. The expression on her face I hope is shame. *This is bigger than we thought. If you help me, we could start a real investigation,* she says.

I walk out. How simple it would be. To blame Japan, the war, the dictator, another violence. What Warden and Teacher did was theirs to own.

You said Teacher's name was Chung Byungchul, right? I can search for—

Don't, I say, my voice catching. *He's probably dead.* The wall between us. The length of the kitchen behind. The hallway ahead. I touch the living room light switch. Turn it off, on. This scraping inside me.

Warden, then. The Keepers. We could punish them, she says.

We can't, and I am spent—there is no space for her, my life. I picture soft waves, and they infect my dreams in their unruliest forms. *I was right about you*, I say. Narae has sliced my world open. There's no protection left to me now.

She stops at the living room entryway. Watches me flick the light switch. I cannot shake it—there were others, we repeated our own imprisonment, Keepers of our own history.

You don't want to know. Her voice is cold, unrelenting. The girl who was taught to box, to defend with knives, reveals herself. Lean and muscular. *I came here to see, and I won't leave until I understand.*

The first time I entered a car after the Stone Home, in a taxi in Daegu, I pulsed with fear. Speeding through the streets, contained in a leather-clad space with an unknown man. He blinked too much, glancing at me through the rearview mirror. A silver cross swinging from a chain around his neck. He tapped his ring against the steering wheel, and I wanted him to stop, shut up, leave me in peace. The smell of dark leather filled me, animal hide and wax and suffocation.

Let me out, I screamed, the oxygen disappearing in the back seat, my tongue clogging my throat. I would choke on myself. The smell of him. My hands shook, and I couldn't open the doors.

He swerved, crossed lanes of traffic, bumped onto the side of the road. *Should I call an ambulance?* He twisted, one hand on the wheel, the other reaching past the gap between the seats.

The air in my lungs shot like a new bursting as I ran from the car, down the street, around squat buildings, toward the sea.

This is what I remembered. That animal smell. My vision dissolving. My dry tongue.

What's stopping you? Give me a reason. Narae touches my arm. Her mutable face. Her perfectly stitched seams and propulsive grief. Her American demand for clear, obvious answers. Her command to witness.

I could get in trouble, I whisper.

Trouble?

Still, I haven't told her what I've done.

Still, I hate her father.

Still, I unspool our stories for her to judge.

PART TWO

JANUARY–MAY 1981

EUNJU

A week after Inspection Day, as everything and nothing changed, Mina came to me. She lingered by my cot, hesitation thickening her steps. "Is your mother outside?"

I kept clipping my toenails, slivered shards scattering onto a sheaf of newspaper. I tried to subdue my surprise. Umma and the others were gathered in the hallway, talking of what had happened to Bora. In the upheaval Youngchul caused, she had been taken by the nuns without ceremony, without a chance for us to say goodbye.

Mina rolled her pajama pants, folding the fabric in on itself up to the knee. I held my breath, scared that despite all that happened, she still hated me. "I need to cut my nails too."

She smiled with effort. Her eyes pink and swollen. My selfishness furred around my neck. She was mourning, and here I was, thinking of myself. Seven days since the news had spread—that Youngchul had been hauled off to Chapel—six days since the speculations—that he was dead, that something had happened that couldn't be explained away—five days since a man had come with a leather bag—a doctor, they whispered. Then, the announcement: a heart attack. A blameless death.

I rubbed her ankle bone. The sparse hairs. "Remember what he said about spirits?"

"Youngchul-oppa?"

I nodded. One afternoon in Workshop, he had whispered his belief in a consciousness separate from our bodies. He'd said our spirits were nothing like what Warden claimed, we had to believe that much, at least, to survive. He had been kind, full of ideas. His reedy arms and flappy ears and narrow, searching face.

"He squeezed his fingers when he was nervous," Mina said.

"His favorite food was bindae-tteok."

We spouted facts about him, all we could gather—how he missed reading and eating market-stall meals, how, of all animals, he thought he was most like a white-naped crane, and it fit him so cleanly, the long-necked, long-legged elegant bird—because in the end, our time with Youngchul had been brief, and yet he was yoked to us.

Mina wiped her cheeks. With Bora, we could pretend: she'd have a better life. With Youngchul, there was no lie for us to hold on to. "Eunju," Mina said, my name supple in her mouth. "I should have known better."

I crinkled the newspaper between us. My hope so slight. I'd been lonely since she had cast me off, since I'd betrayed her, since our world had shifted with Youngchul's and Bora's leaving.

"Your mother, Bora. I know now what you were saying." Her hands rustled through the air, her crumbling voice as familiar as her movements. "It was unfair of me."

I turned to the barred windows, splintered moonlight. She was saying sorry, in her way. Our grievances with each other trivial, bits of dust. "It could have happened to any of us," she said.

"Not us." I folded the newspaper into a square, the clipped slivers pooling in the middle. "I won't let that happen."

"Will we get out?" Mina whispered, and I cupped her bony ankle, pressed against the only knowledge I owned. Our bodies, here, and our predicament:

We were fractured and dazed and scared. Our minds a slurry

of news. The anticipation of freedom deflating with every day. Where had the journalists and nuns gone? The interpreter, he must have told someone what he really saw. For seven days, men in uniforms came to speak to Warden and Teacher, but there was no investigation, no anger. They didn't question us.

Did they even want to know?

SANGCHUL

In the months after Youngchul died, the anger he'd felt, so vast and elemental, changed. It was as if he'd swallowed the sea, the dark waters flushing through him and leaving only salt—bitter, granular, so blaringly white he saw nothing else. Sangchul formed a whittled white block and kept it deep inside.

He extracted himself—from Taeho and Jae, their useless words of comfort, their pitying glances, from the chatter of a world continuing without his brother.

Hyung had left him for the hallucination of freedom. A wispy belief that floated into the air and burned in the sun.

He would never understand—how Youngchul could have abandoned him so thoroughly. How easily disposable he was, even to his family.

EUNJU

Six months passed, time short enough to fit inside our dreams, yet long enough to unspool in our palms. A new year erupted without celebration, the Stone Home a planet knocked off its axis. I no longer bothered tracking Halmoni's calendar. It was easier not to know. Some weeks, the home ran as usual, and other times, Keepers whispered of Warden seething in his office as we sat through an empty Service. Our double layers not enough to contain our warmth. Our ankles exposed, rattling against the floor. Worse, I hated when Warden read the Bible aloud for hours, rambling beyond the loudspeaker bells so we had to rush through Breakfast, Workshop quota impossible. "What'll it be today?" I asked under my breath as we waited at the Little House door.

Mina squinted at the window. "Why's Teacher got Mosquito with him?"

We bowed as they let themselves in from the January cold, not bothering to take off their shoes. Trailing wet dirt. A stunning, icy wind. Nabi pressed her fingers into my back as Teacher unlocked the cafeteria and kitchen, confirming what we hoped: no Service. "We may have a visitor this morning. Head Keeper will wait here and help Eunju carry two meals to Big House."

"He has a key to let them in?" Halmoni asked, her voice sharp. The room gaped. Keepers never had access to keys before.

"Only the one to the back door, only for today." Teacher sucked his teeth, daring us to consider the possibility of escape. "Anyone outside for more than ten minutes would freeze."

Mosquito smirked, smug, as he was left behind. He leaned his elbows on the counter. "I expect the trays ready in five minutes, ladies."

"Keeper will bring you right back," Halmoni said to me, as if that was what I was worried about. I didn't understand why we weren't accosting him, wrangling him to the floor. "He knows who handles the food here."

"Do I?" Mosquito showed us the silver object that fit in his palm. Halmoni stood closest, but she didn't snatch it from him, didn't gouge him through the neck.

I gripped a knife. Sliced a cucumber into ragged pieces, then turned. The blade wet with green. Mina stiffened beside me. "Don't," she said.

Mosquito retreated to the nearest table with his meager cup of tea. His bat beside him. His breath billowing, even in this heated space.

Umma brushed her lips against my head as she passed with a crate of vegetables, gently tugging my wrist until I slackened. "He's right, you know. It's too cold. We aren't prepared."

Bile gnawed my stomach as Mina and I washed daikons, scratching at lines in the white and green skin. I imagined mine as Teacher as I sliced its head and feet. Using a knife still thrilled me, though Halmoni had allowed us the privilege for the past three months. The feel of the worn handle, the weight and metallic clip as I bore down on the wooden board. We cut the radish into squares and dumped them in a pot. Mina poured a glistening line of sesame oil.

The specter of Warden returned as we plated kimchi, kkakdugi, shigimchi and gaji namul, tofu simmered in soy sauce. His spit-cleaned shoes. The snake that writhed up my back whenever I was in the room with him. Ajumma Lee fetched two bowls of gyeran-jjim, the egg transformed into fluffy clouds. Maeun-tang. Rice. Spoons, chopsticks. Two perfect table settings. "You therefore must be perfect, as your heavenly Father is perfect," Warden had said every evening since Inspection Day. Presentations our only constant. "Or we will all suffer."

"Who do you think is visiting?" Areum asked as Halmoni sprinkled sesame seeds.

"Maybe they're returning Bora-unnie," Nabi said.

"The nuns are sick of her sass," I joked.

"Maybe it's a reporter," Mina mused. "Here to get us out."

"The reporters and police know by now and don't care," Ajumma Lee chided.

"Enough." Halmoni covered the trays with bojagis made of a dense woven cloth. Called to Mosquito. "We're ready."

Umma trailed us to the door and pulled the one hat we shared from its hook. My hair too short, my ears exposed, the winter wind blustery enough to burn through the wool to my scalp. "You bring her right back," she said to Mosquito, raising her voice, speaking to him as an elder.

Outside, the snow soaked through my canvas sneakers and socks. I had no jacket. Through the wind's noise, branches crackled, ice crunched, our breaths turned fleecy. "Do you know who's coming?" I shouted.

Mosquito didn't respond. He had a key, and with that, more power than a Keeper should. Was it Inspection Day that changed him, or was it me? He had led the Keepers in beating the boys. He hadn't joined the call to the nuns to witness the rot in this place. He had ruined our chance at freedom, and for that, I despised him.

• • •

My wet socks clung to my toes, my elbows wobbled from steadying the tray, but Teacher's sneer sucked the tired right out of me. "Get in here, then," he snarled, his jaw stiff and round as he opened the classroom door.

Warden ignored us, his hair a flame around his balding head. The room pulsing as he rotated his watch around his wrist. "You think you can escape this? You forget your place."

"They're here." Teacher pointed.

"As if they don't see what kind of person you are." Warden, his new impatience a pyre. "Children! Did you know that Teacher was raised in an orphanage, no different from our center? I question if he's fully reformed, because if he were, would he allow such indiscretion under his purview?"

"This isn't the time," Teacher cut in.

"You need to control your outbursts," Warden nearly shouted.

The room tilted as the men twisted into each other with their words, a spiky heat thrown back and forth. I untied the bojagis, wiped Mosquito's clumsy spill, a chunk of gyeran-jjim stuck to the cloth, and tried to tamp down my surprise—Teacher had grown up in a place like this, the men were fighting openly. The scent of clams and red pepper flakes filled me, and then leather, musk, too much cologne.

"You will never leave." Warden suddenly too close, his hand hot and clammy on my neck, but his voice leveled at Teacher. A pause, then: "What are we having, Eunju?"

His fingers and his breath and his body. The pressure behind my eyes near bursting. My fanged hate. A darkness, sleek and muscular, sliding its way into the room. No, I wouldn't kneel, wouldn't open my mouth and deliver my tongue if he commanded.

"We need to prepare for the visitor," Teacher said, a relief.

Warden let go with an impatient grunt, dismissing us: "Get out, then."

I gathered the bojagis, the wrinkled puffs of red now stained. Touched a shaved pencil that rolled under one of the trays. Slim, with a point sharp enough to slice.

Outside, I returned to myself, the pencil pocketed at the last minute. Around Warden, I became a no one. Afraid and incapable. But here, with only Teacher, I felt myself fully. My resentment at the relief he had provided only a moment before. He was no better than Warden. I could pare the sinews in his heels with my teeth. Push him to the ground. Claw open his throat. The wash of red on clean snow a marker of what he deserved.

Teacher didn't turn back, so confident I would follow.

I pulled out the pencil. Gripped it in the open air, the cold shrinking the skin around my nails. I carried it between us, a cut flower. A bright and blooming thing.

Like Mosquito, Warden, all of them, he knew I couldn't escape. In my wet shoes and no coat, without a way to get past the wall.

With my sad, sharpened pencil.

Without Umma.

Teacher unlocked the door. "Tell Halmoni the boys will go straight to work."

He locked me in. I touched the window glass. Felt the flush of my shame, my dissatisfaction. My cowardice.

Halmoni found me in my ruined shoes. "What're you doing standing there?" She lifted the snow-wet hat and rubbed my short hair. "Take those off before your toes shrivel into nothing."

She steered me to one of the kitchen burners. "You all right, child?"

"I imagined killing him," I said, watching the flames.

She snorted. "Would have been the death of us all if you had. Kyungoh!" She waved. "Come warm your child."

SANGCHUL

The first time Warden handed him a white bat, the scent of rubber hitting his palms, the heft of the handle a surprise, he understood: power came not from violence but from the fear before impact.

The warmth he felt, when Warden anointed him with a new title. He was a reformer now. Chosen without having to pass a Keeper test. Lucky. He couldn't be blamed, not for accepting a command. He hadn't had a choice.

Only later, in the bathroom with its tiled walls, its metal gleam, did he consider the shame Youngchul would have thrown at his feet. But hyung wasn't there any longer, had decided to wither away without him. So what right did he have over how Sangchul survived?

• • •

Sangchul and Dal stamped their boots, scowled at the herds running around the path. Bored and cold, they competed against each other for the longest breath of air, hoary shocks bursting from their lips. "Pick up your pace," Sangchul yelled at the stragglers.

"Or we'll pick it up for you," Dal shouted.

"They'll get sick and slow production." Sangchul massaged his woolen fingers, achy joints. The Keepers weren't much better off, with thin coats and mismatched gloves. He kicked the snow that had fallen overnight and pictured worms underfoot, wondered whether they hibernated or died or burrowed to retain their warmth.

Dal eyed the herds' ill-fitting sweatshirts, their lips darkening with each lap. A kid with a limp. Too slow. "I'll take care of it." He ran off, pulling his bat out of its loop. *Tick.* Sangchul had heard that was Dal's nickname. A brown pest, flat-bodied and barbed. It fit Dal, the squealer, the hanger-on.

Sangchul scanned snow-furred branches, unexpectedly adrift. Since he had become Keeper a month ago, Dal had been his partner, rising with him. They kept each other present, but the sun moved something in him as he stood alone. A memory, a dream? He panted, the air in his lungs compressing as he realized: he had arrived here with a brother on a day like this a year ago. The January cold unhooking their sense of reality. No. He pushed his bat into the space below his ribs, shut down that line of thinking. There—Taeho and Jae ran along, both pointing to a tree. Sangchul searched the brown bark, saw no animal or insect. As they passed his post, he raised his chin, enough to be taken as a greeting if they wanted. Taeho nodded back. Jae raised a finger, as if testing the air.

He patted the white handle of his bat as no one else on the path met his gaze. Jae and Taeho were the only ones to stir any murk inside him anyway. They understood he had no choice.

They had to understand.

A bird cut through the sky—gray and broad-winged and alone. *One*, he mouthed. Sangchul had always been better at locating those tufted animals above. Their grace and wildness.

He couldn't play their game, but he protected them. He had stopped Tick from beating Taeho on a day when the hours passed like sludge. He had cajoled Cow to be lenient when Jae was sick. He was still their Sangchul, and beneath the heat, the drip of distaste on his tongue, he reminded himself of that fact every day.

EUNJU

Warden's scent lingered on my skin all day, while Teacher left me with a cooler anger, an ice pick to the temples. As we ate dinner, I shook myself like a wet dog, trying to unlatch these men. My mind fumbled toward the women, the ways we had changed. Beside me, Mina sank her spoon into her broth. For weeks after Inspection Day, she had refused to eat, grief whittling her, until Ajumma Lee spoke to her in private. Of what, Mina wouldn't say, but now she ate. She tried.

Nabi turned picky overnight, hating the eggplants' slick texture, whining spinach stained her teeth, while Areum ate anything we were given, scarcity making her an undiscerning eater, every dish licked clean as a winter branch. I knew them. Ajumma Lee preferred fried mackerel. Halmoni ate less and less, complaining of a stone in her stomach.

Umma—I watched her most of all. At first, I thought it was shock that squeezed her appetite, made her seek water, fruit, simple jook. Months later, I saw—how her face paled when accosted by the scent of meat, brows tight as she inhaled through her nose, her deepening yawns, increasing headaches.

We had done nothing as Bora was sent off to some foreign country, with nuns who would sell her baby. "She's better off there than in this place," Halmoni had insisted. We assented too easily, wanting a gentler truth to wrap ourselves in. It was only in her absence that we understood—how we had failed her so wholly.

I wouldn't let that happen again.

I chewed on a piece of gristly meat. Gulped thin soup, sesame seeds. I needed to harness my floating mind. I was sixteen now, nearly woman. I could protect her. Umma looked the same, and yet I knew: her body had betrayed her. Her belly filling with seed.

SANGCHUL

Sangchul and the other Keepers waited for Teacher in a half-moon, scuffing the gym floor in unease. It was after Evening Lockup, when time was supposed to be theirs, yet more often, Teacher demanded these meetings. Mosquito's reveal about Teacher's childhood—that he was without family—clattered between them, a new piece of gossip to kick around. Sangchul tried to imagine the type of kid he had been, how he had ended up here, a fancy title slapped over his name.

"What does he want us for anyway?" Rat sucked spit.

"It's not right," Cow agreed.

Sangchul smirked alongside Tick. Cow would have eaten Rat's shit, if asked. It was pathetic, how easily dismissible he made himself.

"He's cutting into my Closet Time." Crow grinned at Mosquito, and Rat snickered too, but Sangchul couldn't. He imagined the relentless dark, the force of a bat spreading his legs. The boy Crow, Mosquito, and Rat lately preferred—a small, pug-nosed slug from Shirts. No, he wasn't sure if he'd ever find that joke funny.

"Aren't we here because you didn't make quota?" Tick leveled his gaze at Rat.

Rat bared his teeth. "You were my squealer first."

"I'm your equal now." Tick fiddled with his sliding glasses.

He was all bluster. The kind who sought the highest power in the room, and it was no longer Rat, but Mosquito.

"Enough." Teacher entered the gym, slapping his notebook against his thigh. Disquiet slid off him, and Sangchul understood: Teacher's fear, not knowing if they knew about his past, the desire to squelch any laughter from them first. "We need to increase production, and one Workshop is consistently behind. What good are you if you can't get them to work?"

Rat pouted. "I already got hit at Presentations. Isn't that enough?"

Teacher pulled Rat's lip—hard, enough for Sangchul to grimace, tuck his tongue over his teeth. He wondered if that string between the lips and gum would tear, tender tissue giving way. It was true, Keepers were now put on the Presentations line, liable as everyone. But Rat didn't seem to recognize there was no reasoning with Teacher. "Calves," he commanded.

Teacher didn't have a switch like Warden, so he used his baton instead, thin, sharp licks replaced by a harsher punishment, less controlled. It almost made Sangchul feel bad for Rat, yet the other part of him admired the way Teacher instinctively identified the one who smirked the most.

After, Sangchul felt the shell of his pride harden as Teacher tossed Mosquito two cigarette packs for keeping them in line. He and Tick should have gotten some too. They were in Leathers together, and they had met quota. These days, Mosquito only rotated around the three Workshops, a Head Keeper who managed nothing, Teacher's best and only squealer.

Back on the second floor, Mosquito returned to his single Head Keeper's room without acknowledging the others. Crow slipped into the herds' dorm, addicted to the extra beatings, the power that came with the dark, while the others headed to their Keepers' cots.

Sangchul went to the showers, where he could coax hot water from the few pipes that hadn't frozen.

He stripped by the door, holed socks last. The skin showing in spots reminded him of Youngchul, how he stuck out his feet as he slept, calluses like snowy hills. Sangchul sprinted across tile, cranked hot water. Inside the plumes, he rubbed chickenfleshed skin. The sack of himself. All day, Sangchul had avoided thinking about hyung—his probing gaze, how he would have squeezed his fingers and tried to stop him when Sangchul swiped a boy's bowl at Dinner.

Sangchul rubbed his throat with a bar of soap and found his razor, a new luxury given when he passed to reformer. His herd was feeble, complacent. Clumsy as they slapped glue onto leather soles, messing up tasks a child could complete. *Don't worry*, he whispered to the grout between the tiles, the hyung in his mind. This was only an impasse, a second self that didn't count. The real Sangchul would return once he was free.

The steam was suffocating, a wet bind around his lungs. *This work will stain you from the inside*, Youngchul would have said, but Sangchul knew better.

One day, he would cut into himself until he found his weakness. His most disgusting self. He would reveal its dark shine in front of the others, his old friends, and he would break that part down until it was nothing, only a seed in the ground, a bit of glass to be forgotten by spring. Outside these walls, he would be forgiven.

EUNJU

Hatred has a particular taste and heat. It's not metallic sharp, as I once thought. But astringent and sweet, like an underripe persimmon. A film on my tongue. When I hate, that fuzzy taste coats my mouth until my throat is dry, until I can only think of water.

To patrol your peers.

To hurt the ones who are your younger form.

Every time I passed him, my mind filled with violence.

Mule. That was what we called him.

That traitor, brother-lost and unforgivable: Sangchul.

2011

The Sincheon River beckons with its sloshing waves, funneling winds. I greet the woman who runs the corner pharmacy, bow to the halmonis who have spread out on the wooden platforms, sharing gossip and tea. Summer insects buzz as I think of them—who among us survived. The ache I'd feel seeing Halmoni with the old women, or Mina ambling down the street, clasping hands with a lover.

Hours ago, in my apartment, Narae had laughed and laughed. *Appa was one of them?* Trilling, uncontrolled. *That's what he made me come all the way here to learn? Even in his death, he can be so selfish.*

Maybe that sort of laughter is a more honest reaction. Maybe that Inspection Day, I should have laughed at the nuns, the harm they caused by looking away.

I reach the river and search. I don't see her. *I'll meet you at four,* Narae had said, her face clouding as she thought of her ruined father. It's too late now. My path is clear: a stone wall, Daegu's 83 Tower. The past and present colliding. It has been two weeks, and Narae has opened a valve in me. I don't know how to shut it, all these wants I had hidden from myself.

Narae, with her concern and shiny strength, with her beautiful linen clothes and meager teacher's salary and easy touch, so American and forthright, her love of beer and impatient desire to better those around her—what will I do without her, when she leaves?

SANGCHUL

Puttering through a game of cards, Sangchul and Tick swiveled on their stools, warming themselves through distraction. It was the start of February, Workshop stuffed with the cranking sound of metal, the rancid stench of lubricant. It was exhausting, really, monitoring the boys. At least they had a discrete task, goals to keep them busy. Sangchul's fingers itched with the memory of work. So, when he and Tick heard a panicked yelp an hour later, a new metallic scent raking the air, it was almost a relief.

Tick dropped his cards. "What now?"

Sangchul recognized the yelper's accent. One of his boys. He pulled himself up with a groan. Seated by the conveyor belt, the boy cradled his hand, his blood bright against the dark. "I punched through my skin."

Sangchul squinted. "Those hole punches are tiny."

"Looks like he needs bandages," another from his herd said. Wide-mouthed with narrow eyes, his whole face off-balance. Triangle Head.

"Clean up that mess instead of sitting there glaring." Sangchul grabbed his hat. "I'll be back in five minutes." He sucked his teeth as he escorted the boy outside. In truth, he was thankful for the excuse to stare at something besides the tops of dirty heads, even if the wind burned. "You'll be all right," he said as they crossed the field, remembering to be kind.

The boy cupped his elbow, blood spotting the snow-melted ground below.

Sangchul turned on the spigot at the side of Little House and rummaged through the jars for a bandage. He'd forgotten his gloves, knuckles reddening in the cold. At least he wasn't bleeding. The kid was fine anyway, a minor cut.

"All right, Minho?" A voice behind them.

Sangchul turned—and there was Jae. He nearly lurched from the surprise. His old friend. Hatless, the heat spiraling out of his crown. His sweatshirt too tight around broadening shoulders, a boy grown taller in his absence. A copy of his kid, with his hand raised, as if elevation would help them heal faster. He couldn't remember the last time they had spoken.

Minho turned on the spigot. "Got a hole punch through the skin," he said with a shrug, pretending he hadn't been whimpering a moment before.

"Look at that," Cow said as he followed behind. He pointed to the meat of Jae's palm. The glint of a fishhook. "Exact thing happened to you, remember?"

Sangchul tensed.

"Watch him for me. Gotta piss." Cow loped away before Sangchul could agree. As if he were still a herd boy. As if Cow wasn't the ineffectual one, the Keeper the others made fun of most.

"You're well, Sangchul?" Jae asked, stepping closer.

"It's Keeper now," Sangchul said softly.

Jae's face tightened. "Does it hurt, Minho?"

Sangchul handed his boy a bandage. "He's fine."

Jae bypassed him to reach the spigot. A ribbony gush of water splashing at their feet. "You know, Hangyeol in your group is sick."

Sangchul bristled. They hadn't spoken in months, and this was what he brought up first?

"If you can, be lenient with him." The authority in Jae's voice, the intimacy. Sangchul imagined Minho whispering to the others as soon as they returned. Their delight in watching his command splinter. "It would be the kind thing to do."

Sangchul stepped back, clarity boxing him in the throat: Jae would never consider him a real Keeper. He would forever be the younger, undeserving brother.

"Hangyeol's young, only thirteen, you know?"

He shook his head, confused. Wasn't that what he wanted, for Jae to see him as before? He blinked, not understanding the architecture of his grief, grasping for the bright barrel of anger instead. He barked at his boy: "Find your ointment so we can go."

Jae raised his palm. "Can you pull it out?"

The easy touch between them was gone. Sangchul no longer remembered these calluses, these uncut nails. The smell of Jae, a warm musk that chewed up his insides. How unfair it was, that Sangchul could be accosted by this scent, when he couldn't recall hyung's. He pulled the hook out quickly, the squelch making him wince. It was true, he had once injured himself in this exact way, but that felt like an era ago, when it had been summer, when hyung had been a tether for them all.

"You know," Jae said, a faint frown on his face, "there was a kid who went from boy to Keeper back to boy."

Sangchul couldn't believe it. Jae's nerve. His idiocy, really. Speaking to him like this. He picked up the dirtied hook from the ground. Wet now, still red. Curled it slowly into Jae's good palm, until his eyelashes fluttered from the pressure. If Sangchul squeezed enough, he could create twin marks. "You don't get to talk to me however you want, slug."

He pushed his kid onto the path. It wasn't his problem if Jae ran, if Cow had left him unattended.

"It's possible," Jae called after them.

Sangchul turned, despite himself, as Cow rounded the corner, that goofy grin on his face. He waved, as if his boy hadn't yelled at a Keeper from across the field.

When they returned to Leathers, Sangchul paused at the door. Mosquito had arrived on his afternoon rounds, his shoulders sloped with ease as he chatted with Tick. Disappointment bloomed in Sangchul—in his gut, behind his eyes, prickling his fingertips. He strode to his herd. They worked quicker when scrutinized, as if he held actual power. They punched holes into limp brown hide, and the abstract strips, once animal, rolled down the belt to the others.

Sangchul nudged a boy. This was the one Jae said was sick, scrawny with curly hair. The boy peered up, his teeth and eyes and nails jittery. Pink-cheeked.

Sangchul wasn't bad. He was reasonable, kind. "I'm giving a quarter of your quota to Triangle Head for mouthing off, and a quarter to that one for putting us behind schedule," he said.

The boy wiped his nose. "I—I can manage."

He tossed the straps to the others. "Don't get your disgusting snot on the leather."

Tick slung his arm around him when he returned to the stools. Mosquito smirked. "Sloppy Keeper, sloppy herd."

Sangchul shut his eyes, pressure enflaming him. "What did you say?"

Mosquito shifted, his hand reaching for his bat.

Sangchul jumped. His neck, the nerves there, bright with pain. "What're you going to do?"

But Head Keeper only laughed, a sudden bark, and settled back into his seat. "You're not worth it, Mule."

EUNJU

"What happened out there?" Taeho whispered as soon as Jae returned with a bandaged hand. "Did you talk to him?"

We had watched through the Fishhooks window as Mule and Minho came back first, trailed a minute later by Jae and loping Cow. Jae fumbled now, his hand clumsy and gauzed, the lines slipping from their positions on the shaft.

"Oh, let me help." Mina reached over and wound the line. "Talk to us." Jae ran his tongue along his teeth, jaw gritted, his anger unnatural. I glanced at Mina, who shrugged. Jae must have spoken to the traitor. I was sure of it. Why else would he return in a mood, refusing us?

"I don't want to think about Mule anyway." I pushed a completed package to Jae and took ten hooks, ten lines. I had plenty.

We had circled the topic of Mule for months. His seat between Mina and Taeho empty, a melancholy mirror to the space between Jae and me. The lost brothers. Mina had tried to bring him up once, but her thoughts were thready and easily knotted. Me, the words congealed in my throat, all I would have said to him if I had the chance. My mouth filling with a cutting sweetness.

"I miss him," Taeho said. Blinking those gentle eyes. He tossed Jae a pack and took some of his lines and hooks too. "I wish he'd come back to us."

"I don't," I said. "Without Youngchul-oppa he's heartless."

"I don't know." Mina pulled her line taut. "He was grieving. Maybe he wasn't thinking clearly." It was like her, to try to parse a reason, a salvageable belief. I wasn't as kind. Sangchul had revealed his true self, and it was ugly, cracked.

"When Youngchul-hyung was facing the choice, didn't we want him to stay?" Taeho asked.

"That was different," I said.

"How?" Mina asked.

I shrugged. Youngchul had yearned for better. Sangchul, I knew. He and I were alike, and with that came repulsion, the darkest disgust.

Jae stared at his bandaged hand. "He decided to become Keeper even after what they did to hyung." He clenched his fists. "I thought that in the end the Keepers were one of us, but what they did on Inspection Day—stopping us from breaking down those windows, from our chance to get out?" He shook his head. "There's no forgiving that."

He was right, and I was glad. It felt good to denounce Mule, to watch Mina's and Taeho's surprise, because if Jae thought so, thoughtful as he was, it must have been true, and whatever Mule had said—I had already decided: unforgivable.

SANGCHUL

Finally, some luck. After Jae's demand that afternoon and Mosquito's taunting, at least Teacher saw Sangchul's worth. Chosen to lead Rewards for the first time, over the other Keepers who had been reformed longer, glee lit Sangchul's face. "Thank you for this opportunity. You can trust me," he said as they waited at the back door of Big House. Teacher ignored him.

"I'm here." A voice came from behind, crisp and sullen, and Sangchul's excitement fell away like a cut stalk. Of all the days. He didn't turn, not wanting to look at her just yet, the cold forcing its way through as Teacher let them out. His shoulders constricted. What was it about her that made him steel himself?

"Can we get going?" Eunju asked.

He pulled off the hood of his jacket so there would be no mistake. "It's your time."

The openness in her face shuttered closed. A sudden and decisive change. Her mouth twisted. "You." She walked ahead, the too-large coat swinging against her hips. Quick steps in thin canvas shoes. Beneath a knit cap, her short hair caught flecks of white.

Sangchul tilted his head. Eunju may have been used to this, but it was his first time. Rewards. Finally, the world above was his for ten minutes. Ribbons of clouds, powdery against the darkening sky. Snow drifting down in sheets, melting as it touched his skin.

The edges of his vision tinted blue. Dark blackberries, deep water. He wanted to smear that color inside himself.

He closed his eyes, let himself dissolve into the air.

Eunju clumped on through a ring of trees. Her movements thick and noisy against the brush. The outside world was too exquisite for her to ruin, the sky already changing to a gauzy plum. Couldn't she feel the possibilities? They could run away, climb the wall. Instead, she forced her anger on him, her tight hold on old betrayals.

He let go of the sky. Followed her as she hacked phlegm. Finally, she spoke: "Why are you here? Where's Mosquito?"

He blinked at her whitening hat. Mosquito, who she'd once claimed wasn't as bad as the others. "Mosquito," he said slowly, "is Head Keeper for a reason."

Eunju veered to the right until, abruptly, the wall rose to meet them. She reached a gloved hand and touched the gray stone. A cold, raw fear filled him. She would disappear through a sieve in the wall. She was a specter, a ghost, no one could hold her. He would be left alone again, covered in a dust of green.

She touched her forehead to the wall. "I hate you."

Sangchul shook loose his thoughts. No. She was only a girl with a scowling face. Liquid loyalties. Didn't she grasp what Mosquito had done to his brother on Inspection Day? His body bent over hyung's limp form, his violence an animal that ate Youngchul whole. The memory clawed through Sangchul in his sleep, leaving him sweat-drenched.

"Mosquito hurts the boys at night. He hurt my brother." He came closer. "You should be embarrassed."

Eunju laughed, a bright streak of color between them. "You think I care about him? You think that's what we're talking about?" A wet circle anointed her forehead, a mark from an unholy god. She pushed past him, back toward Home. "Taeho and Jae hate you too, you know."

He watched her retrace their steps. Her feet falling into old footprints so there was no sign of their return. The wind chilled him through his jacket, into his teeth. He was so tired, and already, it was time.

Before they reached the back door, she turned, the wet spot on her forehead glistening. She spread her gloved fingers. The world had been beautiful for a moment. He tried to hold on to that feeling, that blue light and air and sky. Hopeless effort. It was too exhausting, to pretend. To push away the curdling feeling in his stomach for another day.

"*You* should be embarrassed," she said. "You know that, don't you, Mule?"

EUNJU

Mina needled me about Mule in the bathroom until I replayed his words, the way his eyes flattened into emptiness. "I wish we could purge that bad part out of him. Then he'd return to us," she said, leaning her shoulder on the slick tile wall.

"There was no goodness in him to begin with." I dipped my green mitt in a plastic bucket and rubbed her back, hard enough to make gray rolls of dead skin rise like worms after rain.

Mina sucked her teeth. "Come on, that's not true."

Maybe so, but I didn't want to think about Mule any longer. The cold from Rewards had burrowed into my bones. My skull knotted with phlegm and my throat raw with each swallow. I wet a washcloth and wrapped it around my neck. Still, the chill made my gums hurt.

Mina hugged her sides, so I could get between the blades. "Do you think Jae injured himself on purpose?"

I twisted the green mitt, the fabric harsh beneath my fingernails. "You think?"

"He's usually so careful."

It was true. Jae and I were the fastest, our thickened fingerpads proof of our abilities. He had done it to himself. For what? To talk to a traitor, to try to bring him back to us?

"I don't want to think about Mule for another second," I said.

Mina relented, and we examined the others through the steam. Nabi washed Halmoni, whose arms were speckled with age spots, low breasts settled in her lap. Ajumma Lee scrubbed as she chatted with Umma. The wrinkle between Umma's brows slight and straight as she smiled in response. Something had softened between them since Inspection Day, or maybe since the night I had gone after Teacher, and Ajumma consoled me in the night.

"What's your mother going to do?" Mina glanced at me, and I stiffened—but she and I were friends now, Bora's leaving a reminder of our precarity here.

Last month, Umma had only looked plump, as if she had been sneaking extra meals. Now there was a firmness to her belly, hidden beneath a roomy shirt but obvious when naked. Her breasts heavier, nipples darkening to the color of pat beans. I sighed. When I had told Umma of Warden and Teacher's fighting, of Teacher's orphan childhood, the surrender in the set of her jaw had given her away. She had known, my findings useless.

"I haven't asked." Something kept stopping me, my shame or disappointment. I gave Mina the mitt, and she brushed the line of my spine.

"You know, when a baby is inside you, it pushes all the other organs up to make room. Your lungs go up here, and your stomach, your liver."

"How do you know?" I imagined my kidneys, crowding through my throat until I choked.

"A doctor told me once, from before." Mina quieted. There was so much we didn't know about each other, our previous lives. "You should talk to her."

Through slitted eyes, I watched Umma wash the silky hairs of her armpits. If Jae had hurt himself to confront Mule, I could confront my mother. She needed to know—I wouldn't let her be taken, whoever grew inside her was ours, and we would protect her from the men, because even in this shit-forsaken mouse hole that was our current life, she and I were united.

• • •

I wrapped my arms around Umma, a tentacled octopus, clingy and tight. My head pounded, and I didn't know if it was from cold or fear or anticipation, because tonight, I would remind her of the summer when I was twelve, when we lived in Daegu and ate chamoes for every meal and she fed me stories of growing up without a home, born to a country at war with itself, to a soldier who disappeared, a mother who one day left too. I'd recall that afternoon when she had cradled my chin with a sticky palm and said, "I won't do that to you." I would repeat those words back to her.

Umma slithered down the cot until our faces were level, and I pulled the sheet over our heads. My icy bones. I wanted sweat to bloom between my shoulder blades, dot my upper lip. She brushed my hair with her fingers. "What's bothering you?"

I traced the creases of her neck, a mole on her shoulder. All evening, she had moved slowly, hiding her exhaustion with closed-mouth yawns.

"Tell me," she said, her voice sharpening. "Did something happen at Rewards?"

I was drifting, far from this place and fixed, the world shrinking and obliterating itself until only this room remained. My mind no longer my own, knowledge scattering like shards of glass. "I know what's happening to you."

Her body stiffened, and I squirmed in her silence, how it took up so much space between us.

"You're pregnant," I said, the words coming out like a threat, a taunting. "Is it Teacher's?"

She pinched the skin beneath my chin until the rest of my body clenched. I tried to wrench from her grip, I couldn't breathe, the sheet tight over us. She held my head, as if she could pop it off my neck like a soybean from its stalk. "Don't talk about what you don't understand."

"I don't want your protection, not like this." I willed myself to push into the pain if she was going to be so mean. "How could you let this happen?" It wasn't what I meant to say, blame lighting my words.

"I see you, Eunju, the way you look at me." Her voice shook. I shut my eyes, shame, that shocking burst in the gut. "The women here, the men. Why do you think you're all blaming me, huh?" She pried open my lids. "At least have the honesty to look at me, and know this—it's easier to blame me than the world that made me. This is how I carve a room for us, so tell me what else I could have done."

I clawed off the sheet, coughing, wiping the spit at the corners of my lips, no longer caring who heard. I despised her—for her cruelty, for raging on the street and attracting the policemen's attention last year, for her truth, for giving me this life. Her words barbed me—with my own stupidity, at how shallowly I had seen her—so I groped for the one clear stone I could find in the muck—she was right; it was easier to blame her, to hate ourselves. I rolled over, my throat throbbing. "How many months?" I demanded.

She sighed, touched my spine with one finger. She must have known too, how stupid I was, I only wanted simple answers. "Maybe five," she whispered. "I thought I could gather enough information to use as a threat. I was wrong to trust him."

"Teacher?" I asked, counting out the months. June. We would have until June, then.

"The women will try to protect me. The way they did with Bora, and we'll take their kindness. Still, it won't be enough."

"What next, then?" I asked, my voice sullen. I touched my neck. She really had hurt me. "What about the junk room, with the paint cans? There could be a key, something to help us run."

She shook her head. "What happens if we get caught? The police brought us here once already. We need to think of a way to be let go with their protection."

Fear and disappointment and pity competed within me. Despite myself, I had held on to the hope that she'd come up with a plan, that she knew what she was doing. So tightly I hadn't realized until now. I had trusted her to get us out because she was my mother, because she had saved us before.

"Eunju," she said. "Listen to me."

I pinched my earlobes. She would have a baby, and it would be taken away or live inside these walls. We would rot here, forming tumors and growing old until we were like Halmoni.

Umma pushed the heels of her hands into her eyes. "You have to trust me."

"I do," I said, already rolling away, surging with a desire to never see her again. *Look at what happened when you trusted Teacher,* I wanted to say. *Youngchul died. Bora was sent away. You have his baby in your stomach, stealing your energy and body and mind. Look at me. I tried to take away your power. I made you live this life. I saw myself in you and hated it.*

It was no use. I closed my eyes and asked for the night to sink me—because in our lives, only in sleep could we leave.

SANGCHUL

It's possible. You know that, don't you, Mule? Jae's and Eunju's words spun through Sangchul. The way they accosted him from their smug, virtuous altars. As if they were better than him. What were they up to, speaking to him for the first time in months on the same day? Sangchul scratched his collar as he and Tick climbed the stairs.

"What's bothering you, Mosquito's gruffness? Forget him," Tick chided as they reached Warden's office. It was easy for Tick to placate, when Mosquito praised him above others. He wasn't even a good Keeper, inconsistent, focused on following the scent of power.

"It's not that," Sangchul said as he stopped scratching. Warden didn't tolerate fidgeting, but it was difficult, up on the third floor. While Tick knocked, he peered at the far end of the hall, the shut door with a wooden cross hanging from a nail. Beyond were six cramped rooms where boys atoned for the worst sins. He leaned forward, sure he could hear a muffled voice. Maybe it was only Warden, ordering them to enter.

Inside, Warden flicked two fingers while talking on the phone. They knew what to do. Every week, two Keepers wiped furniture, organized documents, burned extra papers. It was tiresome, easy, and it being winter, Sangchul enjoyed the warmth, the possibility of a compliment.

Tick swabbed the floor, and Sangchul ran a rag around the lamps, shelves, desk. The office was spacious, vaster than two of the dorm rooms combined. Even the lights were different, suppler and more golden here. Gilded frames hung on the walls—a painting of two farmers praying in a field, a Confucian figure in a silk hat. A shelf of Bibles, two crosses nailed side by side. A man who used his faith as decoration. Pity ran through Sangchul; at least he knew himself. He dusted the maroon curtains framing the windows, and in front of the desk, the two plump chairs in a matching shade. His fingers itched with the want to rummage—the contents inside the metal cabinets, the locked drawers of the table with a laid-out set of baduk, black and white pieces as round as eyes.

"My boys." Warden beckoned. Behind him, the snow had thickened into a mass. Still, Sangchul felt the wall, its hold on them as Warden whispered something that made Tick shove his neck forward in delight. Then it was Sangchul's turn to walk around the desk, to regard the room as if it were his own. A hand on his shoulder. Words in his ear: "I witness—how you are learning to curb your anger, wield it for goodness." Sangchul nodded, a pool of warmth filling him. "You haven't been left behind because I am here."

"Thank you, Warden," he said, and he meant it, even before Warden handed them each a red-and-white wrapper. Sangchul bowed, his fingers already ripping the crinkled-cut edge. Inside, a chocolate-covered disc with marshmallow filling. Sweet and crumbly with that gooey white give.

"Eat them by the fire. Take these, while you're at it." He handed them a stack of folders.

For a minute, they sat by the fireplace at the far end of the room, wolfing their Choco Pies, licking their fingers, catching each crumb. The skin on Sangchul's face tightening from the heat, crisping from the flames. He enjoyed this work; tossing orders for bags of rice, sets of linens, crates of vegetables, receipts for more than they ever truly seemed to receive. Boxes of soaps. Memos. Tick burned beside him, quiet. They were both happy, listening.

Warden was on the phone again. "You only need to take a handful." His voice slipped into supplication. "There's no scandal here. Those are only silly rumors, made by those jealous of our success." He laughed, a false, billowy sound.

Trouble? Tick mouthed, a bit of cake stuck between his front teeth.

"We're at capacity, is all," Warden continued.

An ant crawled across Sangchul's foot. The tickle a startle, a swift black body clambering away. Eunju's small, scrunched expression came to him—how she had placed her hand on the wall, owning the spot completely. Spit filled his mouth as he opened another folder. A name scrawled on top, a photograph glued beneath: a young face, staring straight at the camera, fearful. He knew this boy. Twelve years old and gone after Inspection Day. *Fenced*, the other Keepers called the sudden disappearing. Warden had told them he had been shipped off to another orphanage. A doctor's stamp. Previous health condition: *weak heart.*

"What is it?" Tick whispered.

He sifted through the pile, each photograph revealing someone who had left. Their real names, no numbers in sight.

"Maybe he doesn't need them anymore because they're gone to the adult reformatories," Tick said. His voice sounded warped, too buzzy and close.

Sangchul flipped through the folders. His hands slick, the sheets marked by his fingertips. Weak lungs. Bronchitis. Flu. Exhaustion. A doctor's stamp on each page. Tick nudged Sangchul's shoulder. "What're you doing?"

If these boys were in this pile, so was— He shook Tick off, eyes prickly with smoke, Warden cajoling on the phone—and then, he found hyung's face. The long, slim nose. Ears that stuck out at the sides. Eyes pinched at the corners.

He had come in with a weak heart, the paper claimed.

Questions crowded him. Tick shifted until Sangchul was in his shadow. Clamped a hand on his knee. "You can do this."

A new hope slammed against Sangchul. This guy with his thick swinging neck and plastic glasses was his only friend. There were two of them, their bodies hardened and lean. They could take Warden together. "We could—" he started.

"Sangchul," Tick warned, fast-blinking in the heat. "Burn these."

When he didn't answer, Tick grabbed a fistful and tossed them into the flames. Sangchul nearly seized him—but what was the use? What would they do? Run down the stairs and bang on locked doors?

Warden's voice returned to him, through a tunnel. "You don't understand how difficult it is to train these children. They're true heathens. Teacher Chung isn't competent." A stiff pause. "Of course. I'll try harder." The end of a conversation, a bruised grunt. A shout at one of them to come, pour the soju.

Now, Tick mouthed.

Sangchul forced himself to pick up a few sheets. They were only photographs. Square bits of image. A few words scrawled onto a page. Maybe they had been transferred to the adult institution, despite their young age. He crumpled one and rolled it into the fire. The edges caught, singeing as the paper curled. Tick left, calling to Warden that he was coming, he would be right there.

Alone, Sangchul watched the fire lick the walls. He nudged closer to the heat until his eyelids felt like they'd fall and land at his feet. Two colorless petals he could slip under his tongue or flip between his fingers like coins. Warden wasn't in control either; he reported to someone else.

Sangchul threw the rest of them in. It didn't matter. The faces burned all the same. He saved only one—a photograph peeled from its paper. The back gummy, small enough to hide in his palm.

• • •

In the middle of the night, Sangchul stepped out of the Keepers' room. The body that contained him felt brittle; he could take a hammer and crack himself open. He wanted that—the unleashing of whatever was left inside. He stopped at the stairs. How easy it would be, to fall, let go. He unfolded his palm. The photograph made it true—Kim Youngchul had once existed.

Sangchul jolted. In the dark, a flicker of hyung's face, a shadow image.

"Hey," Tick called, too close behind. His voice webby with sleep.

Sangchul doubled over. His cheeks wet.

A hand on his shoulder. "You should return to bed."

He looked up—the image gone. "Hyung?"

"Come on, it's late," Tick soothed.

He let Tick direct him back to the room. He lay down. The sky was a slant shade of green. He blinked. That unholy light, that color—he had been so stupid. After Youngchul had returned from Chapel, one morning in the bathroom, he'd realized something was truly wrong. Hyung's cheekbones protruded, bruised an ugly mossy hue. Sangchul had turned away, too afraid.

"No one cares about us," hyung had whispered.

"I need you," Sangchul had begged. Selfish, ignorant, to the end. If only he had known what would happen. It was too late now. Youngchul's life had been reduced to a flicker of a face, a phantom wish. *A weak heart.*

2011

A photograph? Narae asks, recognition softening her features. She fiddles with her shirtsleeve, knocked off guard.

Do you know the one? An impossible hope floods me. To see Youngchul, even in faded form.

No. She flicks lint from her fingertips, beckons us to pause at a crosswalk, and I cannot tell if she is lying. Daegu blares around us, pedestrians passing by. *Actually, I found something.* She pulls out her phone. She is walking me to work, her presence pressing on a bruise I didn't know I had. She scrolls through lines and lines of comments. *It's a chat group.* I brace myself. *These people on this forum say they've been abused in centers like yours. They want an apology.*

She looks up, only to make sure I am listening, that the light has not turned. Ever since she found out about Youngchul's death, Sangchul becoming Keeper, she has acted this way. Purposeful, veneered. As if intent can create resolution, and she can make up for her father's mistakes. As if that's why he instructed her to find me. She cracks her neck. *There's a man protesting in Seoul. I want to meet him. Will you come? He believes it's all connected to the 1988 Olympics. They say the dictator was trying to clean up the country's image before the Games.*

I could go to jail, I say.

You were a victim. She shakes her head. *Whatever you did, it'll be forgiven.*

It's my turn to shake my head now. How naively she sees our justice system. Isn't she a teacher? Isn't she an American?

EUNJU

March began with another snowstorm, Umma's rounding belly. In the kitchen, she gutted fish, hacked meat off bone. I washed laundry in water swirled with bleach, the skin around my nails peeling in strips. Icicles had formed in my hair during the walk from Service to Little House, and they thorned me with poky aches.

"Perfect medallions," Ajumma Lee instructed, commanding in place of Halmoni, who had woken with a stomachache.

I grunted, sliced carrots haphazardly, an orange pendant rolling off the table like a drunk.

Mina, cutting cucumbers, popped the carrot in her mouth. That bright crunch, that earthy smell. "Come on," she teased. "Is this really so bad? Besides, we'll probably be back in Workshops tomorrow."

I shrugged. All week, she'd been trying to cajole me, filling the air with chatter as Teacher assigned us to Fishhooks some days, and some days not.

"Did you hear?" Ajumma Lee nudged Umma. "Some of the boys were bussed out in the middle of the night."

Mina raised her brow. "What do you think that means?"

"What do I know?" It was never what we wanted. I scooped the cut carrots into a bowl and brought them to Umma. "What next?"

Despite myself, I stared at her stomach. Umma, allowed to rest in Halmoni's corner as needed. Umma, left in Little House to cook during our weekly trips to clean Big House. Umma, with three months left. She pointed. "Scale the fish."

I sighed. Pushed a short, squat knife against a freshly dead mackerel until flecks of iridescence sparked the air. The cold, wet smell of the ocean. I felt heavy, the space between my eyes dammed. We would be here forever, gutting fish until we died.

She hummed, and though I knew it wasn't true, she looked like a woman resigned to this life. "Oh," she said, a note of surprise. She placed my hand on her stomach. A kick. An insistence from inside. I pulled back. "See?" she said. "Don't lose hope, Eunju. She needs you."

I shivered at the strangeness of our bodies, at the flecks of fish clinging to Umma's shirt, and then—as if the world were mocking me, I felt a drip between my legs. I shook the last scales sticking to my palm. "What is that?" I arched my back, already knowing.

Umma stared at the stain. "Your period's come."

"Her period?" Ajumma Lee, beside her, smacked her lips. "Well, finally!"

The news spread through the kitchen, no matter that I didn't want everyone to know. I squeezed, but that only made the trickle leak faster. Umma steered me past the others' knowing smiles, down to the supply closet where she grabbed cloths, to the bathroom by the front door, where there was a single Western toilet reserved for guests. She entered first, and I snared her reflection in the mirror. Her tight, drawn face. In her oversize sweater, she looked young. Not yet thirty. Not yet a mother at all. She sighed. "Let's see."

I pulled down my pants. A dark brown sludge wet my thighs.

Umma handed me a cotton handkerchief, two pairs of underwear. "They won't let us wear corsets. You'll have to change the cloth every few hours. There's a stack in the closet."

I clutched the cotton in my hand.

"It happens to us all," Umma said, softer.

"Not to the boys," I said.

She snorted.

"Is there medicine?" I pulled up my pants, wanting at least that dignity as I crossed to the toilet in the corner. The stench of funk and metal erupted from between my legs as I sat down. So this was what it meant to be a woman.

"You'll have to be careful now. Do you hear me? No more Rewards. You meet quota and that's it. I don't want you alone with the Keepers."

I stopped folding the handkerchief, anger seeping out of me as swiftly as the blood. I imagined myself as air, a piece of stone, a dead cicada. "Rewards is my only thing."

"Not anymore."

I scraped at a clot stuck to my thigh and tried to shape words she would understand. "It's the only act I can guarantee for myself."

"Do you know what can happen to you now?" she pressed. "You think I'm harsh, but nightly, I fret. What he'll say, what he'll do about this baby. We have enough to worry about, so don't add to my headache."

The heat in my temples quickened. "We could file the bars on the windows." I slid off the stained underwear and tugged on the new pairs. "If everyone takes shifts, we could be out of here in a month."

"If one person tells, we'll be sent to the back woods," she said.

"Why would anyone tell?"

Umma braced herself against the sink. "Do I really need to say? How easily do you think one of us could break in Chapel?"

I remembered Youngchul, the scabs on his wrists and ankles, the bruises that revealed themselves when he bent over the workshop table. Bora's belly. Umma's—the kick I'd felt against my palm. "Meet me the next time I win Rewards," I said. "We could run away. We could kill Teacher."

Umma's breath caught in her throat. "Even when a tiger is biting, we keep our minds. That's how we survive."

I sopped the blood with a square of newspaper kept at the side of the toilet and fitted the cotton into my underwear. I wished I could gather the iron scent to shove in Umma's face. "You wouldn't have cared if it happened to me before, but now that I'm bleeding it counts?"

She sighed. "Don't be stupid."

"I'm not." My tone petulant. I couldn't help it. This blood, the stink, the rags I'd have to wash with the rest of the women. The pink water, the rusted stains on the cotton left behind.

"Eunju," Umma said, trying to draw patience, as if from a well. The effort clear in her voice. "I'm telling you, I'm working on it. Warden has a bank account in Australia. Teacher maimed a boy as a child. I'm gathering information. You listen to me."

I pulled up my pants. She was no better than the men, taking away my Rewards. What did it mean, for us to categorize violence only by its consequences? "You already have a baby inside you. Don't treat me like one." I pushed past her to the sink. The water was icy, hit straight to the bone.

She loomed over me, any reserve of patience thrown on the floor. Her exasperation a mirror of mine. "I'm your mother, and you do what I say. You hear me?"

SANGCHUL

At Breakfast, an electric current hissed through the room, fear and thrill competing within Keepers and boys alike. Sangchul saw Jae and Taeho in his periphery, and he flushed with the urge to whisper what he had heard—Honggi attempting escape during Morning Run, Crow darting after him—no, they would figure it out on their own. He needed to focus on himself. A boy had tried the impossible, the Keepers would be blamed.

"Is Teacher feeling ill?" Halmoni asked Warden as he herded them in, her voice softening into the register she used only with him.

"Never mind that incompetent," Warden shouted.

Sangchul fidgeted at the end of his table. Everyone tucked their voices into their throats. Still, the room was too noisy. A constant clatter of plastic and metal. He felt a nagging scraping across his neck, but they were inside this airless, stuffed space. Never mind. Honggi, that idiot. He had caused a mess—for Crow, Teacher, all of them.

Tick mouthed something. Sangchul shook his head. He was lousy at reading lips. A lanky boy at Rat's table spilled soup, and Warden glared. Sangchul swiped at his neck, distracted by a tingling sensation, a gust that wasn't there.

Warden rotated the watch on his wrist. "Lick that up. We don't waste food here."

Rat pushed the boy's crown until he hunched over, his tongue pink, trembling.

Sangchul knuckled his collarbone. The Keepers weren't supposed to go beyond monitoring when Warden was around. He demanded a veil of ignorance when it came to their methods. No veil meant a different Warden, one Sangchul didn't want to know, but it was contagious, the retributions, like puffed rice popping in the ppeongtwigi man's cannon at street markets: Mosquito shoved one of his boys, Tick yelled at another. Even Cow prodded Jae for tending to Taeho, who seemed sick, all snotted and red.

Why didn't the herds kill them, take the chopsticks and ram them through their eyes? There were more of them, and yet they ate, worked, obeyed. He didn't understand anymore, how this place warped the mind. He squeezed the sharp corners of the photograph in his pocket and stared at the women. They too were weak. Using their knives to cut fruits instead of Warden or Teacher.

Where am I?

Sangchul turned, but no one had spoken. He touched the table in front of him. No, he was only speaking to himself. Yes, the women *were* weak, except Eunju. She could do it, if she had a chance. A clear path. He wanted her to feel the unease of his watching, to appreciate how he wasn't hitting, only guarding with his presence. One of his boys had taken two spoons, and he had confiscated the extra utensil without force.

Sometimes, when he saw Eunju, he pictured Youngchul. Where she was sharp, wide-cheeked, he had been long and narrow; it didn't make sense, yet it was in the way she provoked him. A flicker of guilt, a tightening in his throat. The very outline of his birthmark burning, like this sensation now. He couldn't shake it. When he thought of her, he rolled Youngchul's name around his mouth.

What is this place?

Sangchul stopped. He heard the question, clear as a bell. The herd ate without speaking, Eunju wasn't looking his way. He squeezed the photograph in his pocket. He was tired, agitated from the news. He needed sleep, that was all.

A wing against his skin. A voice in his ear. *Answer me, brother.*

Youngchul?

Then, there, diaphanous as paper, like a face pulled from a photograph—it was him. Hyung in miniature, flattened and alive, wrapping around Sangchul's neck.

What happened to me?

Sangchul almost laughed. Caught his throat and turned it into a choking sound. This wasn't the time for guilt. He grabbed stray banchan. Sucked down strands of soybean sprouts. Concentrated on the taste: sesame oil, a sunny yellow crunch. He felt a tickle, wind settling into the crease beneath his chin. For months, his insides had felt too full, a mess of organs. But this voice? Ridiculous. He swiped a bowl of half-eaten rice, his stomach crampy with insistence, the voice thrumming louder in his head: *Brother, brother, brother.*

EUNJU

Patchy gossip wormed through the boys, but I couldn't latch on to any meaning, couldn't parse through my own pain. It felt as if fishhooks were lodged in the pink muscle of my womb, churning clots to mark me as a woman. When harried Cow left to check on Crow's herd in Workshops, Mina leaned forward, all pitch and eager want: "So what happened? Tell us everything."

"Honggi tried to escape," Taeho said, the glee in his voice competing with stodgy phlegm.

Even I fastened onto that news. "Did he get out?" I asked.

"We don't know. Probably not," Jae whispered. "We need to be careful."

"He must be in Chapel by now," Taeho said.

"What'd he do? How'd he get caught?" Mina beheld her fishhooks. Ever since Inspection Day, she got like this. A tremble in her voice at sudden change.

Honggi. A square-faced boy who favored kongnamul muchim, once asking for more sprouts. He was quiet, melancholic, the kind of person I would have glided over in my mind, and he had attempted what I couldn't. What none of us had.

"All right, cut the chatter." Cow walked in, his hair sticking up, as if he had run his hand through it in a rush. "We've got a lot going on today, so I'm relying on you to meet quota."

I stared at the lines splayed out before me. If I couldn't escape, I could imagine. I massaged my stomach, and Mina clucked. "You're on track. You'll meet it."

"I want Rewards," I said, loud enough for Cow to hear.

She sucked her teeth, half playful. "Greedy."

At the next break, I gasped from relief as Mina ground her palms into my hips. "Let yourself rest, stubborn girl." She swept my back and shoulders, comforting and cautious. "You'll feel better in a few days."

I know that, I wanted to say. It wasn't the pain I resented. My body hadn't given me a choice, and now my powerlessness threatened me.

She drew a circle around her face. "You're holding all your tension here."

I blew air at her and turned to the boys. "So, what else do you know?"

Jae refused to speak until Cow left the room, and then it came out in one hurried breath: "He pretended to be sick during Morning Run, and he punched Crow and tried to scale a wall."

Taeho held a hook to his eye and blinked through the hole. "There was screaming and a chase, and we didn't see the end, there's a chance he got away."

Jae ran his tongue along his teeth. "I heard Mosquito towed him by the hair."

"He punched Crow?" Mina asked, and we stilled to imagine: Crow was the most muscled Keeper, tall and angry with a high, cawing voice. Honggi, with his fawn hair and shadowy despair, wasn't a match.

A noise came from the windows. Outside, Cow squeezed his chin dimple as he spoke to Rat. Mosquito joined them, pointing to the third floor of Big House.

"They're in trouble," Jae said.

We got back to work, quota pressing in, as well as how livid Warden and Teacher would be—not only at Honggi for attempting escape, but at us all, for considering it a possibility.

"Scaling the wall." Mina sighed. "You have to team up to try a move like that."

"Or be a really good climber," Taeho said.

I watched them, my friends. A boy had tried to leave this place. "The more people, the harder it is to organize. Maybe it's easier alone," I said.

Mina twinged. "How could one person get out of here by themselves?"

"He's coming." Jae glanced at the Keepers dismantling.

"Do you think they'll get in trouble?" Mina asked in a whisper.

"I hope Mule does," I said.

Mina snorted, but Jae and Taeho pretended like they hadn't heard.

Later, as I groaned over the table and clutched my bowled pelvis, I thought of Mule. The satisfaction I'd feel if he were punished for abandoning us. Pain sliced through me. "How do people do this every month?"

Mina touched my forehead. "It's better than the alternative."

"Being a man?" I asked.

"Being pregnant."

My cheek soaked up the table's metal cold. Umma's hardening belly. Bora's new life. Mina and I were supposed to feel lucky. Our bodies were our own. We were the two girls allowed to leave the kitchen. We were here.

She tucked a strand of hair behind my ear. "My mother used to tell me to carry it as a power."

I flipped to my other cheek. A source of power. If only Umma had said something similar. She seemed to believe it was a weakness, a diminishing, and now those same thoughts roiled through me.

SANGCHUL

The boys whispered about Honggi in Workshop, their voices a rebellion beneath the conveyor belt's cranking, untraceable to one body—but Sangchul didn't care anymore about what Honggi had done or what would become of Crow. There was a ghost on his neck, and he couldn't bend or look down, afraid he'd somehow crush his brother.

"Teacher will take it out on us," Tick moaned. "Damn Honggi for this mess."

Sangchul tried to keep his face calm, neutral. "It isn't our fault."

Mosquito sucked his teeth. His cheek spoke for him anyway, a plummy bruise the remnant of a punishment from two nights before, when the Keepers had bickered in front of Teacher. If they were out of line, then Head Keeper wasn't fulfilling his duties. An easy satisfaction had crept into Sangchul then, but he twitched as he saw the mark now.

What happened to me?

Where am I?

Sangchul shoved himself off the stool. Grasped each boy's neck until they emitted a pathetic puff. His head churned, the chemical scent of glue grinding into his temples, and he held in a scream.

The smells, the quota, this voice, the attempted escape—it was all too much. How little the herds knew—the Keepers were in trouble, not them. That was what he needed to focus on, not this delusion in his head.

Mosquito had told them on the walk over—Honggi had gotten to the wall, managed to get footholds in the gaps, and he and Crow had pulled him down by his pants. The boy's head knocking onto the ground, catching on a bed of rocks. How unfair it was, Teacher's rage, when they had caught the slug before he had taken flight.

"You're right." Tick adjusted his glasses, responding to Mosquito. "If it weren't for you, he'd have escaped."

Sangchul watched, his hold on their conversation already lost, the vise around his temples tight. Tick and Mosquito walked to the other end of the room. Youngchul slid from his neck to his ear. Shouted into it: *Tell me what happened.*

While he fought an imaginary voice, Tick and Mosquito were forming an alliance. It didn't make sense. That was the real dogshit. Their lack of loyalty to the rest of the Keepers. Jealousy jagged through him. He needed to keep busy, distracted. He checked his watch. The black face slid up and down, too big, but he loved its circular flatness, how the numbers glowed brighter than their surroundings.

"Meeting quota?" Teacher appeared at the entrance, knocked over a stack of empty shoeboxes without reason. "I need you in Fishhooks," he spoke to Mosquito. "It might be an extended observation."

He left without acknowledging anyone else. The smell of his sweat, musky and tangy, lingering in his emptiness. So, Crow wouldn't be returning today.

"You think he's in Chapel?" Tick asked. "What if he gets fenced? Can that happen to a Keeper?"

"We don't know." Mosquito tapped Tick's shoulder as he headed to the door. "You're in charge while I'm gone."

Anger unbolted in Sangchul. A ghost, a gust. Something clattered, followed by the scrambling sound of panic.

"What now?" Tick sighed as they turned to a mess of spilled glue. "Again?"

One of Sangchul's kids wiped at the slick with the bottom of his shirt. Clumsy, idiotic. "It fell on its own," the boy said. "I didn't touch it."

The glue oozed across the conveyor belt, pooling into the metal pocket and over the edge to the floor. A tacky, gloppy paste. It was hyung, wreaking havoc. No, Sangchul bit his cheek until he tasted blood. Ridiculous.

Tick frowned at Sangchul, the dare in his voice clear. "I'm responsible for quota now."

"Mind your group," Sangchul said, irritation darting through him. "I've got my own."

This pathetic kid, waster of product. Sangchul grabbed him, and the boy's hair slipped through his fingers. He corkscrewed the curls tighter. A slug who didn't take advantage of the showers, who remained as dirty as the streets he had once lived on. He squealed like a pink, fat thing that rooted the dirt for bugs. His head slammed into the metal rim, the stool, the ground. He flailed, Sangchul's nails scraping scalp. A hit for the wasted product, another for slowing them down, another for making Sangchul hurt him, another for the blood.

Who are you?

"What?" Sangchul wrenched, done.

The other boys had risen off their stools, another infraction. He threw a ruined shoe. "Get back to work. Don't try to help him."

Sangchul stared at his watch, the white numbers, the second hand ticking forward, the cut glass reflecting his face in its own.

How could you?

He rammed Youngchul's voice to the back of his head. His brother was gone, and it was stupid of him—to hold on to his photograph, imagine him alive.

EUNJU

Gossip seethed through the cafeteria at dinnertime, from the boys, us, the Keepers huddled at the doors. With Teacher's and Warden's absences came speculation, a perverse excitement that washed away the morning's dread. Mina and I explained what we had learned. "He punched a Keeper?" Nabi's voice, high and wondering.

I picked at a strand of spinach as they chattered. The bite of sesame against the iron green, the burst of garlic, a good distraction. So much talk of Honggi, and all I could envision was the wall, how it must have felt to climb above the Keepers' skulls.

"I heard Warden and Teacher were heading north beyond Workshops." Areum lowered her voice, the scar on her brow shiny and white.

"Unnie." Nabi nuzzled me. "What's over there?"

I tried to remember. I hadn't walked that way in months, not during Rewards. Pink-throated azaleas, a wire fence. "Nothing, really," I said. "A closed-off area."

Ajumma Lee arched an eyebrow at Umma. A cramp clenched my insides, and I set aside my rice bowl. Even at a time like this, my body wanted to announce itself. "I can't think of this as a power," I said.

Mina brought a potato stem to her lips. "Does your mother know you won Rewards?"

I leaned closer, the din around us like spikes in our conversation, Honggi's name bouncing from group to group. "Not yet."

"The Keepers are angry." Her voice slowed, a sign she was nervous. She glanced at the empty space we left for Bora, and a new possibility opened up in me, like an anchovy releasing its flavor into broth. It had always lurked beneath, but only now did I taste it. I had thought Teacher was the father of Bora's baby. Maybe it was one of the Keepers.

Mina hesitated. "It might be better if you renounce Rewards."

I shook my head. Our bodies—we were full of blood and power. We were so prone to hurt. Rewards was mine, and I wouldn't let that go: the taste of the air, the ache in my ears from the cold, the wall I returned to, memorizing the cracks between stones, a path up and out.

SANGCHUL

He leaned against the cafeteria's double doors, neck blazing, while the others speculated about Crow's absence. He had feared that Jae and Taeho would see hyung, but Youngchul's decapitated head only flickered for him. He tried to calm his skittering pulse, this sensation of being tethered.

"He's going to get fenced." Rat chewed his bottom lip, the beauty mark at the corner disappearing beneath stained teeth.

"He caught Honggi. Shouldn't that count?" Cow asked.

"Whatever he gets, he deserves," Mosquito said, massaging his elbow.

"Has that happened before, fencing a Keeper?" Tick peered over his shoulder at the cafeteria. "Maybe we should quiet them."

Where am I?

Sangchul tried to shake off hyung. For months after his leaving, Sangchul had imagined his brother—a winged creature, a hovering apparition—so hungry for his presence. But he had grown used to solitude, and he didn't need this sudden pecking. The others were talking about a Keeper getting fenced, and he didn't understand what that meant, exactly. He needed to concentrate, make sure he knew who was in danger, and that it wasn't him.

I can't find my body.

The thing on his neck, this air-thin slip, clawed into his skin.

Sangchul coughed. The photograph—he would burn it the next chance he got. In Warden's room, he'd toss it into the flames.

Mosquito stared, head cocked. Sangchul straightened, tried to smile, no, they were worried about Crow being fenced. Sangchul cleared his throat. "We need to be so good they don't notice us," he said.

Mosquito scoffed. "Is that why you beat a kid for no reason?"

Sangchul bit his fingers. The boy had been hurt more than he'd intended, more than a spill of glue was worth.

"They're preoccupied with Honggi, you'll be fine," Tick said.

Sangchul shrugged, feigning indifference.

"I saw Teacher and Warden heading behind Workshops," Rat said. "We need to worry about that. What does this mean for the rest of us?"

Cow squeezed his chin. "That's not good."

"I don't understand." Tick shifted on his feet. This time, Sangchul met his gaze. He didn't either. What was behind Workshops? What did it mean, exactly, to be fenced? Why hadn't anyone mentioned what seemed palpable—that Crow was partially to blame, having taken Honggi for Closet Time too often for any boy to endure without retaliation? Before he could form the words, Mosquito whistled, a sudden hollow. The room quieted, and in the silence, they heard the sounds of Warden and Teacher approaching.

EUNJU

I stared at Teacher anew, this man who could harm me. That scent of musk and wood chips I had smelled on him the day of my arrival textured with something else—ice, a knowing. I had won Rewards, and he and Mule were waiting for me at the back door of Big House. Teacher sucked his teeth as he let us out, glancing over his shoulder at the gymnasium where Warden corralled the others: "This wasn't my idea, keeping Rewards. Not today."

Free, I felt the contours of my body beneath my coat. I had changed the cloth in my underwear three times. Still, fishhooks tore through the muscle of my womb. Of course I knew the capabilities of men, but with bleeding came a fresh discernment. I held my elbows and bent into the wind. Mule, beside me, spoke to himself, his head cricked at a slant. Strange, they were all acting strange. Wasn't I too, imagining escape, too scared to try?

The ground squelched, wet, soggy. Tracked through, from whatever Warden and Teacher had been doing. "What's over there?" I asked, pointing. "What's beyond the fence?"

Mule squinted. "What fence?"

"The fenced area, with the azalea bushes." I hesitated. Whatever we knew, he probably did too. "I heard Warden and Teacher were over there earlier today."

An invisible hand moved over his face, until he became someone else. He winced, grabbed his neck, and for a second, unbidden, I saw Youngchul.

"Can we go look?" Mule shouldered me, and I flinched at his touch. A cold anger burned through me—at my weakness, my new alarm, Umma's and Mina's words rippling like stones.

"Don't touch me." I shoved him from behind and then, before he could react—I ran. Sudden and hard and fast, the blood-soaked cloths in my underwear slipping, branches pressing in, skin of my calves stretched tight. Past Little House, north, up.

Mule yelled. A swift wind whipping the leaves. I squeezed between trunks, ducked beneath a bare branch. He yelled again. There, the wall. Its gray silence. My arm outstretched—I grazed the cold stone, a chill traveling up my palm, my elbow, my brain.

"Don't even try it," he shouted.

My knees buckled as he wrapped himself around my legs. I hit the wall. He pinned my arms, flipped me. His breath so close, acrid and sharp against the bone-clean air. My body rigid, tight.

I screamed.

His thick mittened hand covered my mouth.

"Are you stupid?" Mule touched his forehead to mine. I tried to scream again. He jerked back, understanding staggering through him. "Don't move." He pushed himself onto his elbows and rolled off.

I sucked in ragged scraps of air.

He squatted, huffing. "I wasn't going to hurt you," he said.

The taste of iron filled my mouth, and I spat out red. Touched my lower lip, where the wall had scraped me.

"I wasn't," he repeated.

I dragged myself up to seated.

"What were you thinking, Eunju? Didn't you hear what happened to Honggi?"

I stared at the wall, the near-black sky. Honggi had tried to climb. I had only scraped my fingers against stone. Umma and Mina had been right about the dangers of Rewards. Loathing pricked my eyes. "You don't understand what's happening," I said.

He scrambled to standing.

"Do you know what they do to us?" I asked—Bora, my bleeding, the ways I could be punished flashed through me.

He touched the wall. "I only . . . I thought it was a saying."

I pulled up my knees. What was he talking about?

He stepped back. "I thought they were sent off to orphanages or a hospital, to jail, I don't know. To their families. I thought hyung was the exception."

I tucked my chin between my knees. Bora was gone, and with her, a nameless baby, and here he was speaking of Youngchul. "What do you mean?"

"The boys in Chapel, when they're fenced. I thought it was a funny term, like the nicknames." He spoke to the wall, his head aslant, his gaze far from me. What did I care about the boys? I was talking about the girls, Umma, me. Our words darted past one another. I felt the tightness of his grip in absence. The wind howling around us. His ghost-green imprint on my skin.

2011

So he started seeing ghosts, that's what you're telling me? Narae shakes her head, disbelieving. She thumbs the glass front of the restaurant, leaving a perfect marker. We are outside, and I am late again. I ignore the hostess's beckoning, pull at my ear, Narae's words from earlier settling in my mind.

The Seoul Olympics were in 1988, I say. *How could the Home be connected to them?*

Narae leads me to an empty street bench. *They say Park Chung-hee was trying to win the bid to host. These institutions were created as early as 1975.* She shows me her phone. *I've been asking questions.* She rushes before I can protest. *I haven't mentioned you, but if you want . . . ?*

I remember the Olympics, the special stamps. The coaxing and celebrating. I was out by then. The Stone Home ruined.

The police received promotions, and the centers received subsidies based on how many people they held. Narae spits, a crassness I haven't seen summoned.

The Olympics had been our country's unveiling. The Miracle on the Han River. A laugh comes out of me, pinched and wrong, streaked with white. We were witness. Became animals. For that? Pageantry and games?

The fence. Maybe we can find the place, she says. *Order them to dig up the area.*

Impossible.

Are you listening to me? We have to do something. They used you, like a common pig.

I watched the Opening Ceremony, along with everyone else. At a bar, safe within a crowd of strangers, when the doves caught fire, burned alive.

Sacrifice, I correct. *We were sacrifice.*

SANGCHUL

Four weeks, and Crow hadn't returned. Four weeks, and the wall shed new fears, tilting paranoia in them all. Warden and Teacher were relentless. Four weeks, and that wheedling voice, that wind, that burrow in his neck had bloomed—screeching, a monsoon, parasitic.

As Tick opened the door to Leathers Workshop, Sangchul skimmed the woods. Somewhere beyond was a fence, dormant azalea bushes. Dirt and mounds. *Find my body*, Youngchul screamed. Sangchul couldn't. There was enough to worry about, more accidents by Keepers and boys alike. More sniping and squealing. A guttering fear.

Tick whispered in his ear. As long as they made quota, kept the boys focused, they were valuable, safe. Sangchul nodded, though he wasn't sure anymore what was real or true. "Sneakers!" he yelled as they entered their room. No longer sandals, but white-bottomed sneakers with red tongues.

When quota seemed impossible, he and Tick looped laces alongside the others, against all the rules. Then again, what were the rules anymore? The leather was soft and supple, like handling a skein of their own skin, all sensation erased with repetition. Sangchul bent each piece so the holes rose like volcanoes, silver grommets crowning their lips.

Four weeks, and April arrived, hurtling toward them in rainy sheets.

EUNJU

Today, Umma had been chosen for Chapel Meals duty. I could have taken her place, insisted she wash the laundry, clip clean sheets to lines strung between trees. Instead, I was in Workshops, enclosed, far from her looming belly, the men.

"She'll be all right," Mina whispered.

"No talking," Cow shouted.

He was a Keeper who shouted now. No longer afraid of Halmoni's power, his round eyes branded with fear. *He acts like his brain's been scooped out*, Jae joked once. But we obeyed. Worked harder. Honggi was gone, and we knew what that meant.

"What if they take her—" I started. I couldn't help it. Her pregnancy was obvious, even with the oversize sweatshirts and coats. Seven months, a belly extended and round. Halmoni was the Chapel Meals carrier, not Umma. I imagined Warden and Teacher tricking her into a van, whisking her to an unknown facility, far from me.

Cow smacked my face, and my neck twisted with the force. Taeho coughed, a wet, sticky sound. Mina sucked in a sharp breath.

I couldn't concentrate. The lines slipping out of my hands. Chapel Duty. Umma couldn't hide, working at the burners, behind the counters.

"Warden and Teacher must know she's pregnant by now." Mina clamped shut as my fishhooks clattered. Was I deluding myself in thinking we could hide her?

I shook my head. Quota—Warden had increased quota. I needed to concentrate, but my mind was dusty, and everything took effort. An extra care I couldn't muster. Last night, I had seen something beneath the skin of her belly ribbon across. A foot, a hand. A baby was coming, and I couldn't protect them.

The loudspeaker.

Time already?

A clanging—in my mind, the room. Cow was counting the boxes. "Oh shit, oh no."

"What is it?" Taeho asked.

Jae pushed his tongue between his teeth. Mina squeezed her hands together.

Quota.

We hadn't made quota.

SANGCHUL

He needed to touch something, ground himself to the earth. Even if that meant here, this place. Quota. They hadn't met quota. Tick paced the Workshop, gulping air. "What do we do?"

The hours had spun out of their hands, a ceaseless fury of laces and holes.

"There's nothing," Sangchul said. He wanted his voice to sound harsh, adult, but the words split as they left his mouth.

The loudspeaker buzzed.

The others were gathering outside. It was time.

On the grass, headed to Little House, the news candled into a flame, lighting the others in fear.

"You too?"

"But—"

Tick gripped Sangchul's shoulder. "Did you hear?"

Sangchul shoved him off. He wouldn't cry. He would store the feeling inside him, a roiling ball of heat. They would be whipped on the line, Youngchul screaming in his ear.

"No one made quota."

Sangchul stopped. "What do you mean?"

"Listen to me—" Tick's eyes blinking and blinking and

blinking behind plastic frames. “No Workshop made quota.” The whispers roared. Sangchul stared at the patchy grass, a cluster of clovers, a sign of spring, those many-petaled blooms hyung used to suck on whole. The faint sweet taste they left on their tongues.

EUNJU

We darted into the kitchen, the news blistering our tongues. Knees cracking, feet zinging numb. No one had made quota—adrenaline and fear and confusion. Would they lash us all, or were we protected from punishment?

"Umma," I yelled. I wanted her to be safe, walled in the kitchen where the men wouldn't enter. She was standing with the others. Huddled, with Halmoni at the center.

"What happened?" Mina asked.

Halmoni tilted her chin in the air, a cloth plugging one nostril. Umma patted her sides, soothing. "You're all right now."

Nabi clasped my hand, her freckles paling in the light. "Warden hit her." Her words, wispy, evaporated in front of us. No matter the rules here, she was his elder. She was our grandmother. Nabi's shallow voice. "Why would he do that?"

I looked at our entwined hands. Her thin, bony fingers. "I don't know."

Areum towed us to the serving counter. "He came in ranting about cutting the produce budget. Said Halmoni was stealing, eating all the food and getting fat." She pointed at the cafeteria, the aisle that split the tables. A crooked bench. "All of a sudden, he hit her, that bastard."

Nabi worried the hem of her shirt. "She banged her head, a nosebleed."

Mina picked up a cup, someone else's, and water splashed over her knuckles. "I can't believe it," she said.

"I can." He was a pitiful man, and I wanted to make him hurt—for hitting Halmoni, for making us fear him. One day, I would crush his fingers in my mouth, crunch bone between molars. One day, I would make him see.

SANGCHUL

Warden and Teacher locked everyone in for Dinner. Sangchul couldn't figure out what they were planning, but he knew they'd never failed quota before, not all of them. A sharp, jolty hurt in his stomach. *I need you to find me.* "What are they going to do?" Sangchul asked.

"Whip us, throw us in Chapel, who knows." Rat ran a hand through his oily hair.

"What if they fence us?" Cow asked.

Mosquito held his elbows. "They can't replace us all."

"Couldn't they?" Tick asked.

Mosquito looked back at the tables, the swirling chatter, resolve creasing his forehead. "We show them we're Keepers. Show them they can't blame us. Warden and Teacher will see; we know what we're doing."

They dispersed across the perimeter. *My body, I need it.* The rumors lashed Sangchul's arms, the low hollow of his neck. Warden was going to starve them into submission, the gym would be turned into a makeshift Chapel, the Keepers would be replaced in an exquisite ceremony, Halmoni was hurt. Youngchul was screaming in his head.

"Shut your mouths," Mosquito yelled, and for once Sangchul was grateful for his command. The tenor didn't quiet, though, the boys too afraid. There was no stopping them. Warden was going to limit meals, Shirts would be eliminated, Halmoni was dead. They would be fenced. He would join his brother soon. *I can't leave without seeing.* The herds were wild-eyed, foraging for truth. The women were eating inside the kitchen. Why?

Cow snatched a glass from one of Crow's old boys and drank it down. Rat stopped at Tick's table. Knuckled a freckled boy into a soup bowl, taunting his former squealer. Tick nearly lurched, but this wasn't the time, they were supposed to stay united. The herds were herds.

"Five minutes," Mosquito announced, though Warden and Teacher hadn't returned.

Sangchul smacked the closest kid's head. This one was lazy, motivated by food. He should have done a better job, encouraged the others during Workshops. *Are you listening, brother?*

Behind him, a hard slap. Tick sneered, "Slow at work, slow at eating, you dumb shit."

"I'm not— I didn't—" A familiar voice.

Sangchul turned, but time was fraying before him, sparking his vision. *I need you.*

Tick stood over Taeho, hitting him in the face with his own hand. Sangchul watched, silent and nauseous. Tick had always seen Taeho as weak. He searched for Cow, but he was at the other end of the room. Peering with round, dumb eyes.

"Hey—" Sangchul shouted.

They looked at him. Taeho, half falling off his bench. Jae, holding on to his friend's shirt. Tick, who kept going.

"I was only eating—" Taeho tried to explain.

"Sangchul," Jae pleaded.

Tick stopped. Confusion and a laugh ruining his face. "*Sangchul.* Hear that?" He seesawed between them. "Calling on an old friend?"

Mosquito thrust Jae out of the way, flanked Taeho as if he were a threat.

"Easy now," Sangchul said. "They're coming soon."

Mosquito raised his voice, so the whole room could hear. "Sloppy at work, sloppy at dinner. See what happens when you idiots miss quota?" He wrenched Taeho off the bench. Batted him in the gut.

Tick joined. "By us. By Teacher, Warden. You'll get hit every night until you meet quota." He panted, caught Sangchul's eyes. "You understand?"

Taeho was yowling, a high and spiny sound—and a flash came to Sangchul. A pig rooting in the mud. What was he doing on the floor? The world tilted, segmenting into parts he couldn't lock together. A boy on the ground. A bat cracking a face. *But I need you.* Tick and Mosquito—Sangchul was right—they were squealing together, crowding him out.

Jae stood. "Sangchul, they're hurting him."

It was too much—the wailing in his head, this bleeding body, and Sangchul thought of Eunju's red mouth, and then, yes, the fence. Fenced. He had thought it was a term, but there was a part of the land closed off from the rest of them. There, bodies were buried, marked with a certificate. He hadn't known about the area, what it meant to be disappeared. Or had he? He couldn't bring Youngchul to his body, the truth too frightful, too foul. He couldn't do anything.

"Sangchul!" Jae shouted again.

"It's Keeper." Mosquito raised his bat, walloped Taeho instead.

Sangchul searched—for Teacher, Warden, his brother, an elder. Halmoni—where was Halmoni?

"Leave him alone," someone shouted. Who, he didn't know, but Rat was already on him. The Keepers' anger a storm, the air sparking. The stink of animal among them.

From the ground, someone called his name. What was Taeho doing on the floor? Sangchul shook his head. *But I need you.* Taeho's eye was bleeding. Not the skin around it, the eyeball itself.

"Sangchul," Mosquito mocked. "This one's calling for you."

"Hyung," Taeho whimpered. "You said."

Tick laughed. "You've lost your mind. You think we're your hyungs now?"

Sangchul tried to block the sounds—the crunching, the crying, the wind, the animals. *But what about me, don't you see I need you?*

"This one's been slowing his team down for weeks. He thinks you can protect him." Mosquito's voice returned, his shoulders slack, the only sign of violence his heel against Taeho's cheek. Tick, panting behind him. "Will you?"

Someone gave him a bat. Someone shouted. Someone called him hyung. Sangchul got down on the floor. Pressed himself on top of a body. Taeho, or no, this was only a boy. It was only a back. A spine. He turned the head so the eye was hidden, squished against the floor. It wasn't fair, for them to have to look at that sort of wound. He held the flesh down.

"Hit him." A command.

Sangchul slammed. A shirt. A rib. A head. A crackling sound, sun-crisp leaves. Somehow, he had a bat in his hands. Summer, he had once known summer. A neck. He erased himself with another. A sound with another. *I need you.* An image with another. *I need you.* Another. *To find me.* Was he crying? He didn't know.

He was anyone.

Any body.

Any animal.

Someone called a name.

Someone called him Mule.

EUNJU

Taeho was on the floor, and I could only witness from the counter, from my island of women. We were failing him. Behind me, Umma screamed, "She can't breathe." Halmoni heaved in the corner by the sinks. Nabi and Areum ran over. I stayed hewn to the cafeteria, edgeless heat, thrown cups, smashed bowls, Mina by my side.

Out there, Tick was kicking Taeho, Jae crying, tossed aside. Then, Mule was walking over. Youngchul's brother. "Look," I said, hope rising.

Mina moaned, knowing before me. A passage of words between the Keepers, a look. Then, Mule was on Taeho. Twisting his neck with force. Mina hid her face in my shoulder.

Nabi came for us. "Halmoni's sick."

"They're going to kill him." I was screaming. They pulled me away, into the kitchen.

Halmoni, our grandmother. I tried to shift focus, my mind too clangy, full, a bell ringing behind my eyes.

"Is it a heart attack?" Areum asked.

"Shock, maybe," Umma said.

Halmoni gasped, and we grabbed buckets of cold water. Wet washcloths for her limbs. Nabi cried. Of all of us, she was Halmoni's closest child.

"Someone shut those boys up," Ajumma Lee yelled.

"Help her," Nabi screamed.

Finally, Halmoni lifted her spotted cheeks. "What are they doing to him?"

• • •

Teacher led the boys out, ignoring the taste of iron in the air, Taeho limp on the floor. The Keepers left too, without punishment, subdued, whatever had been festering inside them unleashed. Warden remained by Taeho's body, called Halmoni until she lifted herself from the chair and obeyed. He grabbed her hair, the mask slipping off his face. A small, angry man inside. He pulled it back on with effort. Smiled with his teeth, without heart. "You are useless."

"The boy's hurt," Halmoni said, her voice like ice cracking.

Warden toed Taeho. "Chapel's full. You'll clean him."

"The Keepers, they were—" I started.

"This boy is clumsy, stupid. He did it to himself."

Warden didn't look back, and in the empty space that followed, I wasn't sure if I had spoken at all.

We carried Taeho to our table as Nabi ran between us and Halmoni in the kitchen, searching for bandages, thread, anything that could help. We splayed him, and Ajumma Lee pushed two fingers into his throat. "He's breathing."

Umma ran her hands over his body, lightly, marking the shape of him. "Bruises, but no broken bones." She said it as though we should be grateful. It wasn't fair—his right eye. A crust of blood, the ball roving beneath the thin skin of his lid. He moaned and blinked too fast, too slow. Then, we saw it—all wrong—the black pupil stretching out of its circle and into the brown iris, as if someone had stuck a pole into a puddle and dragged it across sand. I whipped away, bile rising in my throat. Revulsion crawling through me, a betrayal.

"What happened to his eye?" Nabi screamed.

"Don't look," Halmoni said, suddenly arrived, a length of gauze in her hands.

Umma palmed his chest, the shallow up and down of his breathing. "Focus on this."

His head lolled, mouth open and dry. Taeho, sweet Taeho, was empty.

"Let me." Halmoni took over with the charge of a woman who understood her injuries. She hovered a finger above the right lid, the black iris draining into the brown.

"Can you fix it?" I asked. His eye, it wasn't possible.

She touched her pinked cheek, then his. Her shock stripped. Her nostril tinged red. She had been bleeding too. Her voice, aching. "The eye's ruptured."

We circled him, and Halmoni prayed before beginning her healing. I wiped my face with my elbow. Already, my grief was turning into a blaze. We were living among monsters, and I would find a way to make them hurt.

"Clean him." Halmoni pointed to a split along his jawbone and another above his brow. Ajumma Lee washed, rubbing at a trail of yellow around his lips. The smell sharp, anodyne. Halmoni threaded a string into the eye of her needle. "It's coarser than I want, but it's all we have." She cupped Nabi's head. "Don't look."

I forced myself to sit by his side, hold his hand instead of run. When the needle pierced his jaw, he moaned.

"It's all right, Taeho." Mina smoothed his forehead.

Halmoni worked slowly. The needle sliding beneath the skin and back up, looping over the cut like a bridge over water. When she finished, she knotted the string with her teeth.

We cleaned him—his ears, neck, limbs, fingernails. The way we'd clean a newborn, someone we loved. Only Halmoni had the strength to tend to his gaze. "The vision's gone."

Ajumma Lee cried into her apron. Nabi wept. We all knew

Taeho, with his guileless softness. His favorite color was gray because of the river beside his house, where he liked to dip his feet. I imagined the silt there, those fine dark pebbles, his favored shade. He loved the tenderness of galbi, that glossy smoked meat, the sweet pain that crackled behind the ears when sucking on hard candies. Out of everyone, he was the only one who held on to his past life, who shared stories without greed or pride or shame, so convinced this was a mistake, that the world was better than it was.

"He needs to wake before Warden returns," Umma said.

Halmoni wrapped a cloth around his head. Someone made ginger tea. I fed him spoonfuls that dribbled from the corner of his lips. Ajumma Lee sang an old healer's song, and we listened, trusting words had the power to charge his body, an exquisite belief.

Time ticked. The room darkened. Halmoni patted him. Lightly, across the chest, the soles of his feet. The areas of his body we hoped hurt the least. "Wake up now, Taeho. Return to us."

We prodded, whispered, cradled his head.

Slowly, he groaned.

Slowly, he blinked.

Slowly, his lips bubbled open and shut, and he cried.

SANGCHUL

No one could save anyone else, not here. So, he had kicked a body. Mosquito ranting in his ear. *Again. Harder. Now.* Youngchul asking and asking. *I need you.* Suddenly, the body at his feet had turned into nothing but a gray shirt and shoulders, a muss of dark hair.

In the night, he looked down. Found himself on his cot. His empty hands, backlit.

A clean feeling moved through his chest. A wing. He stood. Found his way through the shadows, out the door, down the hall, into the showers.

Relief. That was it. He was feeling the pure sweep of relief.

EUNJU

The next day, we shuffled around hugging our bellies, bracing our bodies for news. Teacher didn't take us to Service, no one came for Breakfast. There were shouts outside, but we couldn't figure from where they came. We scoured the kitchen, cooked. Then, Teacher knocked the wood-beaded curtain in the afternoon, commanding us to haul ten buckets of water without explanation.

Halmoni led us outside, where the sky was drained of color. The buckets sloshed against my thighs as we stopped in the center field. The Keepers, kneeling with their hands raised. Shirtless in the spring chill. There were only five of them, and yet they held such power.

"Two each," Teacher said. They would hold them up for the rest of the day. No food, no bathroom. If they spilled, another punishment. I set my buckets in front of Cow.

As they struggled to hoist them by the handles, Teacher went on about Workshops, how unessential the Keepers were. Bony chests, trembling arms.

"Come on." Halmoni rounded us away. She was fragile from last night's fall, but in front of Teacher, she gathered herself to her fullest height.

Inside Little House, we waited. Watched windows. I imagined them failing—Rat keeling over, Cow crying, Tick's glasses clouding from effort. Mosquito would falter, and Mule—my fury a full blast in my chest. Buckets raked skyward for a few hours was measly, not enough. For this to be their whole punishment, no. I wanted eyes plucked out of skulls, legs trampled to slush.

Teacher appeared as we prepared dinner. "They're to return the buckets to the spigot outside." He pointed at Mina and me. "Go collect them. What're you doing, just standing there?"

Mina cupped a peeled potato like an animal skull, white and porous. We were making food to feed you, I wanted to say. Instead, "That's all they have to do to atone?"

Halmoni pushed me behind her. "I'll talk to her."

He wiped his hands on his pants. "Dinner needs to be ready on time." He had no idea, no grasp of Little House. We had been cooking all day, too much, unsure of what to do. With hours stuck inside, speculating about Taeho and his eye.

Outside, Teacher positioned us by the pump. "Don't say another word."

He left us, as if it were normal to be unwatched, alone, as if the Keepers hadn't proven they were dangerous. It wasn't only the rules that were changing. The adults were slipping too.

Mina and I studied the trees, and I wished they could predict our future. I concentrated on a cluster of yellow buds bursting from a branch. Spring was here, and with it came animals, blooms. "I want to go back in," she said.

I hardened my face. One of us would have to be strong, then.

They came one at a time. I gave them my ugliest sneer. When Mosquito neared, Mina retreated. I had been alone with him during Rewards. Once, he had watched as I lay down in the field and consumed the stars. He followed me to the wall without complaint.

He didn't call me half-breed. I had mistaken him as different—for what, for treating me with ten minutes of kindness, a dignity we couldn't afford?

Mule arrived last, the buckets heavy at his knees. Mule, I could manage. Mule, I could hurt.

He poured the first bucket into the drain. Slow, purposeful, his eyes closing, expecting a beating. The words curdled in my stomach. He was made of nothing, a husk who had never been like his brother. "I can only be myself," he said.

Mina laughed, a streaky sound.

"We have no power either, you understand?" he whispered.

I wanted to cackle like Mina, burst the gnawed air inside me. Taeho's ruptured eye, the black oozing pupil. "Do you know what you've done?" I circled him. "Taeho, who defended you, even after you became a Keeper. You're worse than Mosquito, Teacher, Warden—"

He pinned me to the corner of the wall, a flash of heat against new cold. "You don't know."

"Let her go." Mina tugged at his shoulders, but I knew his strength, how easily he'd tackled me in the snow. The weight of him jamming me down. How he had twisted Taeho's neck. I kicked, the fear solid and white in my throat. He would crack my chest and wrap me around the sides of the building. He would hurt us both. "Sangchul, please," Mina begged.

"You don't know." His eyes round, nearly wet, his voice a whisper, a stone. "Look what Mosquito did to my hyung. Look what he made me do. He's the one who hurt Taeho, not me."

I couldn't see, my vision crackling. Throat, lungs, a head floating away from the rest of me.

A racket of sound. A crash against us. The whoosh of air across my cheek. Release. Mina flung a bucket at him. Hit him right in the neck. He wrenched away, clawing at his collarbone, the pail clattering at our feet.

SANGCHUL

Eunju thought he was more than capable of hurt, that it was a part of him, and maybe it was. What he said was true though. He had no power. Why couldn't she see? He wanted to wring the answer out of her, render his reasoning and have her understand. He found his way here, just as she had. "Look at me," he tried to say. He heard other words come out of his mouth. Felt the pressure of his hands on her neck, spine. How easily he could wrench her down and hit her temple against the spout's curved lip. She was tiny, supple in his grip.

Look at this control, he wanted to say. *I could hurt you, but I don't.*

Mina called his name. He felt the weight first, and then the wetness. The spatter of water against his ear. The tin against his throat. The bucket overturned, his head ringing.

They flung apart. Her springing from the wall as if he had truly wounded her. "One truth doesn't erase another," she said, raspy, almost to herself.

A shout. Teacher, calling from the lawn. He would be in trouble now. He turned from the girls, their righteous anger, their sloppy understanding, and he left. Through the trees, back toward Teacher. Youngchul screaming. *I need you. I need my body. Find me, return me.*

"No—hyung, I can't help you." He said it aloud: he wanted

it to be a clearing. Youngchul had abandoned him, and Sangchul had no desire to search for his remains. He stumbled. A choking, bringing him to his knees. A whirl, a ghost. *Do you see? Witness, brother.*

Sangchul looked at the land hyung had brought him to. A week after Inspection Day, Jae and Taeho had held Sangchul up by the arms and stopped their run at Youngchul's favorite tree. The one with the near-black branches that curved toward the sun, a blown umbrella. While Jae unraveled a goodbye prayer, Taeho squatted and placed a single stone between two roots—a perfect black pebble, as round and smooth as any manufactured thing.

Sangchul touched the roots of hyung's favorite tree. *Listen to me, brother.*

He searched for the stone.

He remembered, and he willed himself to forget.

EUNJU

Mina and I didn't speak of Mule to anyone, even when Halmoni scolded us for breaking the bucket, for putting ourselves in danger, as if it had been our fault. In the evening, Umma pressed. "I saw you when you returned. What happened outside?"

I refused: Mule's grip, his delusions. "I tripped, that's all."

She eyed me, wary. "They're losing control. It's not safe here."

"It wasn't ever safe," I said.

She moved my hand to her stretched-out belly button, and I felt a push from within. "Taeho's beating, the punishment outside." She spoke, seeded with urgency. "We're not waiting for a plan anymore. Tomorrow, we leave."

I swallowed. "How?"

"We'll figure it out as we go. I don't know how to protect us here."

"What about everyone else?" Mina had thrust a bucket at Mule's face, risked herself as I flinched against the wall. "We can't leave them here."

"I'll confront him tonight with what I know. It might be enough to let him release us." She held her moving stomach. It came to me with bright force—she was scared, a slight quake beneath her calm veneer. "I don't know what he'll do now that I'm nearing the arrival date." She closed her eyes. "He's always wanted a son."

"Don't go." My voice was thin, whiny, like a child, not like someone she could depend on.

"Listen to me." She grabbed something beneath her shirt. Pressed it into my palm and leveled her gaze. "I stole it from Halmoni last night."

A key.

"It opens our room. If I don't return by tomorrow, you figure a way out. You run."

A simple silver key like any other. No special marking, not made of brass or jade or iron. "How did you get it?" I asked.

"When she got hit, when we were tending her. Warden, he was upset about me." Her voice impatient. "You understand?"

She had been patting Halmoni's sides when Mina and I returned from Workshop. She had been telling Halmoni it would be all right. Umma was ruthless and sneaky and resourceful, and I loved her. "Let's go right now, before Teacher comes."

"There isn't time." She raised my chin. "We'll leave together. I'll convince him. The key—it's only a reserve, a just-in-case if I don't come back. You understand?"

She held me, and I wanted to believe her. I tried to conjure goodness—an image of us on the other side of the wall. Two figures running in the night. We would go to the market I loved, where the halmoni with cloudy eyes gave us hodu-gwaja for free. Those hot, spongy spheres with their walnut crunch, smooth red bean paste. We would go to the stream I once trampled in my underwear, my dress looped into a crown on my head. Hope seeped into me, sweet and aching. It would be worth leaving them behind. Outside, I wouldn't know them. Halmoni and Mina and the others. I would scour my mind clean.

SANGCHUL

They hoisted buckets for hours until hunger shook their visions and their arms gave way, melting into pulpy slop. They'd hoped that punishment was enough, but Teacher commanded Mosquito to his knees in the gymnasium after-hours, snarling, "To blind a boy at a time like this. You have no self-control. Should I replace you? Has your time come?"

So, this was how it happened, Head Keeper dethroned. Sangchul tried to confirm with the others through a nod. Youngchul's floating head skittered across his cheek; he swatted his own face.

Mosquito swished his palms, his forehead on the floor. "I didn't blind him, I promise you."

"You're the Head Keeper," Teacher shouted. "If not you, then who?"

As Mosquito turned his cheek, licking his lips, Sangchul didn't see desperation, or imploring, but shrewdness. Unease, a ghost on his neck, as he tried to figure what Head Keeper would say next. Mosquito raised himself to kneeling, slowly, not like one being threatened. A clear voice, almost wry, as if it were obvious: "It was Sangchul, sir. A brawl with an old friend. They were in the same group once. We watched, sir, as they attacked each other." He glided into the lie with a smirk. "He was the one."

Sangchul pinched his throat, and Youngchul cackled in his

ear. It was Tick who had started beating the boy, not him. He had come to stop them. He had come to help. He waited for someone to protest—no, Rat's and Cow's mouths were stuffed with wool.

Teacher grabbed him by the neck.

"He's lying." Sangchul tripped as he was forced to his knees. "Taeho was provoking another boy, so Dal went over. I didn't—" He rubbed his palms together, a hot dread rushing through his veins. "I didn't come until the end."

"That's not true," Mosquito said. "It was him. We all saw it."

Teacher held them both by their hair, and Sangchul felt the strands rip from his scalp. "He's only covering for himself, I promise," he begged.

"Dal?" Teacher demanded.

Tick. His Workshop partner. He would tell the truth. Sangchul gazed at his friend. His smudged glasses and blinking eyes. They had come up together, and that meant something.

Silence lingered, thick, excruciating. Finally, Dal spoke. A whisper, meek and stained. "I didn't get involved."

Fury seized him. It was unfair. Taeho's eye. He had seen it before he ever got on top of the body. They were cheats, deceivers. "I was at the opposite end of the room," Sangchul nearly yelled. "How could I have been the one?"

Teacher pulled him by the ear but spoke to them all. "If an inspector ever asks, it's Warden who commanded this, not me, you understand?"

EUNJU

Umma looked the same from behind, a one-hearted woman. She'd kissed my head and told me to be brave. With the key in my hand, I watched her go. The hours I'd have to wait, Mule's fingers around my neck. My blueing lips and suffocation. Umma, disappeared. Outside, in our before-life, she had protected me, and I could never repay her. I pushed myself up, slipped the key below my tongue. This bud of fear in me, I needed to crush its new leaves. I would go out and prepare, see if there was anything I could do.

I took the long way, past Mina's bed, the muscles in my calves tight with the want to embrace her, tell her I was sorry to leave her behind. I crawled to the smooth curve of her neck, her slack mouth. Whispered, called her name, before I knew what I was saying. "Will you help me?"

She startled awake, caught a gasp in her throat as I revealed the key between my teeth. We approached the door together. The fit of it, in the lock. Umma's cunning. Halmoni had been hurt, and yet she had thought of me.

Suddenly, we were in the hall. My feet sticky against the floor, too loud in its slappy tread. We passed Halmoni's room to our left, the bathroom to our right. The hallway light catching us in its orb.

The sleep washed out of her, Mina squeezed her questions into my hand. When I didn't answer, she led me as if she had been the one to wake with a plan. In front of the room Teacher once shoved us into, there was no sound. No whispers, no movement.

I stopped, that feeling mauling me again: Sangchul's grip on my neck, Teacher's on Umma's, the air squeezed out of us. We were clay, unformed vessels. Umma could have been taken already.

"You're stunned," Mina said, pulling me with new strength. "I understand, but it'll fade, that feeling. We could get out, Eunju. We have to check the front door."

On the main floor, we listened for any sound—Umma with Teacher or a Keeper on guard. She had never told me where they went, and she wasn't here. I followed a cold sheet of air to the entrance of Little House. Mina tried the lock. I stared out the window. Shadows textured against the night. She pointed to the only light, golden and coming from the third floor. Silhouetted, Warden placed a glass on his desk. Turned and looked straight at us.

Mina ducked.

I stilled. It was too dark. Backlit, I was nothing, a no one.

Mina yanked my arm, but I wouldn't move.

Witness, he had said.

Let him see me, then. The thought passed through me, delicious and violent. Let him come. I would force him to his knees, pull out his tongue. He would sweep the floors in bare feet.

He turned, greeted by a new silhouette at the edge of the pane. A woman.

I sank down.

Finally, I saw clearly.

It was Warden, not Teacher.

Warden, who hated mixed-blood, who acted the priest, who allowed the Keepers to color boys with bruises. Inside Umma was a child made of him, that man who shamed us with his words, who controlled Chapel, who called us half-breed whore and scavenger daughter.

"Do you hear me?" Mina wiped my face. I hadn't and couldn't, Warden crowding my mind. His leather and false-God-fueled scent, the man who held us here, he would use us up until only the chaffs of our bodies remained. I looked at Mina. My cheek cold from the press of glass.

"He's the one."

SANGCHUL

Sangchul walked alone, his hair wet and throat raw, body wiped clean. He listened to the sounds coming from the herds' rooms, the closet. Even Cow had gone in. What had happened in the cafeteria was no different from what occurred here. He was a bringer of truth, then.

He walked without aim, turning Mosquito's dishonesty around like a puzzle he couldn't break—how quickly the others had latched on, how quickly Sangchul had been sacrificed. The Keepers didn't seem to understand—Teacher only wanted to protect himself. His mind churned, too bright and noisy for sleep. Beneath the lies, the fear. No, Taeho would be all right. He was sturdy, and Halmoni could heal anyone.

Maybe Sangchul would check, to make sure.

Slowly, silently, he ascended to the third floor. If Warden found him, he would confess: he was pitiful, worthless. He couldn't find Youngchul, but he could locate another. Past the rooms they weren't allowed to enter, there at the end of the hall—he touched the cross hanging by a nail. Jesus swung, and Sangchul wanted to ask if He approved, if what happened here was right. His fingers hovered over the knob. Perhaps Taeho was fine. Perhaps no one was in Chapel. Perhaps Chapel was a lie, and they were all lost. Anything felt possible.

The sound of feet, voices from the wrong side of the door. Behind him, coming up the stairs: "I could be your witness. We could file a testimony together." A woman's voice, plaintive and thorny. "You don't have to be beholden to him."

"It's too risky." Terse. That voice, he knew: Teacher.

Sangchul slipped into Chapel and closed the door. Peering through the gap between the frame and the floor, he watched their feet.

"Byungchul, please. Do you want to be in this system forever? You could have a life."

A pause, feet scuffling. The woman continued, her voice hushed. Sangchul caught only stray words. *Australia. Wife. Bank.* Teacher laughed. "You think we're similar?"

"I'm saying, our pasts. We can do it together, I promise you." Her voice made Sangchul wince, how it wavered between strength and pleading. Teacher sighed. Their feet came together.

Finally, Teacher spoke. "Who would believe you? Look at him, lauded and medaled. And you? Bastard child that breeds bastard children." A sneer. "You have no power, Kyungoh, and you never will."

A knock. A door, opening.

"You're late." Warden's rough-cut words. "Get in here."

A shuffling, a woman disappearing, and then, Teacher stood alone.

EUNJU

Waiting for Umma's return by the front doors of Little House, I told Mina everything—about Warden, his shoes, our leaving tomorrow, the stream we'd visit, the hodu-gwaja, the ghost of Mule's hand on my throat, and how I needed to prepare. "Come with us," I said.

"How?" Mina started toward the kitchen as if this freedom weren't strange and Teacher couldn't return any minute. I felt an awe for her. She was flighty and careless, and people misjudged her. I had misjudged. Her strength was tensile. She tried the kitchen doors, locked.

"The room upstairs," I said, a memory surfacing. The night Umma had been choked by Teacher, before I understood the fear that came from violation. "The one with boxes and paint cans. I think the door's unlocked. Maybe we can find something there."

Mina led us up, and relief descended at her assurance. She jiggled the knob until it opened. "Look at all this stuff." She smacked her lips. A pleasure bloomed in me. I had been right.

"You'll come with us?" I asked.

She plucked through the landscape of scattered piles: mismatched sneakers, a wobbly globe on a cracked base, stuffed animals, a red plastic lunch box, a floral dress with buttons running down the center, a tin of white gummy erasers, cans with faded pictures of peaches and tomatoes and corn. She held one up and tried to sound out the English letters. "Why aren't these in the kitchen? Does Halmoni know about this room?"

My mind snagged on her silence at my question. I sidestepped a box of textbooks and clasped her arm. "Tell me you'll come."

She showed me the can. An unbearable, smiling peach. "How are you going to leave?" She shook her head, gentle. "I don't know if it's possible."

"We'll figure it out." I shrugged, a flare of annoyance. She was the impractical one, not me.

She tucked her hair behind her ears. "I'll come, if it happens. Of course I will."

I nodded, jeweling with happiness. With her and Umma, I could do this. I could leave the rest behind.

"Let's find something useful in this junk," she said, and I remembered the time, what we were doing here.

We searched. I unearthed a canvas knapsack, and we shoved in items that seemed worthy. The dress. A white sheet. Mismatched gloves. A can of corn. A nail file to pierce the lid.

"What about this?" I found a jackknife hidden inside a drawer with broken knobs. It was black, with a serrated edge. I pushed it against my arm and flinched.

Mina wound toward me, stepping over a dead roach with crusty legs. "Careful."

"We could hurt them," I said.

She shook her head. "We should leave undetected."

Annoyance crept in me again. She was careful, and Umma would agree. I closed the knife, the blade slipping into a slot in the handle.

"Did you hear that?" Mina crouched, her shoulders crowding into her neck.

Outside, two voices braided in the night. Teacher and Umma had returned. I steadied behind the door, Mina beside me, and we held our breaths. Footsteps passed. If he came in here— No, he wouldn't find us. He would return Umma and leave. He would go back to Big House.

I clicked open the knife. Mina grabbed my ankle.

With the blade pointed at the door, we waited.

SANGCHUL

Under the blue wash of dawn, he stared at his gray pants. A grassy stain on the knee. A thread unraveling at his crotch. A white scar in the center of his palm. The cot blanket crumpled beneath him.

After Teacher had departed, Sangchul had faced Chapel. Without a light, he'd made out the shape of the rooms in the dark. Cramped single cells like closets lined up in two columns. Square latched openings at the base, where trays of food could be pushed through. It was just as they had imagined—the Keepers, the boys, those of the Stone Home.

The slots opened, one by one. Floating mouths, chapped lips, darting eyes.

"Hello?"

"Who's there?"

"Taeho?" Sangchul asked.

"No, it's me."

Shadows, supple and twitching, warped and wilted. A skittering sound. A groan.

It was too dark. He saw nothing. He ran out.

EUNJU

I pointed the knife—my elbow locked, body rigid, Mina's grasp on my ankle grounding me to the earth. A creak as the door opened—blackness, the blade startling in my hand, the relief of knowing who, her egg-shaped goiter and hunched shoulders—Halmoni.

She flung the door wider. I jostled against a box, and Mina reared like a cat, all curved spine and light feet. "Have you lost your minds?" Halmoni hissed.

"We thought, we thought—" Mina started.

She grabbed my collar. "Are you going to kill me with that thing?"

"It's mine." I gripped the black handle, but she had elder strength, all bone and willpower. She forced the knife from me and closed it with a practiced ease.

"Teacher would have cut your throat if he found you here." She hauled us out, lowering her voice as she marched us back to the room. "Are you as idiotic as they claim we are? He would have cut my throat too."

Mina tripped. "You wouldn't tell him, would you? You wouldn't put us in Chapel?"

"What do you think, child? What should I do in this case?"

"It was my idea," I said.

Halmoni wrenched us higher by our collars. "You think I

don't know? You and your mother are the same, believing others will shield you."

I wanted to laugh—she didn't know us. Umma and I didn't rely on anyone. It wasn't true, I started to say, then I saw Mina. Her earnest face. Her gravelly voice. The way she had thrown the bucket at Mule. Her hand on my wrist as she dragged me downstairs to try the doors, to listen and wipe my cheeks. Maybe I was wrong.

From her pocket, Halmoni pulled the key that locked us in every night. "You thought I wouldn't notice your mother taking my spare?" Light spilled onto us as she unlocked the door, and on the other side, Umma clutched her belly, her worry a sound, wordless, in her mouth.

Halmoni barreled toward her until their noses almost touched. "Have you cooked your brains in soup? You think this is the time to steal from me? How am I supposed to do my job, keep you safe?"

A pitiless veneer took over Umma's gaze, a look from the old days, and glee fired in me. This was the mother I knew, crystal-edged and fierce. "You lock us in at night. Don't pretend you're our protector."

"Who stole?" Ajumma Lee asked, rising from her cot. Nabi roused, and Areum woke too.

"Listen!" I pushed between them, then turned to the others who were starting to circle us. "Something's wrong here. Warden and Teacher, the Home. That's why Mina and I snuck out. We're planning an escape."

"Eunju," Umma warned.

I nodded to Halmoni, who held the key. "Why act like slaves when we have our own building, when they don't supervise us at night?"

"She's right," Mina said, quiet.

"What do you want us to do, break the windows and smash the bars? It's impossible," Ajumma Lee said.

I approached her, our skeptical one. "If we worked together, we could be free."

"Nabi," Mina said. "I'll help you find your family."

"These are fantasies." Umma laughed. "They're confused, foolish girls."

But I wasn't, no longer. Umma had wanted to threaten the men, and that was her ruin because they were incapable of shame. Warden and Teacher thought Little House would keep us docile. Umma should have known: we couldn't get away without the help of the others. I clasped Areum's hand. "You could get a job as a bus conductor, like you always wanted."

"How would we do it?" she asked, tentative.

I hesitated. The feeling that netted us together was fragile, I didn't want to admit that we had no plan. "I've been thinking of options."

Ajumma Lee laughed. "Your mother's right. You're talking about dreams."

"We could break down the door," I said.

"We'll come up with a scheme together," Mina said. "Make ropes, or figure a way to dig under the wall. It won't happen if we sit here and bicker."

"We have the kitchen knives," Areum suggested.

"We could use the burlap sacks," Nabi offered. "Or our bedsheets."

"I can cook extra for us to store," Ajumma Lee conceded.

Slowly, hope spread, but Halmoni remained silent. Alone on a separate cot, heavy, the key between her fingers. I knelt at her feet. She had been here for years, and I knew nothing of her past. "You don't have to lock us in at night," I said.

"The doors to the outside are locked anyway. The kitchen too." She coughed.

"We'll find a way." I rested my head on her lap. "We could leave this place together."

"What good would it do for me?" Halmoni's question came out low and limp, vinegared with despair. She slipped her fingers through my hair. I had no answer for her, with her goiter and old age, bereft of family. To the world, she was only a waste of air, food, resources.

"Halmoni." Umma knelt beside me. "Think of Bora, what we could have done if we tried earlier. Are we any better if we allow them to do what they want?"

"We don't have a choice."

"We haven't tried." Umma leaned back on her heels and held her stomach. "You know who did this. He'll take my baby away, and he won't stop. Who will be next? What if it's Nabi?"

I followed the disorder of Halmoni's unsteady breaths.

We waited.

"I'm too old for this earth," she finally said. Brought her hands to her face. "You can do what you want."

I lay my chin against her knee. "You'll help us?"

"You relentless child." She sucked her teeth. "I'll do what I can."

2011

Narae grabs the knife from my kitchen table, face drained of color. *This*, she says, flicking it open. *You found it. So how did it end up with my father?*

She wears red today, a sheath in a shade too close to blood, and I wonder if a part of her already knows.

Unnie?

I left the knife with him by accident, with you, I say.

I can see her mind whirring—I am telling her too much, too fast, hoping to finish before she leaves me, because surely—she will, won't she?

There won't be anyone else for her to blame.

I don't know what to think. She paces, her hands at her temples.

I steward her to the kitchen, where I've left a basket heaped with yellow, dimple-shaped mung beans, their ends matted with dirt. *Here*, I say. *Wash and pick these. Keep busy.*

Sukjunamul bap. I will make sukjunamul bap and we will eat it with swirls of sesame oil and soy sauce, a fat poached egg. We will eat, and tomorrow, I hope, she will be ready for the end.

SANGCHUL

An eerie green light streaked through the sky, and then was gone. An apparition, a warning. He watched from his cot, unable to sleep. He had gone to Chapel, and yet he hadn't found Taeho, hadn't been able to confront himself. What did the truth matter, anyway?

Truth was murky, colored by desire, how humans wanted to bend the world to their understanding of order. Truth was he'd remembered and forgotten at the same time. Recalling and erasing as he turned the boy's head, punched the body, clenched the earth, searched for a stone.

Truth was everything splintered on Inspection Day. Sangchul didn't understand how Youngchul died, how a body could disappear, how it all could have gone so wrong. So many times, he'd imagined that afternoon from inside others' minds, as if that panorama would help. He pictured walking out the back entrance toward Little House, where the women waited with an elaborate meal. They had planted large flat stones to create a path from here to there. He wondered if the nuns noticed the upturned earth around the edges of the stones, or if they strolled without looking, netted by their belief in the Home's essential goodness.

What did the nuns hear? Warden's precise explanations of the rehabilitation program. Teacher's heavy tread as he spoke of their education. The rustle of wind through trees, a stretch of resin scenting the air.

A sudden fissure. A screaming.

One nun, the youngest, perhaps, could have noticed the disturbance. At the back of the group, she would have scanned the building ahead. But Little House was quiet. No, behind her, a home that was too dark and imposing with its barred windows. Her chest would tighten at the thought of the children. Then—another yell, spiking the air.

There, on the second floor. A smudge of a face. What is he saying?

He screams and screams.

The group stops, pivots. Like a sudden growth of mushrooms, more faces, a muddle of noise. Wan boys begging in a language she doesn't understand.

"This is an example of the mental illness we handle daily," Warden might have said, an unsteady smile on his face. Teacher, more easily rankled, would have been sweating if examined closely.

Would the explanation have been enough to placate, a salve that numbed further questioning? Perhaps this young nun of Sang-chul's mind might have demanded to see the boys.

The truth lay somewhere in the middle of his imagined scenarios. They were afraid of uncovering what they didn't want to know. As Warden rushed them to Little House, the nuns would have grasped at easy explanations. Isn't this why they had come, after all, to help the orphaned, homeless, and disturbed of South Korea?

These vagrants, poor children. Yes, some of them would be unbalanced, dragging their past violences along. The nuns would tamp down their hesitations, the flag of suspicion in their stomachs.

When they returned home, they would make some inquiries, but here and now, they would believe this smiling, perfectly average-looking man in the nice suit. The easy answer wasn't always false, they would have reassured themselves. The easy answer could be the truth.

EUNJU

At sunrise, it was almost like nothing had changed, the agreement we came to the night before fine netting, so delicate we were afraid to touch. After Service, Halmoni gathered us in a circle in the kitchen, using the cardboard seats saved from Pentecost. She brewed, poured, and we sipped on tart, sweet plum tea. Finally, she nodded, the taste confirming it. "If we're going to do this, we need to be smart. Start planning right away." She stayed me with a look as I opened my mouth. "You think this is yours to own, but the elders are taking over." She turned to Mina, Areum, and Nabi. "It's the only way to protect you if they find out."

"Halmoni—" I started.

Umma shushed. "Enough."

The elders dismissed us with directions to prepare the rice and vegetables. I slunk away, irritation gathering in me. At the sinks, I blasted scallions beneath cold water, sheared roots with my hands.

All morning, the elders concocted ways to weasel the kitchen key from Teacher, and all morning, Umma barely spoke. I left the room last night against her orders, told Halmoni of our plan, united the women. I did it all for her, and yet she didn't acknowledge me. When breakfast was ready and the boys didn't arrive, she directed me to the supply closet by the stairs. "Come," her only command.

We squeezed into the tight space, my head bumping a shelf

of dish towels. "We could knot these together," I said, reaching, wanting to be helpful, included.

"I told you the key was just in case." Umma grabbed the towel. "What were you thinking?"

I stopped. The spininess of her words like little darts I hadn't expected. She should have been scared, regretful, relieved, grateful—but angry? "I was worried you weren't going—" I started.

Umma unbuckled, sliding to the floor, her breath flapping around the room. I hadn't ever seen her cry. "You could have been hurt."

I shook my head, confused. I thought she was upset at me for including the others. This was a new fear. "Umma?"

She blinked at the bare bulb above us. A slow, shuddering breath, her elbows knocking into a clatter of brooms. "I taught you to live through the world alone."

I knelt, so we were pressed together on the floor. All this time, I thought of her as impenetrable. Alone because she wanted it so. I expected more from her, constantly, because she was my mother.

"Do you remember the last time we were in this closet?" she asked. "I was angry with you for hitting Bora. Back then, I thought leaving the women behind wouldn't have harmed them. I thought they would take you away from me, with their shame. I was wrong."

It seemed a lifetime ago, that conversation. I remembered my anger, the way it filled me like a sickness. We had changed. My rage whittled into a sharp object I could control. I would wield it for us. I came to her, my fiery, soft mother. "Together, we'll get each other out."

SANGCHUL

The morning air was damp from sudden rain, heavy and suffocating. An accusatory drop landed on Sangchul's shoulder as he watched the boys run around the path. They veered far from him, as if he would beat them right there, worse than the other Keepers. *Mule* a whisper that wound through the trees, swept along on warm wind. He noticed Jae's loping stride. Pressed lips, scrunched shoulders. A need stirred, despite himself. A desire to join him, to point at the creatures making their way to the surface of the earth, erasing Taeho's absence with talk.

Sangchul knew he should have been grateful that Warden and Teacher hadn't punished them further, but restlessness swelled in him like an abscess—because in the end, it hadn't mattered that no one had made quota. There was no toppling of Head Keeper, no revolution. They were pawns, knocked around at whim, unable to rely on even the guarantee of punishment.

Sangchul and Tick led the sweating herd to Workshop through the sticky heat—west through the muddied expanse of the field. "You know what I'm craving? Gyeran-jjim," Tick said, trying to force conversation. "Isn't that your favorite?"

Sangchul squinted at the sun, ignored his partner. Mosquito

had lied to Teacher, blaming him for Taeho's blinding, and Tick had followed along, flipping so easily.

Tick stopped at the edge of the field where the trees ended. Ahead lay Workshops, those ugly squat structures they'd remain in for the rest of the day. "You would have acted the same, you know."

Sangchul laughed. Tick had made a choice, crawling up a ladder that didn't exist, sacrificing a friend along the way. He pointed at the herds waiting for their enclosure. "I'm not a coward."

Tick spat. "Without me, you're alone. Don't you get that? I see you, with your snotty looks. You underestimate me."

Sangchul rubbed his eyes as Tick walked away. An atmosphere of rot, a sensation along his skin like heavy air. He hated this—the unknowing ghost whispering in his ear, the Keepers' lies fermenting in him.

Vigilance. He had his vigilance. His herd would make quota. He would show his worth. There, by his feet: a scattering of white rocks, as sharp and pale as teeth. He picked up three. Sunk them into his pocket. The weight and sound reassured him. He was here. He was only doing his job.

EUNJU

Beneath a pool of hallway light, Areum plaited Nabi's hair. Mina and I watched, knocking our knees together. It had been two weeks since we'd agreed on escape, halfway through April, and the elders convened in the room where we slept. "To plan this outrageous idea of yours," Halmoni said before closing the door in my face.

"I want bibim naengmyeon," Mina moaned. "My mouth is watering just picturing it."

"What about you, unnie?" Nabi asked.

Hotteoks. Jjajangmyeon. Bindae-tteok. Apollo Candy. I wanted it all. First, the yellow-and-white-striped skin and crisp melon flesh of my favorite fruit. "Chamoe," I said. "Cold, sliced chamoe."

Areum tugged a braid as she spoke. "How do you think we'll do it?"

"A tunnel from the kitchen to the wall," Nabi said.

"A standoff with the Keepers, knives out." Areum touched her scar. A boy had once threatened her with a broken bottle. She had retaliated.

"We could poison them," Mina joked.

"We should kidnap Warden and force him to unlock us," I said.

"Halmoni will tell us," Nabi said, decisive, "and I'll go back to my family."

"I wish I had someone waiting," Areum said. Out of all of us, I had thought she was most like me, but she revealed her wants now, thoughts I would have kept hidden.

I stared at the orbed light as they imagined their futures, letting the brightness burn until I saw ghosts. Umma's pacing form in the closet, her rounded stomach—fear hammered through me. It was my job to buoy her, and fast—her stomach growing each day, Warden an unpredictable specter. A baby had never been born in this place, and what they would do, we didn't know. I wanted to tell the girls of my dread as Mina chattered about hairdresser school, avoiding the topic of her five sisters and the parents she had run away from, the fact that we had no money, no place to stay.

Mina. Would I see her again? I leaned on her shoulder. "You can visit me whenever you want," she said, knowing my thoughts as intimately as her own.

"We'll live together and wake and cook when we want and no one will hurt us ever," Nabi said.

"I'm not cooking another meal. We'll buy our food from street vendors," Areum said.

We would, we would, we would. I couldn't imagine the after so clearly, every corner returning me to a white wall. I only wanted to know how. Strip sheets and knot them with burlap sacks to form crude ropes. Poison the men in their sleep.

"Come on," Mina teased.

I smiled. Umma and I had traveled through towns holding hands, sidling up to ajummas who spared us rice and sweet potatoes and hodu-gwaja in paper bags. She had never had any friends. I was different from her now.

"Can we play dari-bbaegi?" Nabi asked.

We shifted together, interlacing our purple-pajamaed legs, picking a song. Tomorrow, I would tell them of my terror. Tonight, I would sit here with my friends. I would pretend we had already won.

SANGCHUL

During Dinner, he lifted a spoon. For no reason besides that he could. He stuck it in his pocket as they walked out, and it jangled against the rocks. The sensation of the jagged pieces against the smooth handle reassured him. He was here.

He pressed into the rounded metal now as the Keepers stared at one another. They were waiting in the hallway. For what, they didn't know. Since Taeho's blinding, two weeks had passed without incident, until today—Presentations canceled, Keepers ordered to remain in this corridored space while the boys were given a free hour in their rooms. Warden and Teacher were planning something, and unease skittered among them. A slickness across Sangchul's chest, like a monsoon wind. He tried to peel Youngchul off like a sheet of sunburned skin. *Why won't you help me? Return me, brother.*

"What do you think they're going to do?" Tick shifted his feet.

"I hate this waiting," Rat said.

Maybe, in another life, Sangchul would have found it funny, how differently they responded. Cow pulled out a hwatu set and asked if they wanted to take their minds off what they didn't know. Denial a potent sedative. Rat scratched his oily scalp. Tick, that shape-shifter, stuck to Mosquito's side, and Sangchul wondered if he had ever really known him. It didn't matter. Mosquito was the rot among them. The traitor looked back at him coolly. Sangchul bared his teeth as Warden's voice floated down the hall: "Keepers! Gather the boys. We have an announcement."

Inside the room Sangchul once slept in before he became a reformer, Warden vibrated with conviction. "You have been spared Presentations because it is time for us to be merry and glad. 'For this thy brother was dead, and is alive again. He was lost, and is found.'"

With those words, the room skated away from Sangchul, an impossible hope flaring—Youngchul? He searched for his stones, the curved spoon. They had heard this story in Service before, a prodigal son who was embraced when he returned. Warden twisted words until they were stippled with holes. Why couldn't Sangchul hope, then?

No. Youngchul was dead, and Sangchul was delusional. It wouldn't be him. *You.* Dread. Dark and flooding and slippery as hanyak. *You see.* The smell as strong—bitter herbs, dank mushrooms, sour bark. Warden pointed to the door. *You.* Teacher entered, and behind him, a shadow of a boy. *See.*

Someone called the boy's name. Someone shouted. A rolling relief, and a new taste in Sangchul's mouth. His molars loose. The boys clapping at the return of their own.

See?

Crowned in white bandages, he limped to his cot, arms outstretched for balance. Unsteady, the fat wicked off him, skinny to the bone. Sangchul could look only at fragments, searching for the parts that remained the same, but Taeho—he was altogether changed.

Slowly, Taeho unwound the bandage. *See?* His fingers fluttered around the ends of the gauze, a slow unspooling.

A cry, from someone else.

Where his eye had once been was a stitched hole, a sunken cavity. A small pink mouth opening, shutting. *Do you see?*

See why I need you?

Somewhere inside Sangchul, a pit dislodged.

He got to his feet. It wasn't fair, and he wouldn't accept it. This blame, this ridiculous guilt. He wasn't responsible for that—the empty well, the eyeball gone, the lashes closing in on a hole of air. No. This he wouldn't take. Impossible, to blame him for that atrocity.

2011

You are ruining me, Narae says.

For so long, we were used. Our country, our people, I say. *Thirty years after a civil war perpetuated by colonizers, our halved country was still struggling to rebuild.*

I don't care about that. She covers her throat with spidery fingers. *You're making him seem like a monster.*

Tell me, then, I say, bitter. We sit on opposite ends of my couch, our toes nearly touching. I do not want to hear how Sangchul changed, but Narae holds herself tight. This is her father, and I am hurting her. *Tell me*, again, softer.

And so she does:

She called him Appa, and he called her his little wing.

He could recognize any tree, spruces, alders, oaks, murmuring their names as if he were casting a remedy, an incantation.

On her seventh birthday, he wore one of those paper crowns from Burger King, though she knew it embarrassed him, to act silly in public.

He kept sliced Wonder Bread in his car, for ducks in ponds.

He cut apples into the shape of bunnies, to make her laugh.

He slept with the knife on his bedside table, to protect her, he said.

On his birthday, they ate bindae-tteok, the only dish he knew how to cook.

He drove with one hand on the wheel, the other holding hers, so she wouldn't feel alone.

SANGCHUL

For the fifth day in a row since Taeho's return, Mosquito's boys tripped, knocked their heads on rocks, scraped their palms on tree bark during Morning Run. How strange. Sangchul smiled. It felt good to hold their bodies down, to mold bruises onto skin. At Breakfast, they stayed quiet, and he saw it as proof of their respect of him over their own Keeper.

Mosquito grabbed him on the way to Workshop. "Enough."

Sangchul smirked. "They're injuring themselves."

"Leave them alone." Mosquito shoved.

He shoved back. "Sloppy Keeper, sloppy herd."

Mosquito spat at his feet. A green pat of mucus. Shiny in the morning sun, irregular and white-edged.

Sangchul clutched his spoon's stem, his three lucky rocks. Satisfaction splitting his face. Those boys, with their bruised fingers and starlit gazes. Their heads spinning from all those morning falls. They only had Mosquito to blame.

In the afternoon, they heard shouts outside Workshops. Tick peered through the window beyond the conveyor belt. "Come look."

Sangchul trudged over despite himself. There, behind Shirts, Teacher leered. "You said one-fifty yesterday," Rat complained on his knees. "How can we double that today?"

"Where's Mosquito?" Sangchul asked.

Tick shrugged. "Probably inside minding the boys."

It was disgusting, how Mosquito was protected. Sangchul touched the pane with a finger to block Rat's oily head. "So he gets all the blame."

"He shouldn't talk back," Tick said. "Always tempting Teacher's anger."

"Do you see that?" Sangchul pointed.

For a flash of a moment, what looked like a tooth on the ground between Rat's arms. Shining as bright as the moon.

"See what?" Tick asked.

It was gone. Eaten up by the air. Rat's face in the dirt. Teacher walked away, and in his absence, the clouds tore open, revealing a gush of light. Sangchul started laughing. A brutal burst from his chest. The force making his hands tremble. Tick stared. It was too much. He felt nearly insane, his laughter infecting the room, the boys giggling into their pots of glue, confused and delirious and gaping at their bleating leather hides. They were all crazy with truth. Who were they to say what was real? A ghost that whispered like a wing, a rat in the shape of a boy, piles of shoes and shirts and fishing lines packaged into boxes and shipped to customers in colonizer countries, oblivious men and women who had no thought as to who made these products at all.

EUNJU

We heard the news—Taeho was back, blinded but alive. For weeks, Ajumma Lee braised eggs in soy sauce, a special treat for his return to the cafeteria, and each morning, it remained uneaten. Instead, Warden ordered a tray of rice and the day's soup to be deposited in Teacher's classroom. Halmoni shook her head when she returned. No sight of Taeho. As we braided sheets and raided the junk room for any items to bring on our journey, we cycled through the rumors:

"I heard he fainted on his way to the cafeteria, so Warden lets him eat alone," Areum said as she examined a can of black beans.

Mina sniffed. "Why would he be so generous?"

"Maybe he's not out yet," Nabi offered, passing a can of cut yellow fruit. Pineapples. Inside these miniature trees, a golden sweetness, difficult to believe. "Maybe it's a lie."

Maybe, maybe: Taeho was afraid, the extra meal was a decoy, he was in Chapel, he was a ghost.

Then, on a clouded morning in the early days of May, Mina halted at the Fishhooks door, and I stepped on her heels. For a moment, I didn't understand. There was a new boy? My chest tightened—that seat was supposed to remain empty; we were waiting for him to return. She ran forward, calling his name, but no, she was wrong. That hunched figure—he couldn't be.

Taeho. I had expected a scar, or an eyeball that roved. Impossibly, a return to his normal self. This was worse. Someone had sewn over the globe's absence, a sunken flap of skin, and left a small, pink breach. He blinked, and the lashes curtained open and closed.

The back of my throat filled with electricity. The black pupil that had seeped into the brown of his iris, the white threaded with red, all gone. Someone had pulled it out like an onion bulb from the earth. I touched my own lid, and shame struck me. Here he was, and all I could think of was myself. "You're back," I said, gazing at the space above him.

"We missed you," Mina whispered. "You look good."

The farce of that statement, the embarrassment of the lie. She jumped to hug him, and he fell into himself with a yelp.

"Don't touch him," Jae said, nearly standing.

I took my seat, absorbed myself with fishing lines, metal hooks—these simple, clear objects I knew so well. I avoided him at the corner of the table until the tightness in me unwound. It was easier to work, pretend. Mina couldn't help herself though. "I'm sorry, Taeho. How are you feeling? Have you been eating? Are you in pain? When are you returning for meals? Ajumma Lee made you a special dish. Do you want to know what it is?"

Finally, Jae sucked his teeth. "Enough."

She reddened. "Sorry."

"Stop saying you're sorry and focus on your work." Jae clutched a hook. Terseness didn't suit him, but the last few weeks had changed us all. "Taeho doesn't need your pity."

"I wasn't—" Mina started, and I kicked her under the table. She was too much sometimes.

We filled cardboard packages. Taeho worked slowly, his fingers stiff. Three times, Mina opened her mouth. She was tenderhearted, her care coming out in a tributary of words. I kicked her again, worried she'd split open our secrets. I wasn't as kind. I hurt for him, the scabs along his jaw and browbone. The round cheeks gone. One half-moon eye sunk into a pale face. He was a different person now, and I was afraid.

Whenever Cow shifted, Taeho stopped. Stone-still. Then, a break in the clouds. A shout rattling the window. Instead of freezing, Taeho crawled under the table.

"It's all right," Jae soothed. "It's Rat and Teacher. No one's coming for you."

Mina squatted beside him. "We're here, Taeho."

Only I remained seated. The table spread out before me, glistening with lines and hooks, like some underwater painting.

Below, his crying a vibration I could feel through my palms.

I didn't want to witness. I was a terrible friend.

"Taeho," Mina said.

"I can't, oh nuna, I can't—"

Relief unbuckled me. His voice, it sounded the same. He was here, returned to us. I would open my eyes and we would be all right.

"Taeho," I started.

And then, he wailed.

SANGCHUL

Warden's face cracked open with the notice of a new inspector, his teeth showing through like mung beans. "This one will be sensible. This time it'll go well." His skin, sallow around the eyes. A soju reek lifting from his pores. "Tomorrow, we prove the rumors of your incompetence aren't true. We return the Stone Home's good name."

In the gymnasium after-hours, the Keepers kneeled with their hands raised, a preemptive punishment. Sangchul searched the windows for a round moon, pinprick stars. A wing around his neck. *I can't leave until I see*, the words tattooing him from within. *Tonight, will you take me?*

Warden spoke to Teacher. "I will hold you responsible for any mistakes."

"They know what to do," Teacher said in a cool voice.

They had been fighting, Sangchul was sure of it, but he couldn't focus. His arms hummed as the blood drained from nails to wrists to elbows, pooling in the wells of his armpits. They'd be bloodless by the end. Each limb plucked at the joint, hung from the air to dry into jerky. *Tonight?*

Warden smacked his lips at Rat. "He can't be seen in this condition. Are you trying to ruin us, or are you as stupid as ever?"

Teacher breathed through his nose. "You should have told me about the inspector earlier."

Rat spoke through a swollen lip, his eyes tiny points lost between puffy cheeks. "I can do my job. I'm all right."

"I'm surrounded by idiots." Warden barked out a laugh. "Keep him in the room or put him in Chapel, I don't care. You handle this."

A warm gush sparked down Sangchul's fingers as Warden left and Teacher released them. *Will you let me see?* The wing tightened around his neck. "Soon," he whispered to the ghost, wanting him gone. *Yes?*

Teacher cocked his head. "Remember what I told you, remember the story." He nodded at Mosquito. "You'll be the inspector's guide. We'll walk him through Workshops. He'll see what we're really doing here." He held on to Rat with disdain, as if he had punched himself in the face, and stared at Cow, Tick, and Sangchul. "We'll be two Keepers down, which means you three will have to manage Workshops on your own. You understand?"

You'll really help me?

"We know what to do, Teacher," Tick said, his voice jumpy with excitement.

"I'll say I fell down. Teacher, please. I'll make whatever quota you want," Rat said.

Teacher fisted Rat's shirt tighter. "Tomorrow will be pristine."

Tonight?

"Teacher," Sangchul said.

When?

"Teacher." Sangchul stepped toward him. "Let me be the guide." He wasn't sure if it was Youngchul's voice tearing through him or Rat's pleading or the stones in his pocket forcing him to speak, but he was ready. He could be more, for them. "Head Keeper can manage Shirts. Dal can stay in Leathers. It makes more sense. I can be good at this."

Teacher laughed, prickling, warped. "Are you stupid? You blinded a boy. Another person we need to keep in Chapel for the day, another body we need to account for if the inspector inquires. Why would I ever make you the guide?"

Now? Sangchul held his breath as Teacher walked on, no longer concerned with the boy who blinded another. So be it. He gripped his small treasures, the smooth curve of the spoon, the rocks. These odd talismans that countered the stone ring of Youngchul, invisible around his aching neck. They reminded him: he was here, and the others—Teacher, Mosquito, all of them—they were wrong. He would show them.

EUNJU

Mina cried on the walk back to Little House, and as soon as we were inside, she ran to Halmoni. "We have to take Taeho and Jae with us," she shouted.

Halmoni carried a vat of soup to the serving counter. "Can't you tell I'm busy?"

"You're not listening." She wept openly, her fists jammed into her pockets. "You'll see him and realize."

I watched the other women as the boys arrived, their reactions passing down the serving line as Taeho came into view. Mina had warned them. Still, Nabi ran into the kitchen, Ajumma Lee made a sound, Umma bit her lips.

As we ate, Mina tried once more, whispering to the elders. My silence left a hive along my arms. My palms red from the shame of not having the same conviction. "It's not possible," Halmoni snapped in the bathroom. Mina sunk her face into a bowl of water and blew fat, sad bubbles. She knew Halmoni was right. We had to be ruthless. The Stone Home had made us this way—stripping us to the bone until we had only ourselves to hold on to. Still, Mina was unreasonable, brave.

Halmoni gathered us in our room that night, around Bora's cot as if her specter could protect us. Mina and I clasped hands. Though her eyes were swollen, she had stopped her begging. Umma leaned against the wall, her legs propped. Stomach huge. When had she become so pregnant, so obvious?

"Let's leave tomorrow," I said without thinking. "Before they can hurt us the way they hurt Taeho."

"You saw what they did to him and you want to risk their anger?" Ajumma Lee sucked her teeth. "I say we give up on the idea altogether."

"What about the baby?" I demanded.

"The inspector's coming tomorrow," Halmoni cut in. "Our best chance is a week from now, when we'll have an eyebrow moon." She pointed to the window, too bright. "We need to finish our preparations."

"A week?" Nabi whooped as if we were in a film, and the thought of a cinema, being in a theater like any other ordinary girl, startled me. Seven days was too soon, not soon enough. So much could go wrong. I felt the current pull out beneath me, revealing what I had hidden in the waves. Umma's watermelon belly, my fear.

"How?" I asked.

We had braided ropes into ladders and amassed food. We had packed blankets, extra clothes, lighters. We hadn't discussed a way.

Halmoni spread her hands on her knees. "We'll take the knives before Teacher locks the kitchen." She glanced at us sharply. "We don't want a confrontation. We want to be far gone before they find out, but we should have protection. Once they're asleep, we'll use the paint cans to break the doors."

"What if they hear us?" Areum asked, running a nail along the edge of Bora's cot.

"I don't know." Halmoni sighed. "I don't hold all the answers."

"If they catch us, will they put us in Chapel?" Nabi asked.

"I don't know, child."

We were thinking of Taeho; I could see it in their expressions, their tics of worry. Halmoni pinching the fabric of her pants, Areum smoothing her scar, Nabi humming.

"We knew there'd be risk," Umma said after a pause. "We knew it'd be dangerous."

"Isn't there another way?" Ajumma Lee asked.

Mina dropped my hand. The gauzy hope we had carried for weeks was disintegrating. We couldn't let it go; we needed it to leave something pearled in its wake, resilient. "We can do this," I said. "It's worth trying."

"We don't know how the sound will carry, so we'll have to be fast. We'll run to the wall. It's our only choice," Halmoni said.

"We'll meet at the place Eunju-unnie described?" Nabi asked.

"We'll climb together." Umma stroked her stomach.

Ajumma Lee eyed that same round dome.

I sat straighter. The truth of Umma's circumstance was clear, and with it, our own. "We could rig a pulley to the closest tree for her," I offered.

"Heft Kyungoh up and hope." Ajumma Lee flung a bit of nail at the floor. "I don't know."

Umma sat straighter. "I'm agile."

Mina spoke for the first time since dinner. "There's a baby inside her that will be born in this place if we don't act."

Halmoni nodded. "We do this together."

A pulsing, silver pride rang through me. Without Umma, we wouldn't have believed in escape. We would have gone on with our lives, stupid and obedient. They couldn't leave her behind.

SANGCHUL

Midnight. The other Keepers, asleep. Rat, locked in Chapel. The dark, unbearable as he waited for Youngchul to uncoil from his neck. Sangchul got up from his cot, the seething in him fermented. Across the hall, he knocked. Mosquito opened the door in an undershirt and sweatpants, as if he were anyone. Sangchul peered—a single bed, a dresser, a barred window. A towel, dank and mushroomy, hanging from a hook. The outline was the same, though the details shone. A thicker blanket with hemmed edges. Two cigarette packs by the window, stacked. Wrapped vanilla wafers. A desk and stool. "What do you want?" Mosquito demanded.

Sangchul shoved, a sharp thrust—and as Mosquito stumbled, Sangchul sensed that he too was falling—passing a border he couldn't see, only feel. Warm and moist, a breath of air. They fell onto the cot, the frame sliding across the floor from their doubled weight. Plunged off the other side, Mosquito landing atop him. Catching his throat. Clawing. Sangchul swung his legs until they knocked into the desk, the stool.

He pinned Mosquito down.

There was nothing special about him, and that was what Sangchul wanted him to see. "You lied," he said.

"You didn't?"

But he hadn't. *You're.* He was sure of it, so sure—he pried open

Mosquito's mouth, the slippery lips and teeth. Shoved three rocks inside. His talismans. Jagged earth against muscle pink. *Forgetting.* Mosquito coughed, tongue thrusting to keep his airway clear. Sangchul clamped his jaw, plugged his nostrils. Mosquito kicked, and Sangchul fell. The spoon tumbling from his pocket. *Me.* The spoon. He reached for it, sightless. Mosquito gasping, a fish, a skewered boar. He jabbed the pointed end into Mosquito's side until he could straddle him again. *Listen.* Yes. He knew what to do. He pressed his knees into the stomach and crawled up the body like a rope, a wall.

Mosquito's lashes gummed closed. "Don't." Something wet on the floor, teeth or stones, he wasn't sure. He pushed them away. *You.* He grabbed the head, his thumb against the nostrils. Ready, he slipped the silver rim between spindly lashes, right into the hole. The body reacting. The acorn jelly squish. Red. Blood soaking his hands, his temples, the floor.

The screams. *Lost.* They were too loud, the others would come, but it felt too good to stop, to hurt something so soft, so human.

With his knees against the boy's throat, it didn't matter that he was nothing.

EUNJU

In the middle of the night, I woke to Umma on all fours. Gritted teeth, stifled moan. I felt her stomach, still and hard. "Is it time?"

Her eyes rolled, as if falling into a dream. It was too soon, a month too early. She shook her head. "The baby's not moving."

I felt sticky with sweat, suddenly charged. "I'll wake Halmoni."

"No." She grabbed my arm. "Stay with me."

I wiped the hair off her cheek. "I'm here."

She pushed her face into the pillow. "Waves," she muffled. "When you were coming, I imagined waves."

"We can picture them together," I said.

The ebb and flow of the tide. Purple and wondrous. White, frothy tails. Their churning echoes. She sank into the mattress, and I held her from behind, as if she were my child. Whispered in her ear the shape and sound of waves.

2011

From my bedroom, I bring Narae a gift, folded in a lidded cardboard box. *You're right*, I say. *There was goodness in him. But there was goodness in us too.*

Who says there wasn't? she asks, wiping her face.

It's time I showed you. I lift the lid and reveal two strips of cotton, cascading lengths of fabric.

Purple and worn, stitched with orange. Dotted with what looks like rust. I think I see it, glass in the weave. A flicker. Then it's gone.

What is this? she asks.

How can I explain?

These are all I have left of her.

EUNJU

Dawn. We pushed the extra cots to the wall, an elevated surface for Umma to roam. She swayed, her nails clawing white paint, and let out a warning sound, a stippled, crackling moan.

Above her, a window turned blade blue.

We were all awake now, ready even if we weren't.

I wanted them to leave us alone, I wanted them here. My skin buzzed, and I hugged myself as Umma rocked her hips.

Halmoni hurried in with blankets, washcloths, buckets. "Fill this with water, soak these." Areum and Nabi ran off. Halmoni set aside a matchbook, a sewing kit, shears. "We might need to break open the kitchen."

"The inspector?" Ajumma Lee asked, prickling and practical.

"I know. We'll see." Halmoni squatted beside Umma. "How are you feeling?"

But I understood the movement of her contractions now, the upward climb and release. "Wait," I said.

She counted. "Sixty seconds, four minutes apart. This will be quick."

"I was quick too." A fierce sort of pride swelling in me. Umma had brought me into the world this way.

At the next rest, Umma pulled off her underwear. Dark hairs, matted with blood. "Another," she said, and as if summoned, her moaning began. Halmoni squeezing her hips, time stretching thin by Umma's ringing voice. When the pain released, she leaned against a pillow.

"Good girl," Halmoni soothed. "You're in control."

"I want to help," I said.

She moved to one side. "Push the other hip. We'll work together."

We thrust our palms against her, toward the center of the womb, and Umma turned inward, a hibiscus petaling closed. The others sat around, a half-moon of voices and hands.

Then—a yelp of surprise, a gush between her legs. A valve released, splashing my knees.

"It's clear. Mina, you take over so I can check her," Halmoni said.

My friend across from me. A quick, wondrous smile. The heels of our palms on Umma's flesh, our bodies swinging to the same clock. Halmoni beside us, between my mother's legs. Fingers reaching up and— "You're close, Kyungoh. You'll be able to push soon."

"Shower." Umma's first words in hours. "Water."

We stripped down, all of us fleshed and naked as the day of our own arrival. Round-hipped with hanging breasts and brown nipples, skeletal, not yet budding, some of us hairy and some of us smooth. We walked to the bathroom together, we didn't need everyone, but we were here. Umma's hard, low belly, a dark line running down her stomach like a sign, her thighs stained red. She was beautiful. She grabbed the first sink and sank into a squat. Mina and I at her sides, ready to press. Our knees crackling against white tile.

"Nabi, make sure she sips when she can. Everyone else, fill more buckets." Halmoni was our director, our midwife, our bringer of life. They formed a line. With each pause, a waterfall of heat across Umma's shoulders, down her spine, to the curve of her buttocks.

Umma looked over at the next rest. Drank water from Nabi's cup. Kissed my head. Again and again. There was only movement and sound. My arms trembling from the steady pushing. Our bodies sticky with sweat, condensation, anticipation. A new moan—rocking high and higher, a bird swooping the sky.

"It's time." Halmoni cupped her wet head.

"I feel him," Umma said. "I know."

At the next hold, Halmoni pried Umma's fingers from the sink and helped her over to the showers. I settled against the tile, opened my legs. Umma nestled against my chest, and I rounded myself, making a home. She propped her thighs, and a bird flew out of her again, soaring to the ceiling, circling our heads.

"You're ready now," Halmoni said. "Follow the urge."

Umma opened her mouth—a scream, primal and unleashed, jolting away from us all. Echoing off the tile.

"Concentrate your strength, Kyungoh. Keep your body loose."

"You can do this."

"We're here."

"You're in control."

She closed her eyes. The bird transformed into a bear, that deep, dark growl, all musk and earth. Burrowing, and then, a rest.

"Breathe," Halmoni said. "Push when you feel that pressure."

"I want to see," Umma said.

Witness.

Nabi brought a small mirror, angled it so, and Umma bore down, a bear woman, all flesh and body, our hearts connected, an 웅녀, the origin of our world. There between her legs a pulsing chestnut, a thatch of hair, widening and widening and widening.

"One more, Kyungoh. One more and you're done."

A scream, a concentration, her fingers squeezing mine. The sky rent open, blue and light, air and waves.

I whispered into her ear. She was my mother, and she was all-powerful. She was witness, and we were here. She opened her eyes. There, between your legs, look at that. One more, yes, and there—a face, a body, an arm raised in power, ready to scramble into our world.

Oh—

A baby on her chest, slathered in white, eyes closed, not yet screaming, Umma shaking.

"It's a girl."

A girl, a girl, a girl.

A teeming, pulsing cord. An echo of pain, another push, a placenta of red, an organ as thick and large and beating as any heart.

"My girls."

SANGCHUL

Sangchul jolted awake to a skittering. A roach running across his foot. He tried to scramble into himself, but his body no longer listened to his commands. His wrists raw and tied together. His feet too, a rope around his ankles. His bones ringing with pain.

He blinked, and his limbs disappeared. The dark a texture that left a grit in his mouth. A new fear bulged in his throat, and he brought his fingers to his face. Touched the round hills beneath his lids. They were there.

His toes grazed a wall, his right shoulder butted up against another. Panic squeezed him. He knew where he was. Chapel. That meant— Yes, there, an opening took shape in the night. A slot big enough for a tray of food. He heaved himself across the wet floor, his shirt riding high, his stomach slathering in his own piss. A scraping sort of wound unsealing in him.

He tried to push the plastic flap covering the rectangular gap. His fingers slipped, he was shaking too hard. The walls leered. Afterimages flashed in the dark—Mosquito, on the floor. Keepers, rushing in. Sangchul thrashing at Teacher, drawing blood. The baton, looming. A burst of black. Waking alone, here. He knew then: he would die in this cramped space, and no one would ever find him.

"Hello?"

He touched his lips, unsure if he had spoken. Someone else. He tried the flap again. This time, he elbowed enough to let in a slip of air. He tried to get his face into that empty space, but the breach was only as tall as his hand, narrower than his shoulders. He stuck out his fingers and swept the floor. Crumbs.

"Someone new is in here, I know it."

"Who's there? We won't hurt you."

A rough laugh. "Like we could."

Two voices in the night. He knew them. He saw only dark squares, though they formed whole selves in his mind. Contained in a moving truck rolling across hills, they had come to the Stone Home together. They were together again. Sangchul cradled his bound hands to his chest. The ceiling a blurry, shifting mess.

"Maybe he's hurt," Taeho said.

"Of course he's hurt."

"Hey." Taeho spoke gently, with the kindness only he deserved. "It's me, Taeho. I bet whatever your injuries are, they aren't as bad as mine."

"He doesn't even have an eye."

A dry laugh.

Sangchul didn't understand their banter, their softness with each other in this space, how the hierarchies had collapsed. Taeho and Rat. Boy and Keeper. A crumble of dust in the corner of the room. Sangchul retched.

"These roaches are everywhere." Rat's disgust. "Look, whoever you are, the inspector's coming today, right? What's happened out there?"

"Let him rest," Taeho said.

"Fine." Rat shifted, a scrape of cloth and cracking knuckles. "Later, you'll speak to us. I want to know what's happening."

Sangchul wiped the acid from his mouth. He couldn't reveal himself. He was Mule now. Taeho's face cracking open beneath his heel, the eyeball leaking blood. He knew what he had done.

Time splintered. Hours or days or minutes passed.

"You there?" Rat asked again. "There's a bucket in the corner to piss and shit in. Food will come eventually."

"We hope."

"When Warden visits, you stay silent."

"Don't resist."

Sangchul opened his mouth, a pocket of air tumbling from him. He wanted so much—to ask for forgiveness, reveal himself, remind them of that damned truck they had ridden together to this wretched place, the light slanting through the porthole, unveiling their dirtied shoes, the chained handcuffs, and how repulsed Sangchul had been by their forms, how Youngchul—his hyung, his friend—had defended them, how debased Sangchul was now—but he couldn't speak, and it wasn't the walls leering or the fear or the pain or the roaches or the piss. It was his brother.

Youngchul's ghost on his chest, pressing and pressing and pressing, squeezing the air right out of him.

2011

I wrap the cloths around my palms. Show Narae the orange-stitched flowers, the quilted purple cotton. I raise my hands in the air.

Because of her, we are here together now, I say. *Not because of your father, but Umma.*

I don't want to hear anymore, Narae says.

Too late.

A wave. An eye. A bird.

A wall.

EUNJU

As the sun stripped away the night's blue dark, Umma wanted to be close to the ground, in a corner where she could feel the warmth of the walls. We padded the floor with blankets and then padded her and the baby. She wept a tearful sort of happiness. My sister suckled my mother's breast, a tiny and swollen creature. When she unlatched, I saw the milk—yellow-hued and thick.

"Can I stay with them?" I asked.

"The inspector's coming in a few hours," Ajumma Lee warned.

I didn't care about him, any of these ineffectual men. My mother had birthed a life, and I wanted to burrow beside her.

"She's right," Umma said. "We don't want his attention."

"As soon as Teacher leaves, I'll send someone with food." Halmoni smoothed Umma's hair. "It won't be miyeokguk, but I'll make some tonight."

We were all in a tender mood, the past hours unpeeling the drudgeries of our world to reveal a raw, sweet knowledge. We washed and dressed. Nabi rested her forehead on the bathroom mirror, whispering to herself. Even Mina, forever moving, sat in a daze.

Halmoni led us downstairs. "Teacher shouldn't be late with an inspector coming," she said, knotting her hands in front of her chest. We waited. Umma lay upstairs with a new life—it was unbelievable and my only truth. We had all been brought into the world that way, surging forth between a woman's legs.

"There he is," Halmoni finally said.

Teacher came in quick, the keys jangling against his knuckles. He unlocked the kitchen. "No Service. Be prepared to serve a meal at any time after eight."

I tugged my ear; Mina set her jaw. Something had happened in Big House.

He stopped me as I tried to pass him. "Where's your mother?" Spit hung from his lips. "Today is not the day for tardiness."

"The pregnancy," I said. "It makes her constipated."

"Tell her to hurry. We need a special meal, as much meat as we have." He turned to leave, then twisted, nearly tripping over his feet. "Halmoni," he called, pulled down his shirt collar. At the back of his neck, a ragged red gash. "Can you get me a bandage?"

Halmoni stared, her lips parting. *Be anonymous*, she'd said upstairs. *The less we speak, the quicker we disappear from their minds.* She hurried to the closet, returned with gauze.

He bent forward as if we weren't capable of treachery. "Make it subtle. The inspector, you know." He wrung his hands. Massaged the length of his fingers. "The Keepers are wearing me down."

He didn't say anything more, only stared at us moving through the kitchen. I wiped the counter with a striped rag. Mina brought washed potatoes, and we peeled the skins. He touched the covered wound. "I changed my mind. Keep Kyungoh upstairs. We don't need the inspector questioning her condition."

Halmoni sucked her teeth once he was gone. "Something's happened."

I laid down the potatoes, the airy heap of brown skins. "Can I go to her now?"

"I've prepared this." Ajumma Lee raised a tray with yesterday's rice, doenjang-jjigae, banchan, a cup of hot tea.

"What about me?" I asked.

"Ajumma Lee knows how to help with the breastfeeding." Halmoni straightened the washcloth tucked into her waistband. "You and Mina, look out the window. Find out as much as you can."

Ajumma Lee paused beside me before leaving. "You'll be with them soon."

Mina and I peered out the panes flanking the main doors—left toward Big House, right to the path that rang around the trees. Morning Run hadn't yet started.

"I've never seen anything like that," she said. "You're a real unnie now."

I closed my eyes. The round dome emerging, the final push, and then a body, full-fleshed and warm and alive.

"Look," she said. "What's he doing there?"

Cow fumbled to the Keeper post closest to us, where Mosquito usually watched the boys. Even from meters away, I saw an oval of sweat forming on his back.

"Cow as Head Keeper?" I asked.

Mina massaged her forehead against the wall. "The way Teacher was acting . . . I think—"

I slapped the window. "Don't say it. Don't let it take shape."

"Something's wrong." She stared at me, her cheek flat across the wall, her eye nearly squished. "I know you feel it."

I shuddered despite myself. My handprint had smudged the pane. A ghost, sunlit. Umma's blood, Teacher's gash. A rootlessness stirring discontent. The sound of screaming from beyond.

• • •

Halmoni told us to smile as we welcomed the boys to Breakfast. We'd made two days' worth of food, the banchan fragrant and varied. Rolled eggs spotted with scallions, matchstick strips of potatoes fried in oil, heaps of dark spinach sprinkled with sesame seeds. A platter of bulgogi for Warden, Teacher, the inspector.

Cow entered first, commanding the boys without conviction, his group and Mosquito's surging forward at the same time. He squeezed his chin. "Stop it, get in order!" The line jostled, bickered below their breaths. Tick wrangled the others. There was no one else—no Rat, Mosquito, Mule. Mina and I swapped glances, and she dropped her serving spoon, splattering rice.

There was a thinness to the air, we couldn't suck enough in. Warden and Teacher spoke over each other in loud voices. The inspector stood between them with a notepad and pencil. He wore wire-rimmed glasses, a gray suit. His eyebrows connected at the center of his face. He didn't look like a brute. Still, Warden avoided his gaze. I searched. No Taeho either.

On rice duty, Mina scooped heaping white mounds into each bowl. The boys kept their shoulders high and tight, as if strung by a line through their ears.

"Halmoni, our curious Inspector Kim wants to eat here instead of in the office." Warden spoke, his voice round with false merriment.

Inspector Kim accepted his tray as if he were one of us. I ladled tteokmandu-guk into his bowl. Strands of feathery yellow egg floating above oval tteok and plump mandu. "Thank you." He looked straight at me, and my eyes swelled, a sudden pressure I couldn't explain.

He stopped at a middle table on the right. "Can I join you?" His question carried through the quiet. Warden massaged his wrist. By the door, Teacher touched the back of his bandaged neck.

"Would you like some bulgogi?" Inspector spoke to the small boy beside him. I recognized him, a boisterous one from Crow's Fishhooks who had once been friends with Honggi.

The boy grabbed the meat with his chopsticks. Inspector knitted his brows as Cow shouted at another. Warden smiled. Tick seesawed between the groups, filmy with sweat.

"Do they usually eat in silence?" Inspector asked.

"Teacher Chung is instructing them on manners, how to behave in our society like good Koreans." Warden waved, and Teacher approached the men, his lips set in a line.

"Socialization is important to reformation. I think they've become shy overnight, impressed by our guest." Teacher nodded at the cafeteria, and a chatter erupted from the tables. "See?"

Inspector spoke to the boys around him. Warden and Teacher watched, too intent. Halmoni motioned us to serve ourselves. Quiet. Unobtrusive. We sat, and I blew on my soup. Something clattered—a spoon or chopsticks—and Teacher snapped at a boy with a rash on his cheek. Inspector frowned. Then, a cry. Piercing, winding its way from upstairs.

Halmoni guffawed loudly, just as abruptly, patting Ajumma Lee's shoulder. Her eyes wide. The baby, we needed to cover her sounds. I nudged Mina and Areum, and we followed, our table bursting into a raucous sort of laughter. Another newborn-needy wail. I caught Jae's gaze, and understanding passed over him. He whispered to another. Plates rattled. Too late, pockets of noise.

Teacher squinted at the ceiling. Warden counted us under his breath.

Inspector stood, and I grabbed Mina's hand—if he asked to go upstairs, I didn't know what I would do. Instead, the man brought his tray to the line. Halmoni hurried over and took it from him with a bow.

He bowed back. "Thank you. It was a delicious meal. You're a true cook."

She blushed. A pink across her cheeks that seemed impossible. "Ajumma Lee is the real chef," she said.

"Done so soon?" Warden approached. "Would you like to tour our Workshops now?"

"I think it's time I leave," Inspector said.

Warden blinked, surprised. "I'll walk you."

Inspector nodded, a polite smile on his face. At the cafeteria doors, beneath the framed portraits, he stopped. Turned and cleared his throat. "Have a good day, everyone."

"Meal's over," Teacher said in a flat voice as the door closed behind them. "Leave your trays where they are. Straight to Workshops."

A stroke of silence, then Cow: "You heard him!" The boys rose at once instead of in groups. Some scooped food into their mouths with their hands.

Teacher wove through the confusion toward us. We were already standing, readying to pick up the trays. His gaze glided over to me, then slowly rested on Halmoni. "She's had the baby."

There was nothing to say. Halmoni raised the tray in her hands and smiled. "Inspector Kim seems like a nice man."

Upstairs, Halmoni and I watched Umma from the door. I knew Halmoni wanted to act, prepare for Warden's inevitable wrath. But Umma, in a quilted purple robe embroidered with orange flowers, scavenged from the closet, crooned with a tenderness I'd never seen before. Her nose grazing my sister's cheek. The baby was nameless, clean, and unknown. Halmoni tutted, came close to brush a tuft of black hair. "Warden heard," she said.

"Stay here." Umma rolled to her side, not acknowledging our fear, sleep lidding her eyes. Pale from exertion.

We felt the pull, we wanted a moment of peace. The comfort of this corner. I drew a blanket over our laps and held my sister. So light, bird-boned. Halmoni sang an old folk song, and I wondered whether she had children of her own, what happened to them, and how she ended up here.

A grudging smile. "What're you staring at me for?"

Then—the door swung open, knocking into the wall. Nabi ran to us. "He's coming."

Umma sat up, instantly awake. "Give her to me."

"What do we do?" Nabi asked.

I didn't know. Halmoni puffed the blankets as if that could shield us. "We tell them the truth," she said. "The baby came early. He can't fault us for that."

Warden entered with his shoes on, suit jacket flapping to reveal damp marks beneath his armpits. The stale stink of soju rising from his skin. His red-flecked tie tossed over his shoulder. Umma skittered back like a beetle crossing glass. Her spine pressed to the corner, the baby at her breast.

"Let me see him."

She was there, swaddled and asleep despite the noise. Swollen from squeezing through to the world. I tried not to categorize her features, to find a similarity with the man who had hurt my mother.

Umma squeezed too tight, and the baby started crying.

Halmoni stepped between them. "She came early. She's healthy, and Kyungoh is too. It's a grace from God, Warden. A healthy little girl."

Warden shook, not from anger but something hidden. He looked only at Umma. "A worthless girl who can't keep her mouth shut, like her mother."

SANGCHUL

Still, he hadn't spoken, unable to parse the passing of time. It was noon or dawn or dusk or twilight. Sooner or later, the others would be released, and he would remain in Chapel forever. Youngchul on his chest, licking up his food and water and mind.

Was he crying? He didn't know. Everything covered in wet. Piss and vomit and tears. A spilled cup. A heaving vibration through the walls.

The sound of shushing, the others trying to reach him, despite it all. Talking to each other as brothers, friends.

The dark a release where he could be gilled with grief.

A voice, sometime in the constant night. The sorrow a crystal he could hold on his tongue. "I know who it is."

"Who?"

"Sangchul-hyung."

Silence.

Whispering.

A cleaving in him as he heard the next words—

But he didn't want to be forgiven.

He didn't need that kindness anymore.

EUNJU

Umma rocked over her baby as the women rushed in, Warden's wake leaving a trail of fear. "We have to leave. Tonight. Not tomorrow, not in three days. Tonight." She looked up at me, her face colorless and sheened. "Eunju, make it happen. You're an unnie now."

"No one's taking your child," Halmoni said.

"How do you know?" She bared her teeth. "Don't try to calm me. None of you know what he's capable of."

"If the inspector knows, they'll have to be on good behavior," Halmoni said.

"The inspector! He could take her too." She got to her knees, and the baby opened her eyes, peered at her mother.

"We should wait," Ajumma Lee said. "It won't be good for you to be out in the cold."

"We've been planning," Umma said. "We're ready."

"You didn't see them," Ajumma Lee responded more sharply. "They're in a rage, and they'll be suspicious of any strangeness."

I watched them. Warden and Teacher were loose-limbed, jangly with nerves. Mosquito and Rat and Mule were missing. I wasn't sure.

"I'm scared," Nabi said. Mina and Areum stood silent around her. This was elder talk, but Umma had asked me. I was an unnie now. I touched the baby's tiny hand, wanted to kiss her fingers, whisper beautiful words into her ear and fill her head with goodness.

"I think we should do it," I said. My voice tough.

"Stay out of this," Ajumma Lee snapped.

Halmoni sighed. "We don't know what Warden will do. He could take the baby tomorrow. It's possible."

"Promise me we leave tonight," Umma pleaded.

Halmoni folded the end of her washcloth. Rubbed her goiter. Slowly, she shook her head. "I can't decide for us. There's risk."

"There was always risk." Umma twisted away, her jaw set. "You don't have to come, but we're going. Eunju, the baby, and I."

"Shhhhhh," Halmoni hushed.

"What about us?" Nabi asked.

"It's not the right time," Ajumma Lee said.

"Leave me, then," Umma screamed.

Ajumma Lee raised her hands. "All right, Kyungoh, we understand. Rest now."

"I mean it." Umma wiped her face. She steadied to her feet, and the blanket slid off, her robe opening to reveal red, a spreading stain. Blood, everywhere. Thick and dark and clotted between her legs.

SANGCHUL

The door opened.

Sangchul blinked. The light, its too-bright shine. Was his brother coming to take him home?

A silhouette.

A noise of disgust. A hand on his neck.

A command—"Get up."

Now, brother? Is it time?

EUNJU

I tripped over the flat stones dug into the earth, trying to glance back at Little House, where Umma and Halmoni and the baby remained. There had been too much blood. Too red, too heavy. Teacher prodded my shoulder. I stumbled again. My pulse braying in my ears.

In the gym, I stood beside Mina at the end of our line, Ajumma Lee the head. Nabi cried. We were defenseless without Halmoni, the hours of the day snaking in on themselves. Dinner canceled; the inspector gone. Acid surged up my throat—if Warden went to Little House now, Halmoni wouldn't be able to fend him off herself.

"Presentations," Cow yelled.

"It's only Presentations," Mina said with relief. "That means Warden's here. They'll be all right, Eunju. We'll return to them before anything happens."

The knot between my shoulder blades didn't release. I tried to contain myself. "They'll be all right," I copied, my voice a shadow.

"Taeho's back," Mina said. I followed the tilt of her chin. He stood beside Jae, his empty eyehole blinking.

An image of them before: Jae's and Taeho's rounded shoulders in Workshop. Their quick fingers and smiles. How Taeho shared fat rumors with us, easy and giving, and how Jae protected us in his quiet way. We were leaving them behind. Mina squeezed my hand,

and I knew she was thinking the same thing. We weren't loyal, even though we loved them. They had kept our minds tied to the earth during hours of assembly. A pain burst in my stomach. We could have planned better, found some way to bring them along. Mina touched her pinky to mine. "We're doing the right thing."

"Attention." Teacher signaled, and we followed the plane of his arm to the back of the gym, where Warden walked a swollen-faced boy to us. From half a room away, the stink. The limping form.

I squinted.

"Who is that?" Nabi asked.

A sharp breath. Mina. "His shirt."

There, ripped at the collar. A cloud of a birthmark peering through.

"This is what happens," Warden said, "when you go after your own."

Mumbling cluttered the room, though the boys didn't stiffen with surprise. Only we gripped one another tighter. I tried to escape my body, back to Little House, Umma, and the purple-orange flowered robe and the baby. Warden spoke of respect and loyalty, what hate could do to a soul. Mule kneeled. I remembered my tongue, Warden's shoes, the leather stink.

"Is your repentance over?" he asked.

"No, Warden." Mule's fingers wavered, their tips dark. His pinky nail flapped like a flag, hanging by a thread of skin.

Pity flooded me. The faded color of dried grass, a brittle flutter in my chest. How wayward Sangchul had become without his brother.

SANGCHUL

It was hard to see. His lids heavy and sticky, red shading the corner of his vision. Waxed floors, pine wafting from the open window. Sweat. Piss fumes rising from his unwashed body. He tried to straighten his swaying head. His wrists were full of holes, planks of wood ruined by termites.

"This is what happens," Warden said, "when you go after your own."

Youngchul clung to his neck, squeezing the life out of him.

He couldn't feel his legs, whether he was kneeling or floating.

"Is your repentance over?"

"No, Warden," his mouth said.

A temple punch.

His cheek on the floor. There were so many faces, oval patches with eyes and noses and mouths. They watched, no one speaking or crying or protesting. There, the cluster of girls. He searched for Halmoni, any kind face, but they were too far away. A breeze scampered through the room, scraped his tender skin. Youngchul pushed into his windpipe, his birthmark. The lesser parts of his body Warden hadn't yet hurt.

"A false witness will not go unpunished, and he who breathes lies will not escape." The inspector had gone, and with him, any container for Warden's rage. He roved to the others. "The noise you made during Breakfast, the embarrassment of your ineptitude. The Stone Home is a rehabilitation center!"

Sangchul spat. At least he wasn't Mosquito. He was here instead of disappeared, shipped to a hospital or another reformatory or fenced.

"Get up."

He floated out of his body. A line of boys. Keepers. Cow, cheeks ruddy from the effort of feigning calm, sweat blooms betraying him. Tick and Rat, followers with cowardly hearts. Taeho and Jae, yoked by cleanness. In his mind, they were ageless.

"Arms," Warden said.

He raised them skyward. Warden grabbed his hand. Pulled out his pinky nail at the seam. Sangchul screamed.

EUNJU

The blood. The elders spoke of Mule's as we took off our shoes, Teacher already locking us in and on his way back to Big House, but I could think only of Umma's: thick, clotted, red between her legs. The need to rush upstairs and tend to her.

"What could he have done to get that sort of beating?" Ajumma Lee shook her head.

"I haven't ever seen Warden that way." Halmoni pushed her tongue against her teeth.

Areum consoled Nabi, whose tears hadn't stopped since Mule keeled over. I wanted to scream at them for crying, allowing their fear to take hold. It was the night we would leave, and Umma was bleeding.

Mina touched my elbow. "We'll go to her."

Halmoni braced my shoulder. "We need to see if she's recovered her strength. You need to be calm for her. There's a chance we won't be able to—"

"What's that?" Nabi asked, wiping her eyes, our attentive one.

The sound of grunting, from the kitchen. A metallic crash.

I rushed to Umma, the others following. The doorknob had been broken, and inside, she heaved a bag across the floor. Pale, her shirt and pants drenched. The robe dragging behind her. In piles: our rope ladder, bags of beans, matchsticks, menstrual napkins we'd use to protect our hands.

"Where's the baby?" Halmoni asked, the same time as everyone shouted.

"Ajumma, you need to rest!"

"Teacher could have heard, reckless woman."

Umma pointed to a puff of blankets in Halmoni's corner. The baby asleep, undisturbed. Mina rushed to her. Ajumma Lee and Halmoni surrounded Umma, squeezing me out, but she shook them off. "I won't let them take her away. Even if none of you are with me, I won't."

"We're with you," Ajumma Lee said, using her mildest voice.

"Save your strength, and we'll gather the supplies," Halmoni said.

Their soothing voices, their gentleness. I didn't know if they meant it, I wanted it to be true. We weren't appeasing, we weren't afraid, and even if we were, we would leave tonight.

"Let me." I grabbed Umma by the waist, careful with her swollen belly. At my touch, her resistance fell like a dress, her weight heavy in my arms. We limped to the corner, and I eased her down beside my sister.

"It's time for her to eat," Umma said, her voice changing, focus shifting to this new being, her soft mewling.

"She eats so much." I touched her cheek. Her alien face, not yet fattened.

"Her stomach is as tiny as a pebble." Umma lifted her shirt, and veins shone through her skin. Her breasts, hard and engorged.

Mina brought cabbage leaves, and I switched out the wilted ones in her brassiere. "I'll pack extra for the trip," I said. "Cloth too, for the bleeding." I looked at her lap. "Has it gotten better?"

"Don't worry about me." She watched the baby suckle. "Make sure the others are ready."

"I'm ready," I said. "Isn't that all that matters?"

She nodded, though I wasn't sure she was listening. A wince as she repositioned.

"The bleeding?" I asked again. "Is it all right?"

"It's been one year," Umma said, and for a moment, I didn't understand. "I'm sorry," she started, and I shushed her. One year—since we had entered this place, our lives forever changed.

"Look." I pointed at my sister, her open eyes. Bright black hair and high, soft cheeks. Her pointed chin. Whatever we called her, we would be a trio now. "Where will we go?"

Umma closed her eyes. "I was thinking back to Daegu."

Daegu. Where we had escaped to when I was eleven, in the middle of the night. Where one warm spring morning, we hiked a mountain. We had been hungry, the days-on-end kind that left me delirious. With our worn bamboo mat and a knapsack that hung low on Umma's shoulders, we climbed, consumed by 개나리, those golden-belled blooms everywhere, sating us with their sticky soft scent, until we arrived at a slow river. As I unrolled the mat, Umma picked wild ddalgi, naengi, dallae, minari. We dipped our feet in the rush of water and lay on flat boulders, drying ourselves in the sun. Our bounty knocking against the current, tied up in a bojagi until they chilled, the satisfaction as we bit into bumpy red fruit, crunchy seedpods, hollow stems, peppery leaves. We scooped those found plants into our mouths, dipped back into the cold, and screamed. That whole spring, we took walks shaded by yellow blossoms, and I believed in our permanence.

"Daegu sounds nice," I said, but she had already fallen back asleep.

SANGCHUL

Sangchul woke with a start. His body curled around a desk's metal legs, at first the pain a plane, vaster than any singular sensation. Then, he felt it. The small hurts. His knees like split bones. Ribs spasming. A cut on his brow reopening as he unpeeled himself. Rancid with vomit and mucus and his own dirty breath. The clock ticking above him. He was in Teacher's classroom, and it was past midnight, and Warden was gone. There, the reason for his waking. A shadow at the door: "Follow me."

Sangchul pulled himself to his knees. Crawled to standing. Teacher grabbed his neck. "Faster."

He tripped. Every part of him burning. Out of the classroom and down the hall, to the stairs. The reality of Chapel—no. Dread like bile in him. He didn't want to. *Now?* Not inside Chapel, not with Youngchul gnawing his organs. *Is it time?*

His eyes were leaking, his voice no longer his own. Palms rasping together. "I can be different. I promise, I'll do whatever you want. Please, not Chapel."

Teacher stopped. Elbowed him to the wall and pulled out his keys. They were at the back entrance, not the stairs.

"Look." Teacher opened the door. A gust of red wind. A whisper of trees. Out there was a wall crusted with glass. The soil, dark and unknowable beneath. "Do you remember?"

Sangchul squinted.

In Teacher's other hand, a length of rope. Pale, a rough green. Thick and bristly. The color of dried hemp seeds. He raised it, in the direction of sunset.

At last.

Sangchul felt the cold hand of fear.

"Where are we going?"

EUNJU

Time. There was too much time, hours passing with the light in Warden's room still bright. We banded together where we felt safest, in the space that was ours, where no man entered. By candlelight, we waited. The supplies collected in a pile. Each minute an excruciation.

Umma and the baby slept in the corner, blanketed, while I sat with Mina and Areum behind the serving counter. Ajumma Lee paced the kitchen floor, from the side entrance by the stairs to the sinks at the back. A shifting shadow. Her agitation heightening with each lap. Halmoni scurrying around, as if there was anything left to do.

"I don't know," Mina said, following Ajumma Lee's tread. "Doesn't it feel like we've been waiting forever?"

"You sound like her," Areum chided.

"I'm not afraid." Mina sucked her teeth. "You know I'm no good at waiting." She hovered her hand above our candle. The flame warming her palm until I imagined a hole opening in her.

"Nabi will come with good news soon." I gestured to the main entrance, where she was on window-watch duty, trying to sound confident, but there was a rising tide in the room, Ajumma Lee's pacing churning the waters. I sat on my hands to stop myself from yanking her down.

"What if Warden never goes to sleep?" Mina dipped her finger into the melted wax at the bottom of the candle holder. She waited for it to dry, then peeled it off in one strip.

"Enough!" Ajumma Lee stopped. Her bony fists tight by her sides. "Enough of this silly, stupid plan. Let's go upstairs."

I rose, batting Mina away. Too late. "She might be right," Halmoni said, worrying her fingers. "We can tell Teacher we had to break the lock to get something for the baby."

Umma sat up from her corner. "To give him another reason to take her away?"

"That's not what I meant," Halmoni said, ashen. "We don't want harm to come to anyone."

"We leave today," I said, joining them.

Ajumma Lee scoffed. "Talking back as you do. It's not your decision, child."

Her words scraped through me. I was tired of her, these elders treating me like I didn't understand. Mina grabbed my arm before I could move closer.

"We're nervous." Halmoni shook her head. "Sooner or later, Warden will sleep. Until then, we rest." She drew me away, until we were by the stairs. I waited for her to scold me, but she cupped my head. "You need to focus your anger." She pointed to the others. "They aren't the ones, you understand?"

I nodded, though I felt a heat in my chest, down my fingertips. I nodded again to make myself believe.

"Your anger, it can be a source of protection." She tilted my chin until I met her gaze. "Go, take a walk. Focus your mind."

I did as she told me, touching each surface, harnessing myself. The grease built up on the wall behind the stove, a sticky residue left on my fingers. The scratched plastic bowls stacked on the shelf, and the smooth cool of the ceramic ones tucked behind, only for our special guests. The sink where I punched Bora in the stomach. The knob of the closet where Umma dragged me twice, once to promise escape and once to accept my own. Tomorrow, we would work to forget this place, to erase the Home from our memories, but a tiny flame in me would miss this kitchen.

Nabi ran in as I palmed the wooden cutting boards. Her arms up, her short hair swinging. "Blow out the candles," she whispered. "Someone's coming."

SANGCHUL

Teacher's flashlight cut a line through the land, one Sangchul followed, the rope around his wrists a command. His brother making him stumble. *Is it happening?* It was dark, past midnight, the winds a high whistle, the pines making slippery sounds. He wanted to ask where they were going, and he didn't want to know. He would be whipped, tied to a tree, slaughtered, and left for the birds. He would be made to dig or disappeared. He tried to wipe his face. *Finally?* This inexplicable liquid upheaval in him.

"Open your eyes," Teacher said as Sangchul tripped. He landed on his knees. A rock cutting his palm. Tried to grasp it. He was too unsteady, it was hopeless, there was no more he could do.

Take me. Take me to my body.

They were on the path. The green dust in his face a sign. He saw what would come next. They would follow it to Workshop, the azalea bushes, the fence, the mounds. *Come with me?*

Teacher yanked the rope, stopped. "What is that?" A stitch of sound. "What do they—?"

He was dragged up once more, shoulders sliding in their sockets from the force. Pulled along like the mule he was. Where were they going?

A flickering. A sound.

EUNJU

Nabi had seen a flashlight snaking toward Little House. A figure in the dark. "I told you," Ajumma Lee said, pacing the tiles. She pointed at the handmade rope ladders, the piles of food and materials we had gathered. "There's no time to hide now. We'll have to confront him."

Halmoni spoke. "It's either Teacher or Warden. I'll go into the cafeteria and convince him to go away."

"What if he's suspicious?" Nabi stood unmoving, her eyes drifting to the ceiling, to that second floor where part of her wanted to run. But she was loyal—if not to us, then to Halmoni.

"We don't have time," Umma said with the baby in her arms. Standing, too alert for this afterbirth period. She was supposed to rest, drink hot liquids, sleep.

"Hide," Halmoni commanded. She caught my arm as the others scattered. Mina by the stoves, Ajumma Lee to Umma's side, helping to shush the baby. Areum and Nabi behind the vegetables counter. Even without the candlelight, we knew this space. Halmoni led me to the wood-beaded curtain. From her pocket, a smooth object that fit in my palm. The jackknife from the room upstairs. The one I had thrust in her face when I'd thought she was Teacher. "He must be coming for the baby. If it sounds like trouble, you get her out."

I slipped the knife into my pocket and hugged her, a quick impulsive surge.

"Be brave," she said, her voice shaking, and then she walked out.

I looked back at Umma. She was protected by Ajumma Lee. Halmoni, she was alone. I squatted by the curtain, one hand against cold tile, and watched her feet disappear past the rows of cafeteria tables. Mina crawled to me, pressed her chin to my back, the relief of her near.

The light turned on. Too bright. A sharp breath. "What are you doing here?"

Teacher.

I strained to hear. A cough. A noise of surprise from Halmoni. "Kyungoh's bleeding, and the baby needs to eat every few hours, but I have control, Teacher."

"You're not answering my question."

"I needed supplies. There's so much to be done after a birth. The bleeding and release." Her tentative voice. "Why is he here with you?"

He? Mina clutched my shoulder. I tried to peer through the beaded strands, so close I feared my breath would make them clack together. We couldn't see. The sounds, though, they were enough. The screech of a sliding bench. A thudding. The smack of a body pushed aside.

Mina scrambled back to Umma's corner, dragging me with her. Nabi and Areum behind us. "He's coming," she whispered.

My mouth filled with metal, a coin under my tongue.

"Who's there?" Teacher called.

"I'll go." Ajumma Lee stood. The fear on her face visible, if only I could reach out and grab it. I had never thought of her as brave. She was biting and ungenerous, quick to cast blame, but she was also an elder, and she would protect us. "Eunju, take your mother and the baby out the side door. If we're lucky, he's left the entrance open." She looked at the others. "Go with her or run upstairs."

She parted the beaded curtain and walked forward. "Teacher!" I could hear her false smile. "Are you here to help? We've been making a batch of miyeokguk. Kyungoh's bleeding hasn't stopped. Is there anything you could do? Perhaps you could call a doctor?"

Areum and Mina tightened the baby to Umma's chest with a blanket, ushered her to the side entrance.

"I'm scared." Nabi held her shirt.

"Eunju," Umma whispered, and I hauled myself out of the silence, this strange undoing. I met them at the door.

A whip of air. Scatters of noise, shrieking. Ajumma Lee and Halmoni.

Mina and Areum turned, and something in them united. A stone of jealousy in me as they decided together. "Go," Areum said to us, grabbing a fruit knife. "We'll protect them."

"What about me?" Nabi asked.

"You all go," Mina said. She knew as I did Nabi was too young.

"Eunju," Umma panted. Her face pale and sweating. There wasn't time. I turned to look once more—at Mina with a pair of scissors and Areum with her knife, reaching the curtain.

There was no talk, no bright prattling Mina voice. Instead, Teacher's fury at their arrival. "You?" The sound of cutting air. "Are all of you down here?"

"Come on." I grabbed Nabi's arm.

She shook her head. Pulled back from us. "I can't leave Halmoni."

"Let us go." Umma's gaze was too gleamy, unfocused.

I made a choice.

Past the stairs, the supply closet, to the front entrance. I led my mother and sister, walking forward in the dark. Praying the baby stayed silent, asleep, milk-drunk at the breast. Praying the entrance remained unlocked. "We have to sneak across," I said, trying to pin Umma to me, pointing to the open cafeteria doors.

Inside, a screaming. Beads scattering—the wooden curtain pulled down. I looked through the doors we were supposed to pass, a hook in my stomach refusing to let go. Teacher staggered with Areum at his waist, flung her against a table. I saw it—the reason for his careening—a knife in his shoe. He grabbed Mina. Her scissors already gone. She tried to swing her fists, and he rasped, "You can't hurt me."

He was right. She was too good, my Mina, but there was a coldness in me, deep in my bones, and I knew what to do.

I opened my jackknife, and I ran.

There had been a man. Before Daegu, when I was eleven, in the middle of the night, raging at the door. In the one room that was ours, with our clothes and blankets and a desk with three perfect books. A man breaking the handle and coming in. Umma, telling me to run. Umma, handling a knife. Umma, slashing his face so we could escape, leaving everything she had earned behind. I thought of her strength, that room that was ours the man had taken from us, as I pushed the knife into Teacher's chest. As close to the heart as I could get. A new sound. He grabbed me by the throat, and I remembered the after. How she had sliced her hand open. An alarm ringing, squealing in the air, then the slow realization. That terrible noise was coming from me. Umma's hand on my mouth to shush, to become invisible. The taste of iron.

I wouldn't stay quiet now.

He pressed into my windpipe. The knife still in him. A lever I could push. With all my strength, down against resistant flesh. The edges of my vision darkening. Fat. I found his face. Muscle. The wild frenzy of his gaze. Bone.

Taeho's eye. That pupil leaking into the iris. A drained lake.

I wanted to make him bleed.

He let go, and I dropped to my feet, gathered the air in my lungs like a gift. Blood on my hands, the knife, the floor. It tied me to him, so be it. The wounds in his body, dark and insistent.

A horror, a mess, salvation.

SANGCHUL

Shadowed by the cafeteria doors, Eunju's mother clutched her baby in fear as she saw him. Her high-cheeked face damp with sweat, her strength a shield he wouldn't ever want to pierce. As Eunju ran to the women, Ajumma whispered to Sangchul: "Don't." She thought he could hurt the baby. He was no longer surprised, no longer wearied. He held up his roped arms and bared his neck, as if she could see his brother's ghost coiled there, like a scarf. *I am harmless*, he wanted to say, but that would never be true again.

Then—the highest screaming. They turned together. Ajumma gasped as her daughter stabbed a man they hated. A soul-scraping weeping, the baby squirming on her chest.

He couldn't help her or any of them. Relief and mourning bringing him to his knees. He wasn't the one. He should have been the one.

Teacher lay belly down on the floor, unmoving. Eunju beside him, gasping for breath on all fours. Cafeteria tables strewn aside, benches toppled. Ajumma Lee hauled Mina, who was crying, her ankle twisted, to the kitchen. Areum hovered over Halmoni by the ruined wood-beaded curtain.

Ajumma screamed her daughter's name.

Eunju stood, and Sangchul caught her gaze. Would she come for him next? Halmoni was pushing Areum aside now, grabbing a wet knife from the floor, whispering into Eunju's ear. He knew what she was saying. Warden would come soon, in search of Teacher. Eunju pointed to the kitchen, the women, and Halmoni mouthed *no*. Pointed to the baby instead. Warden would take her, the easiest revenge. A relenting in Eunju—he saw it—in the fall of her shoulders, the way she wiped her forehead, leaving a streak of red. She moved to them, and he turned with his bound hands. The front door, he needed to open the door and go.

EUNJU

We were outside—Umma and the baby and me. We were running. I struggled against myself. *Take them and go, before Warden comes,* Halmoni had said, and I'd listened.

Teacher, lying on the floor. A fish, a splayed animal. They would kill me for what I had done.

"You need to show us," Umma said, ragged and rasping, and I remembered: I was the one who knew this land, not her. I was the one Halmoni trusted.

I carved a path through the trees, avoiding the open lawn, the stench of iron rising from my hands, sharp against the cold air. My attention focused forward to the wall and back toward Big House. *Before Warden comes.*

We had made too much noise. Teacher had been gone for too long. Mule, there was the question of Mule, who had run, disappeared, maybe back to Big House with the news of our betrayal. Warden would come looking.

"Mina," I said, halting.

After Teacher had dropped me, the knife clattering to the floor, he had crawled on his stomach, caught Mina's ankle, held on to it as if he were sinking into the ground. The sound of her bone breaking. He couldn't hurt me, and so he'd needed to find someone else. I had rushed to him. One last push, and he was done.

"We have to go back," I said.

A light behind us. A shout. Umma, clamping a hand across her baby's mouth.

We ran—

Until we reached the wall. We had forgotten the bags, the rope ladders, everything.

"What about the others?" I sank to the ground, my legs, my throat aching where he had choked me. We had abandoned them. "Where are they?"

She turned. Whistles. Another shout. A knife cutting skin. Teacher, on the floor. "I don't know," she said, her teeth chattering. She retched, and I smelled it again. The iron funk. It wasn't coming from me. In the dark, I found its source, swamping the ground from between her legs.

"Umma, you're bleeding."

She shushed me. Tender, this time. She opened my arms. "You need to be brave."

"I can't," I said.

"You have to." She gave me her daughter. This new creature, soft and squished and true. Umma unraveled the blanket from her shoulders and wrapped it around us, tightening her to my chest. This hot, tiny being. I wasn't ready. I didn't know how. I tried to catch her gaze. I couldn't stitch her together.

She doubled over herself. "Listen." Her voice strained, trying to focus on me and her and our circumstance. She pointed to the wall, the gaps in the stone. "You'll have to try."

He stumbled toward us.

"No," I said, my voice pleading and unfamiliar. "Let us be, Sangchul."

He scanned the wall and looked back at us. He raised his hands. A rope.

The baby—she screamed, louder than I thought possible, a beautiful and terrifying sound.

SANGCHUL

Eunju said *no*, as ferocious and feral as the first day he had seen her. Tiny, with her clutch of hair. They were shrouded in darkness, and when that baby screamed, they all shuddered. "They'll hear," he said, taking a step closer.

The quick swish of a knife opening in her hand.

"I blinded Mosquito." But those weren't the right words. He only wanted someone to understand. "I mean, Taeho." He wasn't coming to hurt them. He hadn't been coming for them at all. "I mean, both."

She sliced the air.

He pointed at her mother on the ground. "I can help."

"You?" She came at him, the baby wrapped to her chest, and he lifted his chin—offered the expanse. She could do it, and he would be grateful. He closed his eyes and remembered: Taeho's curved spine, the high squeal of a boy who trusted him, a flash like a coin in a stream. There, and then gone. Teacher's body crusting the floor, Mina's ankle crooked the wrong way, Ajumma Lee and Areum and Halmoni and—a new screaming. Warden. Keepers. They were coming.

Eunju hesitated, and another image came to him, unbidden: Eunju and her mother and this baby tied together and dragged back to Big House like cattle. Warden's reward. His mind, always acting as a Keeper first.

"The blood, there's too much," her mother said.

He started to cry.

A wind from the earth, lifting his shirt, blowing into his eyes.

Eunju pulled back her knife, her face changed. A flicker between them. "The azalea bushes, the fence, you need to go." A whisper, coming out of her.

Yes.

A ghost in the air, slipping away.

He saw hyung—searching for a blue wing, a road that would lead him home. It was her.

"You, Sangchul," Ajumma said, she was talking to him. "Come here."

Yes.

He kneeled before her, his hands bound.

Now.

EUNJU

For a flash, I had seen Youngchul between us. A flying, near-invisible thing. Chain link and leaves. Buds, upturned earth. Stones. The words, summoned from elsewhere. I shook my head. Had I spoken? I looked around—

Umma, forcing an oath from Sangchul as she bled. His neck outstretched, the curl of his birthmark visible, that brown wisp of a cloud. He shouldn't be here, I wanted to scream. The baby squirmed against my chest. We needed to figure out a way.

A shout. Not from the house, closer. Umma beckoned, and I listened, against all I wanted, I unbound his wrists. Together they swung the rope over a branch of the tree above us. Sangchul tied one end around his waist, another around mine.

"You'll have to brace your feet. This will help. We'll hold it steady," she panted.

"Umma," I wept.

"This will have to do," he said.

"You go first, Umma. I'll push you up," I begged.

She sat, heaving. I tried to unwrap myself, to give her back the baby. If she wouldn't for me, she would have to for this new child. The milk, the tending. There was a life here now. She stopped my hands. "I'll follow soon, with the others." She touched the baby's hair, my cheeks. I had always loved her, never enough. "I only need to rest."

The sound of cloth ripping. Umma unraveling the hem of her robe. Tying the strips around and around my palms. "You can do this."

"You'll come right after?" I asked. The desperation in me a sound, a bell in my stomach, ringing and ringing.

"It's time," Sangchul said.

There, in the near distance, I heard it: deep and male and familiar, but I couldn't go, I couldn't leave her.

"You keep running, and I'll wait for the others. I'll come meet you." She pushed me to the wall, the rope.

"Where?" I asked. "Where?"

The baby wailed. She touched my forehead with her own. "You are mine, my first. Go."

Gaps between stones. My feet searching for a hold. I pulled one hand above the other. I climbed with a hot being against my chest, pulsing and alive. She fought me as we rose into the air, and I begged her to be quiet, to not give us away. At the top, I stared back. The slump of my mother against the stone, her chin tilted so she was looking straight at us. Her two daughters. And then, we were gone.

2011

We ran to reach sunlight, to force space between us and the place we once called home. When alarms sounded, Sangchul stood still while I wanted to go. Whoever was holding you won. The baby, you turned pale and weak without breast milk. We begged the nearest homes for water and corn syrup. We survived this way for weeks, moving north through the May warmth. We reached Daegu, and then—

You turn on the light, and I am here, at my kitchen table. My hands wrapped in the cloths Umma ripped from her robe. You stand across from me, but I am sixteen again, alone on the other side of a wall.

No, I wasn't ever alone. You, that tiny infant on my chest.

You, Narae, look at me. The realization furrowed between your brows. *We're sisters.*

I nod—I could explain myself, how I never meant to leave you or her and how I had, my mind emptied with hunger and exhaustion and grief. I want to explain, but my world is dissolving, and I don't know what is my truth, the truth, or his truth anymore.

What I remember: we reached Daegu, and I told Sangchul we would wait for them. He disagreed, hushing you on his chest, convinced I was deluding myself. I walked off in the dawn, before the sky shrugged off its shadows. I only meant to go for a moment. An hour, a day. Grief unspooling my mind, and anger too. I hadn't tried enough, Umma had made me leave, I had failed her and Mina and everyone.

I walked through the woods to the stream, the spot where we had eaten wild plants all spring, surrounded by golden-belled blooms, their honeyed scent heady and delicious. Except I couldn't remember the exact place. I had been too young. I found a shaded, slanted rock. I pretended. Laid myself down like an offering and waited for something to happen.

I woke shivering. The sun gone. The air charged with pine and earth and river water. I hadn't eaten, and I felt alive, my mind carved out of me.

You left me with him. Narae looks away. *That's how he became my father.*

I am sorry. The words, too flimsy for the feelings within me.

No, she says, as I open my mouth. *I don't want to hear it.* You move to the kitchen sink. A cupboard opens, closes. The faucet runs water, shuts off. Dry, heaving breathing. You won't weep. You are tougher than any of us. I stare at the hands on my lap. Cuticles raw from fretting. Burns from years of hot oil, smooth and shiny. A scar on my palm from that glass on top of the wall that sparked in the sun.

I looked for you, I say.

After I woke on that rock, I ran. My shoes crusting with dirt as I squeezed between trees, slipped into streams, trampled new flowers. Finally, I found the ash from the fire we had made the night before, the black smudges on the rocks we had formed into a crescent. Sangchul and you gone. I searched. I called for you. I looked until I couldn't breathe.

I stare at the wall, the calendar from the local bank that hangs from a nail. Beside it, a lone picture, tape fraying at its corners. Cut from a magazine. A woman in an orange flowered dress. She looks almost like our mother.

I want to explain—for so long, I thought I didn't deserve a full life. You see, I'd hated you some days, how you required so much. Your needy body, your pebble stomach, your screeching, and how you put our lives in danger. I accepted the help of a boy I despised, I let him take you away.

I peel the picture off the wall. Tuck the tape over the corners so the wafery paper won't rip. I will show you the closest image I have, explain how I imagined a life for Umma—she had escaped and become this woman, she found you instead. This song churning inside me—will you shun me now, will you say I'm no good?

What I want you to know: I was always trying to find you. When Sangchul located me decades later, I flew to him right away. *Where did you go?* I asked that stranger lying in the hospital bed.

He chewed slowly, the effort it took to move his jaw obvious and painful. Beside his empty bowl, a fish licked clean, its skeleton gleaming. He rubbed his collarbone and sputtered, speaking of Youngchul and a ghost and a bird and blue. The color, the sweep of it.

I was going to come back, I told him, my voice unsteady.

He set down his spoon, his lips wet. *The body doesn't forget.* He gestured to himself, the cancer riddling him. *My penance.*

I sit back down, the picture on the table, and I feel you approach. You, a stranger who came to my door with a request, a knife. My sister, my blood. I cannot live without you now, and it is hope that squeezes through me as you kneel, cup my hands.

A sound, belling in my mouth. Is this relief?

—because I see it now, a swell retreating, silt and stones, the dark wet of the earth, yellow-tipped blooms.

내딸들아,

Yes.

보이니?

You are no longer a wave, but a river, beckoning me in.

EPILOGUE

Narae follows the directions. When she arrives, she is relieved. Where there once was a wall enclosing five buildings, there is an open road. A pale cream apartment building. To the side, an empty playground with a seesaw, its red paint peeling off in strips. A rusty metal slide. She checks her phone for the directions from Unnie and looks up. No Workshops. No Little House. Even the trees are gone. Still, lives stutter open before her.

A memory: her father loved hiding among trees. On weekends, when she was young, they drove to Bear Mountain and walked around throwing sticks. He didn't talk, though he pointed out birds, insects, worms, white-tailed deer. They made a game of it. He brought chamoes. When she tired, they'd sit on a mat he unrolled onto the ground.

Always, he retrieved the knife from his jacket pocket. She loved the lusterless handle and serrated blade, how it knew how to fold into itself so perfectly. She had once grabbed it from him. Flicked it open and shut with a mighty look on her face.

Careful. He took it back and carved yellow-and-white-striped skin. She scooped the goopy white flesh from the cavity. Stuffed the strings into her mouth. As her father pared, she split the seeds between her molars.

Where'd you buy that knife? she asked.

He crossed his legs, and she copied him. The blade wet, shiny. *It was a gift from your unnie, many years ago.*

She stopped. There was no unnie. There was only them, a daughter of a single father, their shared loneliness. She pressed her hand into the dirt and sniffed her palm. The world was tilting away from her. *Lie.*

Maybe I am a liar. He passed her a slice. The slippery fruit, its sweet crunch. *Did you know, I had a hyung once. That's true. He died a long time ago.*

I thought you were like me. Accusation threw her voice high. She broke the chamoe in two. Dropped one half into the dirt and covered it with a scattering of grass.

He handed her a paper napkin. *Let's eat.*

She sits at the bottom of the slide though she is too big for it, her adult hips squeezed between raised railings. She hadn't known he was dying. He had kept his secrets until the end. Her grief is difficult to describe, reedy and choking and unremitting. She unzips her coat and pushes her boots against the playground asphalt. From her inner chest pocket, she retrieves a photograph. Her favorite memento, taken at her college graduation. He wears the white button-down shirt and blue paisley tie he saved for special occasions. He is grinning, full-teethed. A rarity. She holds two bouquets. One given in congratulations, one in thanks, and the extravagance makes her chest twinge still, her frugal father.

For years, she hoarded what she knew of him, trying to patch together a truth. His right pinky joint jutted into a misshapen knob. The left middle finger had once been broken, the line from knuckle to tip angled, unnatural. His palms, heavy with scars. He rubbed his birthmark when nervous, when feeling anything at all. He loved fast food. Burgers and fries, the salty, fatty richness of her youth. He spoke to himself in the dawn hours. He kept a photograph of a boy inside a peppermint candy container in his underwear drawer. Worn down to nothing except a ghostly form. If he could be any animal, he would be a bird. *That's why you're my little wing*, he used to say. Mostly, his answers skirted truths.

I broke them once.

When I was a teenager.

That's a picture of me. What do you mean?

We don't have family there, and we don't have the money anyway.

You speak the language. Isn't that good enough?

He drank. Returned in the middle of the night bleeding. Stinking of soju. Once, he threw a lamp through their apartment window, and they had to move the week after. He spent hours walking through forests and streets alone. He cried. He missed her parent-teacher conferences but attended her competitions, and on the drive home, he critiqued her sparring techniques, the strength of her kicks. He kept her. She was his little wing.

Narae rises from the slide and pulls out the knife. Flicks it open and closed the way she did as a child when she snuck into her father's room. She scrapes the blade against the slide's tongue. A wild, scratchy tribute in the shape of a bird. Strange. It is not him that comes to mind, but Eunju.

With her eyes closed, a picture of a woman on the kitchen table before her, Unnie pulled at her ear. That was how Narae had known she was afraid. But loneliness wasn't their truth anymore—she needed Unnie to believe that.

She cupped her sister's hand, kneeled before her.

I found you, Narae said, and suddenly, she'd tasted a rush of water, golden bells. A new voice, higher than any living sound.

AUTHOR'S NOTE

The Stone Home is an act of fiction, but it was inspired by historical events in Korea. In 2016, while researching an artist's residency called the Gyeonggi Creation Center, I learned of its rumored past as a concentration camp during the Japanese colonial period. 선감학원 (Seongam Academy), as the camp was known, was established in 1942 with the purpose of housing "vagrant" children. In reality, children were abducted, abused, and forced into labor. It is said ghosts haunt the property now.

A few months later, I read Kim Tong-Hyung and Foster Klug's investigative article for the Associated Press titled "S. Korea Covered Up Mass Abuse, Killings Of 'Vagrants,'" which exposed human rights atrocities at institutions throughout South Korea in the years leading up to the 1988 Seoul Olympics. They found that these abuses, most notably at one of the largest facilities called 형제복지원 (the Brothers Home), were orchestrated and covered up by the government for decades. I was struck by how the colonial institutionalization and abuse of children had been reenacted by Korea's dictators. Questions plagued me: What does it mean that state-sanctioned violence happens time and again? How do we confront our capacity for evil? Whose stories are silenced in our history, and how does that erasure contribute to future crimes against humanity? I began writing—not to find clean answers, but to wrestle with the unknowability of ourselves.

In 2022, after years of advocacy from survivors, South Korea's Truth and Reconciliation Commission acknowledged the government's role in the detention of innocents and human rights violations at Seongam Academy, the Brothers Home, and other facilities throughout the country. Survivors are still waiting for a governmental apology and reparations. More information about the survivors' fight for justice can be found in 한겨레 (*Hankyoreh*), 연합뉴스 (*Yonhap News*), 조선일보 (*Chosun Ilbo*), and other Korean news agencies. Articles in English can be found at the Associated Press and the *New York Times*.

I am indebted to 한종선 (Han Jong-sun), a survivor of the Brothers Home and active protestor, who spoke with me on April 23, 2018, in Seoul, South Korea. He bravely sparked a broader conversation about the Brothers Home's abuses in 2012 via a sit-in in front of South Korea's National Assembly. His willingness to share his story and his acknowledgment of my novel endeavor were invaluable.

The following texts were foundational in considering the historical, cultural, political, and psychological context of these institutions and humanity's capability of evil: *The Gwangju Uprising* by Choi Jungwoon, *Sex Among Allies: Military Prostitution in U.S.–Korea Relations* by Katharine H. S. Moon, the City History Compilation Committee of Seoul's texts, *DMZ Colony* by Don Mee Choi, *Trauma and Recovery* by Judith Herman, *Man's Search For Meaning* by Viktor E. Frankl, and *Into That Darkness* by Gitta Sereny.

ACKNOWLEDGMENTS

I once again want to thank 한종선 (Han Jong-sun), who spoke with me for hours about his experiences at the Brothers Home. I am thankful to my aunt Jackie Kwak for accompanying me that day, acting as both a cultural and linguistic interpreter when needed.

Deepest gratitude to Katherine Fausset, my steadfast and brilliant agent. Thank you for encouraging me to take my time, and for your enthusiasm about this novel from the very beginning. To everyone else at Curtis Brown, including Jazmia Young, Sarah Perillo, Lizzie Johnson, and Holly Frederick.

I am thrilled to be teaming up again with the powerhouse Jessica Williams, who understood my vision and pushed me further. Thank you for your constant belief in my writing. To the whole William Morrow team for shepherding this book into the world, including Julia Elliott, Eliza Rosenberry, Sharyn Rosenblum, Tavia Kowalchuk, Ploy Siripant, Peter Kispert, Taylor Turkington, Andrea Monagle, and Liate Stehlik.

Thank you to Hokyoung Kim for illustrating the cover of my dreams. Thank you to Emily Jungmin Yoon for allowing me to use "Let Us Part Like This," originally published in her collection *A Cruelty Special to Our Species*, as the epigraph for this book. Together the cover and the poem act as the perfect opening for *The Stone Home*.

Gratitude to the Jerome Foundation, Sewanee Writers' Conference, Jentel Artist Residency Program, and Brush Creek Foundation for the Arts. Thank you to Min Jin Lee and the National Book Foundation for the 5 Under 35 honor.

I began *The Stone Home* in 2017 and worked through many iterations before finding the right words. Thank you, a million times over, to my community. To my early readers, Lucy Tan and Ingrid Rojas Contreras. To my writing sisters, Nicole Chung and R. O. Kwon, for your support and care. To EJ Koh, for your soulful, inspiring friendship. To the Resistance Workshop: Brittany Allen, Alexander Chee, Mira Jacob, Luis Jaramillo, Tennessee Jones, and Julia Phillips. To Taylor Hahn—how lucky we are to be on this writing path together. To Kirsten Saracini—for our craft walks in the park, which helped me see my characters anew. To Claire Sylvester Smith, for your ophthalmological advice. To Leigh Kader and Marni Deutsch, for showing me the exquisite, roaring power of labor and birth. To Julia and Alex—I am so grateful to be alloparenting together. Writing this book would not have been possible without childcare—to Ezgi, Aysel, Fatima, and Fatiha, thank you for your devotion to my children. To Yewon Kim, for being the coolest nuna around.

Always, I am indebted to my parents and sister. Without your love, in its many and varied forms, I would not be here. To the rest of the Kims and Kwaks, my blood, my ancestors. To the Chyus, Leonards, and Whitneys—we are family.

Finally, to my greatest loves: Eric, you see the whole of me, and I am grateful for the life we are building together. To 해솔 and 해온, for bringing a new wealth of possibility and love and joy and learning into our family. Thank you for choosing me as your umma.

ABOUT THE AUTHOR

Crystal Hana Kim is the author of *If You Leave Me*, which was named a best book of 2018 by more than a dozen publications. She is the recipient of the 2022 National Book Foundation's 5 Under 35 Award and is a 2017 PEN/Robert J. Dau Short Story Prize winner. Currently, Kim is a visiting assistant professor at Queens College and a contributing editor at *Apogee Journal*. She lives in Brooklyn, New York, with her family.